WORTH
Every STEP

KG MacGregor

Bella
BOOKS
2009

Bella Books, Inc.
P.O. Box 10543
Tallahassee, FL 32302

Printed in the United States of America on acid-free paper
First Edition

Editor: Cindy Cresap
Cover Designer: Linda Callaghan

ISBN 10: 1-59493-142-9
ISBN 13:978-1-59493-142-0

About the Author

KG MacGregor was born in 1955 into a military family in Wilmington, North Carolina.

Following her graduation from Appalachian State University, she worked briefly in elementary education, but returned to earn a doctoral degree in journalism and mass communications from the University of North Carolina at Chapel Hill. Her love of both writing and math led to a second career in market research, where she consulted with clients in the publishing, television and travel industries.

The discovery of lesbian fan fiction prompted her to try her own hand at romantic storytelling in 2002 with a story called *Shaken*. In 2005, MacGregor signed with Bella Books, which published Goldie Award finalist *Just This Once*. Her sixth Bella novel, *Out of Love*, won the 2007 Lambda Literary Award for Women's Romance, and the 2008 Goldie Award in Lesbian Romance. In 2008, she proudly announced the return of the Shaken Series with its first installment, *Without Warning*.

To KG, there is no better praise for her work than hearing she has created characters her readers want to know and have as friends. Please visit her at www.kgmacgregor.com.

Dedication

To the adventurous spirit in all of us.

Acknowledgments

When I was thirteen, I fell in love with Africa through Joy Adamson's stories of the lioness Elsa and her cubs. My visit to Kenya and Tanzania in the summer of 2001 was a dream come true. Over the course of my visit, which included an eight-day trek to the summit of Mt. Kilimanjaro, my admiration for the rich heritage of those living in the shadow of the mountain soared. I thank them for their hospitality, and for giving me the adventure of a lifetime.

I appreciate editor Cindy Cresap's hard work in whipping this story into shape. If it makes sense, hangs together and fulfills its potential, it's her fault. If it doesn't, she'll get to say she told me so.

Thanks also to Jenny for the technical edit, and to Karen for her uncanny ability to see words that aren't there, and words that are there, but shouldn't be.

Prologue

Never in her life had Mary Kate Sasser faced such a harrowing challenge, a quest so daunting that not even her months of meticulous preparation could quell her doubts. And this was just the plane ride!

Once they stabilized, she forced herself to loosen the death grip on her armrest. As if holding on would matter should this tin can disintegrate in turbulence at twenty-eight thousand feet.

Not exactly a seasoned traveler, Mary Kate had no idea what a normal flight was supposed to feel like. All she knew was they were bouncing over a third world country with a third world airline, probably in a plane that had been junked by somebody else after flying a couple of hundred million miles. This flight was much rougher than her first leg, a sixteen-hour adventure over the ocean, where she had been crammed in the middle section between the Michelin Man and a woman with a baby. Her attempts to sleep were thwarted either by the big guy drooping into her space, the baby pulling her hair or her own gloomy thoughts about her crumbling relationship with Bobby Britton. The last bit annoyed her to no end. After thinking about it all the way across the ocean, she had finally solidified the decision that should have made her happy. But instead of feeling as though she were finally in control of her life, she had already begun to second-guess herself about what she was giving up. The closer she got to Tanzania, the more she hoped for resolve.

At least this time she had a seatmate who stayed on his side of the armrest. He didn't seem nervous about all this bouncing, and she found that comforting. Her window seat offered little in the way of a view, as they had been stuck in the clouds since Johannesburg. The plains of Africa were down there somewhere, but her first look would have to wait until touchdown, and only then if her prayers for a safe landing were answered.

In sharp contrast to her gloomy thoughts about Bobby and her fears of hurtling through the stratosphere, Mary Kate had never been so excited. Somewhere underneath all those clouds below was Mount Kilimanjaro, the highest peak on the continent, and her ultimate destination. If they didn't fall from the sky in a ball of fire, getting there would be worth it.

She had sucked in every small detail of the trip so far, from the robotic way they had marched through immigration in Johannesburg to the jumbled cadence of Swahili she had overheard as they boarded this flight. This was the experience of a lifetime, and while part of her thought it was a shame to be having that at twenty-four years old, at least she knew she would have it. Hardly anyone back in her tiny town of Mooresville, Georgia, would have an adventure like this to look back on.

The plane bounced again forcefully and she looked around the cabin for any signs of panic. No one else appeared nervous, and the flight attendants were up and about performing what looked like mundane duties. That had to be good news, she told herself, unless they were trained to act nonchalant at moments of impending doom.

With a deep, calming breath, she settled her shoulders against the seat back. Africa was all she had thought about for the past six months, ever since seeing a documentary on public television. She couldn't say why the mountain had called to her the way it had…maybe because Bobby made fun of it, saying it wasn't all that big a deal if a person could just walk to the top. It wasn't as if he aspired to scale the ice walls of Everest. His idea of a summer vacation was Myrtle Beach one year and Disney World the next. Repeat thirty times or until you died of boredom, whichever came first. That was all the adventure he needed, and it reinforced the growing realization that they weren't exactly made for each other. In fact, the whole year they had spent together seemed to her an exercise in trying to fit a square peg into a round hole.

As if belittling her about hiking to the summit of Kilimanjaro weren't enough, Bobby also had convinced himself and practically everyone else that she couldn't manage the trip on her own. He seemed to think a Y-chromosome was required for reading a schedule or navigating an airport or bus terminal. She could still hear him warning her that she would be stranded in the middle of nowhere if she missed a ride, and then be sorry for not letting him come along. What Mary Kate couldn't fathom was why he thought he knew all there was to know about getting around in a foreign country since he had never been farther from home than Branson, Missouri.

Of course, he wasn't the only one who had thought her solo trip was a bad idea. Her mother worried that she would plunge to her death from a cliff, even though Mary Kate had tried to explain that this expedition wasn't like that, that it was more of a steep hike than an actual climb. Then her father read in one of the brochures that Tanzania was primarily a Muslim country, and he immediately started worrying that terrorists would blow up the plane or the bus or the hotel or the café or the tent. And finally, there was her sister Carol Lee, whose biggest concern was that Bobby would break up with her over the whole thing.

No matter how many times she tried to push him out of her head, Bobby kept popping back up. She had told herself a hundred times since leaving Atlanta that she wouldn't spend the next sixteen days thinking about him. She was finally growing clear on what she had to do, and she was ready this time…as soon as she got back to Mooresville, or as he put it, once she got this out of her system.

She was getting worked up again, clenching her fists instead of squeezing the armrests. She didn't need Bobby's permission for this or anything else. Still, it was hard to go against him and her whole family over something nobody seemed to understand. No matter how many times she tried, she couldn't seem to explain why this trip was so important to her. It just was.

At least her mom had come around a little just before she left. Her Aunt Jean was on her side too, saying she had always wanted to go to Africa and see the wild animals. When Mary Kate told her she couldn't afford that part of the trip, that she had scraped up only enough to pay for the climb and the plane ticket, Aunt Jean produced a check for two thousand dollars and told her to keep her mouth shut. So thanks to Aunt Jean, she would have a five-night wildlife picture safari before heading back home.

Her stomach pitched again as the plane did, emptying her head of all thoughts except where she was sitting in relation to the emergency exits. By her watch, they were due to land soon. She hoped that had something to do with why they were suddenly losing altitude. The pilot was saying something on the loudspeaker...the only word she could make out was Kilimanjaro.

Suddenly, half the passengers from the other side of the plane were standing up, leaning over her row to look out the window. Fearing the wing was on fire, she made herself look, thinking that a request to have her ashes scattered over Africa would be timely.

"Holy shit."

The man beside her seemed a bit surprised at her choice of words, which she hadn't meant to utter aloud. Jutting well above the clouds below them was a massive tower, a hollowed crater with a glacial ice cap on its highest ridge. Up until that moment, she had managed to suppress her doubts about whether or not she would make it all the way to Uhuru Peak, the top of that ridge. Bleak and foreboding, it looked about as hospitable as the moon, not at all something a normal person with only foothills hiking experience could conquer. "Did he just say that was Kilimanjaro?"

The man nodded and pointed toward her hiking boots. "You climb?"

"I..." Going with Bobby to Myrtle Beach suddenly had its merits. "I'm going to try."

"Dangerous."

"Yeah, that's what I've heard." People had died on that mountain, most from acute altitude sickness. No wonder. It was just right there under the plane.

She pressed her face against the window to keep the mountain in sight until the plane banked. Then they were engulfed in white again, bouncing hard against the thick clouds on what she hoped was their final approach. Flight attendants were rushing around, picking up the cups and trash, bringing the seat backs forward and tray tables up.

Mary Kate tugged her seat belt another notch and gripped the armrests again, not caring at all if she left imprints in the plastic.

Chapter One

From the vista point on Rabun Bald, the Blue Ridge Mountains cascaded in the distance, giving way to the rolling foothills. Mary Kate closed her eyes and tried to imagine the view from the summit of Mount Kilimanjaro, the one she would see in exactly twenty-one days.

As she started down the steep slope, the loose gravel rolled under her left boot, throwing her off balance. She went into automatic recovery mode, jamming the pole into the dirt to stop her slide. Just as she was congratulating herself for avoiding a fall, her right foot skidded out from under her, dumping her on her behind. Tom Muncie was right about the descent being every bit as tough as going up, and requiring far more concentration. Her knees were throbbing, and the heavy pack had pounded into her lower back with each step until she figured out that adjusting the straps across her stomach helped her carry it higher.

This trial run up the second-highest peak in Georgia had been a success. The blooming bruise on her backside notwithstanding, she had done everything Tom had recommended in the brochure to test herself for the Kilimanjaro climb—two straight days of hiking steep, rugged terrain, fourteen miles in all. She was tired, but not exhausted. With that goal behind her, she was confident there wouldn't be any surprises two weeks from now when she started up the real mountain.

All of her new equipment had checked out. The backpack she had ordered over the Internet was perfect for a day hike. It had a built-in water bladder that held two liters, with a hose that clipped to her shoulder strap so she wouldn't have to reach around for a drink. The deep inner pouch was big enough for a fleece jacket, a rain poncho and an extra pair of shoes and socks, none of which she had needed this weekend, but she wanted to get used to carrying them. Her first-aid kit was stuffed into one of the pouches, along with a few snacks and an extra bottle of water. The webbed pockets on the outside held her camera and binoculars.

The best news was that her feet felt great, thanks to the fact she had worn her boots practically everywhere but church for the last three months. Tom said the loudest complaints on Kili came from hikers who bought brand-new boots and didn't break them in. Now she had done everything she could to prepare. The rest would come down to how well she handled the altitude, which was four times higher than she had hiked today in the Smokies.

She couldn't believe it was almost time to go, her six months of planning and preparation nearly over. She wished she were leaving tomorrow, but that had more to do with getting away from Mooresville than with going to Africa. She was tired of trying to explain to practically everybody why she wanted to do this, and especially why she didn't want Bobby to come along.

If only he had been reasonable last February, when she watched the documentary at his apartment. He had been working on the school budget that night, paying little attention to the television. From the get-go, he said it was stupid, that it wasn't such a big deal to climb Kilimanjaro because practically anybody could do it. But Mary Kate was fascinated by the idea and asked him right then if he would do it with her. He said no, that he would rather spend his vacation relaxing on the beach. Unable to get it out of her head, she checked out a few of the tour companies on the public TV Web site and found one that claimed a high success rate to the summit. Some of the routes had only a forty percent summit rate, and she showed that to Bobby so he could see that it wasn't as simple as he thought. He blew her off again, but by that time she was burning to do it, even if it meant going by herself.

Then out of the blue he changed his mind, announcing just last week that he had decided to come too. He said he didn't want to have to worry about her the whole time she was gone, and if he went, he would make sure they made all the connections and met up with their group. The way Mary Kate saw it, that would have been marginally okay—his natural condescension aside—if he had changed his mind a few months ago and started working out with her and taking the whole thing seriously. The fact that he waited until the last minute to be patronizing pissed her off. And of course, he had made his big declaration during Sunday dinner in front of her whole family, prompting her mom and dad to say how relieved they were. Her sister Carol Lee had practically swooned.

That's when the fireworks started, because Mary Kate had simply said thanks, but no thanks, and to pass her the cornbread. Everyone at the table froze and looked at her as if she had asked for heroin, so she just leaned over and got the cornbread herself. Then they started talking all at once, and after she had her bread buttered, she explained that she wanted to go by herself, that's how she had planned it for five months, and now she was looking forward to doing it on her own. Besides, he hadn't trained at all, and she didn't want to have to keep stopping and waiting for him to catch his breath.

She could still hear him whine, and couldn't resist mocking him, even though he wasn't around to hear it. "It's just a hike, Mary Kate. Anybody can do it." She shook her head thinking she needed to stop thinking about all of this if it was going to make her talk to herself. Besides, this weekend wasn't about him. It was about her making sure she was ready to go.

Her best friend Deb Demers had suggested this place for her trial run. Rabun Bald, at almost five thousand feet, was the ideal place to try out her gear and test her stamina. They had done this hike together four years earlier when Deb was going to college not far from here. Today was almost like old times, except Deb was waiting for her on a ridge down below. They had gone to the summit together yesterday, but Deb had been cussing her out ever since, especially last night when she was soaking in the tub at the motel. No way was Deb going to do another seven-mile hike today.

Other than her penchant for occasionally taking Mary Kate's name in vain, friends didn't come any better than Deb. When Bobby first said he didn't want to go to Africa, Mary Kate had asked Deb to come, but Deb's mother was sick with lupus, and sixteen days was too long to be gone.

The two of them had been practically inseparable in high school, which prompted a few spiteful rumors about them being lesbians, but they weathered that storm, thanks to Mary Kate's mom being a teacher and basically telling everybody to knock it off or else. That had led to a humiliating mother-daughter talk, in which Mary Kate was advised to take a cue from her other classmates and go out with a few boys.

Of course, her mom didn't know then what Mary Kate knew, which was that Deb really was a lesbian, and that she had seriously considered the possibility that she might be too. She had never been all that interested in boys, at least not like most of her friends were. The closest she had ever come to a crush back then was a fascination with Darcy Mathis, the prettiest girl in her high school, and again in college with her roommate Jessica. Her curiosity had led her to test the waters in college with Becky Dugan, a basketball teammate, but the spark wasn't there. It was there for Becky, though, and Mary Kate hadn't minded all that much. Gay people were just like everyone else as far as she was concerned, and she didn't care what people at college thought about her. The people in Mooresville were a different matter, though, because that reflected on her whole family.

She caught a glimpse of Deb's red shirt on the ridge right below and gave a yell. When she arrived at the ledge, she found her stretched out in the shade with a book.

"It's about time you got here, Mary Kate. I already ate your lunch."

"You better be lying, girl. I've been thinking about that sandwich for the last three hours."

Deb pulled it out of the thermal bag and set it on the rock next to her. "Okay, I saved your sandwich, but I ate all the cookies."

"All of them? There was a whole bag."

"I know, but the chocolate chips were melting. I didn't want you to get your new clothes all messy."

Mary Kate looked down at her filthy shorts and shirt, then back at Deb, who was batting her eyes innocently. She poked the side of her boot with the sharp tip of her walking stick.

"Ow!"

"Big baby."

"If you hurt me, you'll have to carry me down on your back."

"I can get you down a lot easier than that. I'll just push you off." Mary Kate dropped her backpack and collapsed beside it, remembering too late her new bruise.

"You got here sooner than I thought you would. Did you go all the way up?"

"Of course I did."

"I guess it's a lot quicker when you don't have to drag somebody else's ass behind you."

"I'm too polite to say something like that." She bit around the crust of the peanut butter and jelly sandwich, saving the creamiest part for last.

"Since when?" Deb unscrewed the top from a sports drink and handed it to her. "You think you're ready?"

Mary Kate answered with a nod and chased the peanut butter down her throat with the sports drink. "I wish I could leave tomorrow."

"It's just two more weeks."

"I know. But I'll be crazy by then. Especially if I have to listen to Bobby keep whining about not being able to come."

"Say the word and I'll kick his ass."

Mary Kate had no doubt she could. Deb was as tough as they come. "Why should you get to have all the fun?"

"Why's he being such a prick about this?"

Deb liked Bobby just fine, but only when Mary Kate did. When she was mad at him, Deb was even madder. That was a true friend. "He's just being Bobby. He's thinks he's supposed to save the day because he's a guy and I couldn't possibly do this by myself."

"I don't know how you stand it. I'd have beaten the shit out of him by now."

It wasn't hard to picture her doing that, and it made Mary Kate laugh.

"Makes me glad I'm queer," Deb said. "I don't need to act all helpless just so some guy can feel like a big man."

"You don't think I'm acting helpless, do you?"

"No, and I bet that's precisely what's bugging him."

She was probably right about that, Mary Kate thought. "Because he doesn't get to play the knight in shining armor."

"Right. I never have been able to figure out what you see in him."

"Come on, you know he's a nice guy."

"He's all right, I guess."

That was probably the highest mark Deb could give him, so Mary Kate took it in stride. "He just avoids you because you beat up his brother."

"Shit, that was eleven years ago."

She laughed again, remembering it like it was yesterday. Deb had caught Corey Britton cheating off her math test, so she changed her answers and got him to copy the wrong numbers down. He got a zero on the test and told his friends it was because she was stupid. He couldn't talk after that because his jaw was wired shut from the knuckle sandwich she fed him, and there wasn't a soul in Mooresville who hadn't heard the story and teased him about it.

"Bobby's not a bad guy. He just has a lot of old-fashioned

ideas, like everybody else in Mooresville. At least he's not a redneck."

"True."

Whether Mary Kate wanted to admit it or not, Bobby was probably the best catch in Hurston County. He was college educated and had a good job as the assistant principal at the elementary school where she taught special education. He was nice looking, he didn't use tobacco in any form, and he drove a car instead of a truck. It didn't get any better than that in Mooresville. And he could be the sweetest guy in the world— except when it came to this Africa thing. On that, he had been a jerk from day one.

Bobby had made his biggest mess by telling practically everybody in Mooresville last year that he had gotten her an engagement ring for Christmas. And naturally, he gave it to her on Christmas Eve right in front of her whole family. That's when the problems started, because Mary Kate wouldn't take it. She told him she just wasn't ready to get married. Her dad took him off in the other room and said who knows what, and her mom said she couldn't imagine what she was looking for if Bobby Britton wasn't good enough. Carol Lee just called her crazy.

Mary Kate didn't want to tell everybody the real reason, which was that she just didn't feel the way she wanted to feel about the person she was going to spend her whole life with. What she wanted was to find a guy that made her feel the way dreaming about Darcy and Jessica had. She wanted to be comfortable with Bobby the way she was with Deb, instead of knotted up about having to say and do all the right things.

The whole Bobby thing was in a sort of limbo for now, and had been since Christmas. They had talked about the ring and Bobby said he would take it back and wait for her to tell him when she was ready. He promised not to pressure her about it at all, and mostly, he had kept his word. He said if he got too tired of waiting, he would ask one more time, but that would be the last. And she had promised if she ever decided for sure it wasn't going to work out, she wouldn't string him along.

Though she hadn't meant for it to, this Kilimanjaro thing was turning into a test for them, and Bobby wasn't faring so well. It bothered her that she didn't have his support for this climb, and even more that she didn't seem to have his respect. Worse than that, he had lectured her about spending her savings when she might want to be thinking about putting together a down payment on a house. And he didn't mean her house. He meant their house, even though they weren't officially—

"You ready to get down off this mountain, Mary Kate?"

She wondered how long she had been staring off into space. "What I'm ready for is something else to eat."

"Me too. This sitting around on my ass all day waiting for you is hard work."

"Why don't you go get the car and come get me?"

"Why don't I just wiggle my nose and pop both of us back to Mooresville without having to drive four hours?"

"That's too fast. I don't want to get there until it's too late for Bobby to come over."

"Just tell him no."

"Don't worry, I will." She had plenty of practice with that recently. Too tired, too much to do, cramps, headache… She had used every excuse she could think of to keep from spending too much time together. That's how bad things had gotten, all because of this trip.

She pushed herself up and offered a hand to Deb. "You want me to carry any of your stuff? I drank most of my water, so my pack's light."

"That's okay. I don't have that much now that the cookies are gone."

"You really ate that whole bag by yourself?"

"Correct."

They walked downhill about a hundred yards in silence. Mary Kate had gotten stiff sitting on the rock, but the muscles in her hips and legs seemed to relax more with every step.

"I've been meaning to tell you something…something about Bobby," Deb said, without turning around to make eye contact.

Mary Kate had suspected Deb had something else on her mind. Deb was usually careful not to butt in or give advice that wasn't asked for, especially advice about Bobby. "What about him?"

"If you decide you want to marry him, I won't give you a hard time about it. I know you're still thinking it over."

"I haven't thought much about it lately. I figured we'd talk some more when I got back."

Deb nodded, watching her feet instead of looking at Mary Kate. "I know I talk shit about him, but if he's what you want, I'll be there for you."

"I know you will, Deb. I've always known that." That was exactly what she wanted from Bobby, for him to be as easygoing as Deb and satisfied to let her have her own opinions. Instead, he always tried to smooth things out and strike a compromise so they could agree on practically everything. In theory, that might have been a good plan for building a relationship and avoiding conflict. But in reality, it felt like he was trying to water her down. "And I know if I get married, you're the kind of friend who would wear a pink bridesmaid dress at my wedding."

If looks could kill, the one Deb shot over her shoulder would have done it.

Chapter Two

Addison Falk skipped through the stalled traffic, tossing up an apologetic hand in the direction of a taxi driver trying to inch forward. An airport traffic cop was closing in on her friend Cyn's Honda Insight, which was parked illegally at the far curb. Addison wasted no time tossing her bags into the hatchback and sliding into the front seat. "Sorry I'm late."

Cyn lurched into the exit lane. "What took you so long?"

"It's Miami," she said, knowing her explanation would suffice.

"How's your mom?"

"All right, I guess. Hector built her a studio and she's getting back into painting again. She says hi." Cyn Juarez, her best friend since middle school, knew her mother because she had come along six years ago on a visit to Peru.

"I bet she was surprised to see how much you've changed."

"No shit." Since the start of her training last March, Addison had lost the extra fifteen pounds she had carried since puberty.

"Did you keep up your training?"

"I ran four miles a day—on hills." Her mother's neighborhood in suburban Lima had proven a greater challenge than the flat streets of Coral Gables. "I got Hector to pledge a thousand bucks, and he'll double it if I get to the top."

Friends of theirs had used the Kilimanjaro climb last year to generate press and raise money for breast cancer. Cyn liked the idea, and had coordinated with Summit Trail and Safari to do the same for the Miami Hunger Coalition. She and her husband Javier promoted it through Mercy Hospital, where Javier worked as a physician's assistant, and Addison had garnered almost twenty thousand dollars from the corporate sponsors she had developed as co-director of the Coalition, a volunteer position she had held throughout her MBA program.

"Javier and I have about six thousand between us."

"Six? You guys had about eight when I left. What happened?"

"It's complicated." She shot Addison a sheepish look. "I'll explain it when we get to your house."

Ten minutes later, they turned onto a posh, tree-lined street in Coral Gables. Addison's home was a two-story Mediterranean, yellow with a red tile roof. A For Sale sign stood at the curb.

"I can't believe your father's really selling this house."

"Believe it. Reginald Falk at his finest." Her father had moved to his native London when Addison finished high school, but kept the house for her while she had attended college at the University of Miami. Now that she had wrapped up her master's degree in finance, he expected her to join his investment firm. Selling the house out from under her was his way of forcing the issue.

"I can't believe you're really moving. Have you gotten any nibbles from the résumés you sent out?"

"If I did, they're lying on the floor," she said. She pushed open the heavy oak door and dropped her bags in the foyer. Someone, most likely a real estate agent, had stacked her mail on a table, but Addison was too distracted to look through it. "So what's this about you losing pledges?"

Cyn drew a deep breath and said in a squeaky voice, "We're not going."

"What?" Addison refused to believe she had heard that. Three of their other friends had already dropped out, and that left only her. "This whole trip was your idea."

"I know, but…"

She wanted to get angry, but something about Cyn's expression stopped her. "Spill it."

"I'm pregnant."

Her jaw dropped suddenly as Cyn's face broke into an enormous smile. "Aaaaaaah!" she screamed, wrapping Cyn in a fierce hug and twirling her around. "Tell me everything…well, not the icky boy stuff."

"I went to get my shots for the trip and the nurse asked me if there was any chance I might be pregnant. I'd skipped a couple of periods, but I thought it was all the training. I said it might be possible, so they did a test. I'm due in February."

"So you guys cancelled. Did you get your money back?" She let go of Cyn and whirled around to grab her backpack, where her cell phone was tucked in the side pocket. "I should call and cancel too."

"You can't. You're the last one, and with our pledges, that makes almost thirty thousand dollars for the Coalition. You have to go, Addison."

"By myself?"

"You were going to be paired with somebody anyway. And you've done so much to get ready." Cyn looked at her with pleading eyes. "Just go. You'll have a great time. I'll feel guilty if you don't."

Addison groaned and dropped into a chair. She thought again about why their plans had changed, and her misery gave way to happiness. "A baby."

"A little Javier."

"Awwwww."

"And I already bought a whole bunch of stuff for the trip. You can take it all—toilet paper, camp soap, water purification tablets."

"You're making this sound like so much fun."

"It will be. Look at it as your last hurrah before joining the rat race."

Addison snorted. "I'll probably come home to find my stuff in the street."

"Then you can come and live with us. You can be our nanny and teach little Javier how to invest his allowance."

"Be careful what you ask for."

Cyn shrugged. "There could be worse things than having you help my kid get rich."

"I can't believe it, Cyn. This is so great. I bet Javier's over the moon."

"He's panicking already. At first he wanted his mother to come live with us."

"Shouldn't you be the one panicking about that?"

"Actually, we're talking about the possibility of moving back to Puerto Rico. Javier has this big idea about raising his son the way he was raised, on a simple farm with his family all around. You know, like your parents wanted before you threw a fit and refused to go with either one of them."

Indeed, Addison knew that story well, though her upbringing had been far from the simple life Javier wanted for his son. Her parents had fought bitterly after their divorce over whether she would be raised in Peru or England. A family court judge had seen fit to ask her what she wanted, and at fourteen, the answer was simple. She wanted to stay in Miami, so her father reluctantly obliged. Her mother married Hector and returned to Lima, and Addison visited over Christmas and summers until college. "Would you be all right with that?"

Cyn shrugged. "I like it there. And I can't argue with how Javier turned out."

Selfishly, though, Addison felt the walls caving in. The house would sell soon and her best friends were probably leaving Miami. Not that it mattered. Her father expected her to start work in London as soon as she finished the climb. This part of her life was officially ending.

"I need to go," Cyn said. "I'm supposed to do a pickup at the food bank and take it down to Homestead. Want to come?"

Addison was exhausted from her long flight. "Not tonight. But I'll call over to the Coalition tomorrow and see if they need me for any runs this weekend."

"Okay. I'll bring that stuff over Sunday night and help you pack."

Alone in the big house, she eyed her suitcase and decided unpacking could wait. A quick perusal of her unopened mail yielded eight responses to her employment queries, five of which were polite rejections. The others invited her to proceed to the next step, which was to fill out the formal application packet.

She no longer had the luxury of time. She had only until the house sold to explore other options before making the move to London. It wasn't that her father's offer was unattractive. His company, Global Allied Investments, financed business development all over the world. Addison's chief complaint was that they focused more on industrialized countries, such that the people who made money were the ones who already had it. She felt they could make a bigger mark by working with third-world governments to launch more small businesses on a self-sustaining scale. Once she made her philosophy known, her father had turned it into the proverbial carrot, promising her the chance to research and identify communities that might benefit from her vision—as long as she also found lucrative opportunities for their investors.

It was the idea of moving to London that gave her pause, though she enjoyed the city. She loved visiting and even had friends there, a group of lesbians she had met four years ago during London Pride. In her heart, though, she was American born and bred. She belonged to its history and culture, just as her father belonged to England and her mother to Peru. Both of them had chosen to go home, and while it felt disjointed to have her parents separated by nine thousand miles, she understood their yearnings for home.

If only she could make her father understand hers.

Chapter Three

"I thought you were just going for a couple of weeks, Mary Kate. I didn't know you were moving there."

Mary Kate held her breath and watched her mother instantly assess the contents of the cluttered room. She could practically see the wheels turning inside her head as she mentally sized up the challenge. In all of Mooresville, there was no better organizer than Mary Nell Sasser. Whether in her kitchen, her closets or her biology classroom, everything was sorted and in its place. Mary Kate had inherited the neatness part, but didn't have her knack for making the most of space. Still, she could have managed packing on her own, but her mother's other, more dubious skill was her refusal to take no for an answer. Ostensibly, she wanted to share some tricks for keeping things pressed and neat, but Mary Kate suspected another motive, most likely a last-ditch plea to get her either to change her mind about going, or to let Bobby come along.

She was tired of having to defend her decision to make this trip. But at least her mom's insistence on coming over tonight gave her an excuse for not spending the evening with Bobby. If she had to argue with somebody, she preferred it not be him. As excited as she was about her trip, she looked forward to returning home and having the stress of the past six months behind her once and for all.

Everything she planned to take on the trip was sorted in her living room according to when she would need it, the cold weather items on the couch, lightweight clothes in two piles on the coffee table, and rain gear stacked in a chair. Anything that wasn't clothing was piled on the dining table. Her backpack and two canvas bags, one of which was a yellow duffel provided by Summit Trail and Safari, sat empty in the middle of the floor.

"Believe me, there is nothing here I won't need. Now all we have to do is figure out how to get it all in these bags."

Her mother made a circle of the staging area. "These bags are plenty big for everything. We just have to arrange—"

"It's trickier than that." Mary Kate held up the Summit bag. "Everything on the couch, plus my sleeping bag and walking sticks, has to go in here."

"All that? How come?"

"They have porters to carry our bags on the mountain, but this is the only one we can take. That's why they gave it to us, so they'd all be the same size. Anything that can't be crammed into this bag has to go in my backpack, which means I have to carry it. Believe me, I don't want to carry more than I have to."

"What is this?" Her mother picked up a balaclava. "You planning on robbing a bank?"

"That's to cover my face when we go up to the summit. It's supposed to get below zero." Well below zero, she thought. She showed off her new gloves and liners, gaiters, long johns, fleece tights and pullovers, and windproof pants and jacket. "And we have to put everything inside these trash bags in case it rains on the trail."

"Well, now that's a good idea. If your bag gets wet, your clothes still stay dry."

"And my sleeping bag."

"When are you ever going to use this stuff again, Mary Kate?"

"I don't know. I might leave some of it there…you know, give it to the porters. Tom says they don't have much."

"You bought all these things special for this trip and you're just going to leave them there?"

"Maybe some of them. Like you said, I'll probably never use them again."

Her mother shook her head, which Mary Kate read as her way of saying she thought it was all ridiculous without actually having to speak the words. At least they weren't arguing.

For the next hour, they folded and rolled, wrapped and tightened, and packed and repacked, until the Summit bag closed with ease. The other bag was mostly for the lightweight clothes she would wear on the safari and things she planned to carry in her backpack on the trail—her rain gear, extra shoes, energy bars and first-aid kit.

"The first thing you need will probably be in the bottom of the bag, Mary Kate. That's the way it always is."

"I know. But I shouldn't have to open the yellow one until we get to camp on Monday."

"How are we going to know where you are? Can you call us on your cell phone?"

"Tom says they won't work in Africa. There aren't enough towers to relay the signal. But there's supposed to be a phone at the hotel where we're staying. I can call you when we get back from the climb."

"That's one call I won't want to miss."

"You better not, because Tom says it costs twenty dollars for three minutes. I'd hate to get your answering machine."

"Twenty dollars?" She said it as if she had been mortally wounded. "And you'll need to call Bobby too. Why don't you just call him and tell him to call us?"

"I guess I can do that. Will you call Deb then?" She wouldn't ask Bobby to do that.

"Yeah, we'll get a little chain going." With the larger bags packed, they began to sort the things she would carry in her backpack on the plane. "Did you and Bobby get everything worked out?"

She hated talking about Bobby to anyone other than Deb, since everyone else seemed more concerned about his feelings than hers. Her mother wasn't as bad as Carol Lee, but after the big blowup over telling Bobby he couldn't come, she wasn't sure whose side anyone was on anymore. "Yeah, he's taking me tomorrow."

"You still mad at him?"

"I'm not mad, Mom. I'm just frustrated. I told you, I don't like him making me feel like I'm some sort of bimbo who can't do anything by herself."

"I don't think he really feels like that, Mary Kate. I think he just feels bad for not saying he'd go with you to begin with. He's trying to make up for it."

"But he could have changed his mind six months ago when I booked the trip. Or even three months ago. Why did he have to wait until the last minute, and why did he have to make it some big gallant gesture about taking care of me?"

"You know how men are. Sometimes it just works best to let them think we can't get on without them."

Mary Kate thought that was bullshit, but she knew better than to use a word like that with her mother, even at twenty-four years old. "Seriously, can you see me doing that?"

"You got me there." She laughed and fell back on the couch, a sure sign she was planning to stay and talk awhile. "Sometimes I can't imagine you married at all, Mary Kate. You don't like to be told what to do."

"Who does?"

She shrugged. "Some people."

Her sister Carol Lee would love it. "Shouldn't marriage be a partnership?"

"It is. And if you get really good at it, you can get everything you want. You just have to train him to give it to you."

"Obviously, I'm not any good at that."

"I wouldn't say that. You got Bobby to say he'd come with you, even though he didn't really want to. It just took him too

24

long to figure it out. Maybe he learned he better not beat around the bush next time."

"I don't want to have to play games like that. And I don't want Bobby thinking he has to take care of me all the time. I can take care of myself."

"I'm sure you can." If there was such a thing as a matronizing look, her mother was giving it now. "But Bobby wants to feel like you need him for that. It's a silly man thing, and he's a little stubborn about it sometimes."

That was the first time anybody in her family had ever said anything negative about Bobby. It took Mary Kate a few seconds for the shock to wear off.

"I don't blame you for not wanting him to go, Mary Kate. But you're going to have to smooth this over as soon as you get back if you want to have a future with him. You can't keep him guessing about whether you're going to run off and do something else next."

"It's not like I have a long list to check off. But this is important to me. I think it'll be great to say I climbed the highest mountain on a whole continent."

"I know. But mountain climbing isn't on Bobby's list. He's ready to settle down and have a family."

She could practically feel her nose sliding out of joint, which meant this conversation was at high risk of becoming just another stressful argument to pile on top of the others. "Can I ask a simple question? Why does it seem like my own family cares more about what Bobby wants than what I want?"

"Is that what it feels like?"

"Not really." When it came to confrontations with her family, she was an avowed chickenshit. No wonder everyone thought they could lead her around by the nose. "I just wish somebody could see my side of this."

"I can see your side, Mary Kate. But I'm still worried about you going off by yourself."

"Then answer me this. Why does everybody think I'm so helpless?"

"Probably because the rest of us would be helpless if we were doing what you're doing. I can tell by the way you've gotten yourself ready to go that you aren't even a little bit afraid. You're probably the only one of us who has courage like that."

It was hard not to grin and blush at hearing praise like that from her mother. "I'm too excited to be afraid."

"That's all right, as long as you remember to be careful. I mean that. Watch where you step, keep an eye on the people around you, and don't let your guard down. You have to come back here in one piece."

"I promise to do that."

"You'd better." She folded her arms for emphasis and crossed her feet on the coffee table. "And then you're going to have to deal with Bobby, whether you like it or not."

"I know, Mom. I'm not going to keep putting it off. It's like you said. I just don't know if I want all the same things he wants. I definitely don't want them right now."

"Then you ought not rush into anything. Getting married isn't something you do for everybody else. It has to be what you want."

Mary Kate thought for an instant that she needed to clean out her ears. She couldn't believe her mother was actually agreeing with her. "I sometimes feel like the second I take that ring, I'll be following a script for the rest of my life. He knows he wants three kids. Dad's already got our house planned for that lot on Grandpa's land. What if I want to travel more and see things? The only way that's ever going to happen is for Bobby to want it too, and I don't think he ever will."

"Getting married shouldn't feel like you're going off to the gallows."

"I know. But it does, and that's why I'm so scared to say yes."

"Do you love Bobby?"

She waited too long to answer for anything else to sound convincing, so she admitted the truth. "I do, Mom. But I don't feel like I always thought I would."

"And how's that?"

"Well...you see how Carol Lee is about Wayne."

Her mother rolled her eyes, making Mary Kate feel ridiculous for using her sister as an example. Every boyfriend she had ever had was The Eternal One as far as Carol Lee was concerned.

"Your sister just wants to be married. I don't think it matters to her if it's Wayne or Corey or the mailman."

"Bad example. But I was thinking the other day about my roommate Jessica. She was crazy about Chuck before they got married. All she could talk about was what their life was going to be like and how happy they'd be."

"Isn't that what Bobby does with you?"

"Yeah, but it's not what I do with him. I wish I did. Then it would be easy."

"The decision part's supposed to be easy. You shouldn't have to wring your hands about it."

"That's what I feel like I'm doing. I know he loves me, but I'm scared the rest of it will be too hard." She had never talked to her mother like this before, and tears were stinging her eyes. "I don't want to let everybody down."

Her mother leaned forward and held out her hand, which Mary Kate took. "You don't have to please anybody but yourself, honey. Not Bobby, not your dad, and not me. If this scares you too much, just take a big step back."

"People are going to think I'm crazy, Mom."

"You don't have to care what people think. Nobody gets to make this decision but you. We're going to love you no matter what you decide."

This was a totally different conversation than the one she had dreaded, and she had to admit she felt better about everything— even Bobby—just knowing she had her mother's support to break up with him if that's what she needed to do. "I don't know what's going to happen. I'm just upset with him right now. Things will probably be okay when I get back."

"You know how I feel about Bobby. I think he's a fine young man, and I'd be proud to have him for a son-in-law. But that

27

won't be worth a hill of beans to me or your dad if you're not happy."

"Thanks, Mom. I feel better just from talking about it."

"You don't talk to me like your sister does. You never have."

Something told her that might start to change a little, especially since she now felt she had her mother squarely on her side.

Chapter Four

"You sure you don't want anything, Mary Kate?"

"I'm sure."

"Not even a jelly biscuit?"

"No, I had breakfast already." The engine idled as they waited to approach the speaker. Out of consideration for the clerk on the other end, Bobby never pulled up until he was ready to give his whole order. It was hard to get mad at him when he usually had other people's best interests at heart, though sometimes his quirks made her crazy.

"If your plane's late, it might be a long time before you get anything else to eat."

"I have some energy bars in my backpack. I'll be fine."

"You don't want to eat all those up, Mary Kate. It's not like they sell them at the corner Seven-Eleven in Africa."

She wanted to point out that he didn't know that for a fact, but that would have been petty. Bobby was persistent about everything, something she had learned to deal with. Still, she was on the verge of screaming at him just to get his fucking coffee so they could go. She usually saved the F-bomb, however, for when she was absolutely furious and wanted him to know it. "I really don't want anything, thank you. Just get your coffee."

He finally pulled forward and ordered a large coffee with four creams and four sugars. He didn't like coffee much, but he appreciated its effects. She took the Styrofoam cup from him and stirred in the condiments as he collected and counted his change.

"This should keep you awake all day."

"I hope so. I have a meeting at the superintendent's office this afternoon."

It was a big deal for him to take off half a day to drive her to the airport in Atlanta. As a school administrator, he wasn't off all summer like she was. His only vacation was two weeks in the summer, and the week between Christmas and New Year's Day.

"I really appreciate you doing this for me, Bobby. I know it's going to make for a long day."

"It's all right. But we could have slept a whole extra half hour if you'd stayed at my place last night. Nobody would have seen us because we would have left before they were up."

Appearances were important in Mooresville. If her car ever sat out in front of his apartment overnight, the whole school would have been whispering about it the next day. That made it hard for them to have much of a love life, but they had managed to spend a few nights together since last summer when they started dating. Most of those nights were before she started training for the climb, and all of them were at his place. He said he felt more comfortable there than at her apartment.

"It worked out better this way. I didn't sleep much last night."

"You worried about something?"

"No, just excited I guess. I got up in the night and went through all my stuff again just to make sure I had everything." She wanted her words back as soon as they left her lips, because she knew he would ask about the—

"Are you wearing the money belt I gave you?"

Damn it. "No. It pinches my waist."

"But you're going to put it on when we get to the airport,

right?"

"Bobby, I didn't bring it."

"Mary Kate!" That was his I'm-about-to-give-you-a-lecture voice. "You didn't even bring it? I bought it special for you."

"It isn't comfortable. I tried it when Deb and I went to Rabun Bald. It gets in the way of the strap on my backpack."

"I can't believe you. Your things aren't going to be safe in that backpack. What if somebody steals it, or…" By the look on his face, his mind was turning over all the sinister possibilities. "Or you drop it off a cliff or something? There goes your passport, your money, your plane ticket."

She wasn't about to tell him they weren't taking those things along on the hike. Tom had explained the procedure at the hotel for safeguarding their things while they were gone, but she knew Bobby would go ballistic to find out she was entrusting a bunch of Africans to watch her belongings. "If the tour company thought we needed one, I'm sure they would have recommended it."

He sighed, too indulgently for her taste, but she was used to it. He always thought he knew best. "Fine. But if you lose something important, you're going to be mad at yourself for not wearing it."

"I hope you wouldn't wish something like that on me just to be able to say I told you so."

"Now that's just silly. You know I'm not wishing anything bad to happen. If I had my way, you wouldn't even be going."

She bit her tongue again. The next sixteen days were hers, and she didn't want to have to spend them thinking about a big fight. "You know as well as I do that staying home is no guarantee something bad won't happen. Look what happened to Paige Riley." Paige was Carol Lee's boyfriend's cousin's wife. "She went out to get her mail one day and got shot by a deer hunter. She never knew what hit her."

"That's just it. We don't have any control over things like that so we have to be careful whenever we can. And that means not deliberately making reckless choices."

Her patience nearly ended then and there. Even Bobby

seemed to sense that he had stepped over a line.

"I'm not saying you're being reckless, Mary Kate. But I love you, and I can't help but worry about you doing this. I just wish you had agreed to let me come too."

She sighed and felt as though six months of frustration came out with her breath. "Why? You said yourself you had no interest in seeing Africa or climbing Kilimanjaro. I'm not afraid to go by myself, and whether you believe it or not, I'm pretty sure I can manage to keep up with my things and get on the right bus, so you don't have to worry the whole time I'm gone."

He fixed his face in a pout, which set her off even more. She was tired of putting his feelings first, always being diplomatic to soften the blow to his ego.

"Really, Bobby. I've been looking forward to this trip since February. I've worked hard to get in shape for it, and I've planned every single detail all by myself. It may be nothing to you, but it's the most exciting thing I've ever done, and I haven't even been able to talk to you about it because all you can think about is how it affects you. You haven't encouraged me. You haven't asked me any questions or shown any interest at all. All you've done is belittle the whole idea and try to make me feel like an idiot who can't even cross the street by herself."

She knew she had finally struck a nerve because the tips of his ears were turning red and his jaw was set like a brick. Her normal *modus operandi* was to bail him out after a disagreement by changing the subject just to take the sting away, but this time she wanted him to feel it.

Bobby waited a full minute before speaking. "I'm sorry."

"Apology accepted." She knew she could have pressed him into groveling, but Bobby usually took criticism to heart, and when he apologized, it was genuine. It made her wish she had told him a few weeks ago that he was ruining her fun. Instead, she had concerned herself with his feelings.

They drove along in silence until veering south on Interstate 285 toward the airport. She already dreaded the awkward parting.

"Your plane leaves at eleven, right?"

"Five till."

He chuckled. "I bet you're not too excited about what happens after that."

She recognized his joke about her mortal fear of flying as an attempt to lighten their collective mood, and she appreciated it. "Okay, that part I haven't been looking forward to as much."

"What time do you get there?"

She retrieved her travel documents from her backpack and thumbed through to the itinerary. "I left one of these with Mom if you want to make a copy and keep up with where I am. My plane gets into Johannesburg at nine o'clock tomorrow morning, which will be two a.m. for you. And then at eleven thirty, I board the Air Tanzania flight for Kilimanjaro. That's two and a half hours, but there's another time change."

"So when I get up tomorrow at seven…"

"I should be landing at Kilimanjaro."

He shook his head and laughed. "Don't take this the wrong way, but I wish I was going just to see you drag your butt off that plane tomorrow."

"I'll be comatose."

"You'll be dragging your butt up the mountain too."

"Maybe not. I have all day Sunday to rest. We don't leave on our hike until Monday morning."

"I remember…something about the plane schedule."

"Right. This flight doesn't go on Saturdays, so I had to go a day early. It should work out fine though. At least I'll be rested up and acclimated a little to the time change by the time we leave."

"And how many days is your hike?"

She would have given anything for him to have asked these questions back when she was dying to tell him about it. At least he was making an effort now, even though it had taken her getting angry to get him to do it. "It's supposed to take us six and a half days to get to the top and one and a half to hike back down. And we summit in the middle of the night, so that means we get there Sunday morning."

"How come they make you climb it at night?"

"Somebody said it was because the sun melts the ice and makes it too slick to walk on. If we go at night, it's easier to walk."

"Except you can't see where you're going. They ought to just give you those pickaxes so you can get a grip in the ice."

To hear him talk, it was clear he hadn't listened to a word she had said about the hike. "I picked this time to go because we'll have a full moon. The tour company said we should be able to see everything, but we'll have flashlights if we need them."

"I hope you get good weather."

"Me too." Just because she had spent two hundred dollars on rain gear didn't mean she wanted to use it.

"Do you know anything about the people in your group?"

"Not much. There are fourteen of us from all over the country, but I don't know any more than that."

"I hope they're nice."

"I'm sure they will be. And I bet we've all spent the last six months the same way, getting in shape and deciding what to take, so we'll have that in common."

They passed a directional sign for the airport, and Bobby moved into the exit lane. Mary Kate was glad they had smoothed things over. She could get on the plane now and push it out of her head, thinking only about Africa for the next two weeks.

"If you want to, you can let me out at the curb. Then you can get back to Mooresville and not miss too much work."

"You know I'm not going to just dump you out on the sidewalk, Mary Kate. I can be a little late. It's not like I don't work nights and weekends at home."

That much was true. The principal at their school was nearing retirement, and dependent on Bobby for things that required details or patience. There was little doubt Bobby would take over soon as principal, quite an accomplishment for a guy who was only twenty-nine years old.

They followed the signs for the parking garage, finally securing a space on the fourth level. Mary Kate's only experience with this airport was a couple of times dropping people off, so she began to feel as if her adventure was already underway.

Bobby opened the trunk and reached for the yellow canvas bag. She grabbed the smaller bag and backpack.

"Mary Kate, how are you going to carry all these bags to the top of that mountain? They must weigh sixty pounds."

"All I have to carry is my backpack. We have porters for everything else."

"That's all? Just your backpack?"

"Just the stuff I need during the day."

"Wow, I don't think you ever told me that part. You shouldn't have any trouble at all getting to the top if you don't have to carry all your stuff."

"It still isn't going to be easy, Bobby. It's over nineteen thousand feet, and we have to do it in temperatures below zero. The last mile of that is like walking up stairs that don't ever end, and the oxygen just gets thinner and thinner."

"But all you have to do is keep walking." He set down the Summit bag so he could put the parking ticket in his wallet and she picked it up, slinging it over the opposite shoulder from the lighter bag and backpack. "I'll get that, Mary Kate."

She was thoroughly annoyed again, and ignored him. "I can manage these. Why don't you find a staircase and try to walk up it for seven hours? It should be a piece of cake for somebody like you."

"Now don't be like that." He hurried to catch up with her, lifting the Summit bag from her shoulder. "I was trying to be encouraging, because I know you're going to get to the top. That's what you want, isn't it?"

"Yeah, but so what? I will have accomplished something that's no big deal to you. Won't I be proud?"

"Man, I'm just stepping in it right and left. I'm not trying to—"

"You know what, Bobby? Talking about this is a bad idea. Why don't we just forget it?" She didn't want to leave this way. He wasn't going to miraculously get it all of a sudden, and she decided on the spot that it no longer mattered. This was her trip, not their trip. "Let's just get these bags checked."

They found the ticket counter for the flight to Johannesburg and joined the line.

"What all are you going to do while I'm gone?" She listened half-heartedly as Bobby described his schedule for the next two weeks—work, Sunday dinners with her family and a couple of recreation league softball games. Her thoughts wandered to the advice her mother had given her back in high school when she first started dating, that guys liked to talk about themselves, so she should try to think of interesting questions. Since women had trained them to be this way for generations, it didn't seem fair to complain now.

They finally made it to the front of the line, where Bobby had the good sense to stand quietly as she handled her own check-in. The agent said the flight was on time and would begin boarding about an hour before departure.

Then she watched her bags disappear through the X-ray machine, hoping they were headed where she was. There was plenty of time to kill, but she was eager to get her trip officially underway. In her mind, that didn't happen until she was on her own. "So I guess I should head on toward the gate."

"Yeah, and I need to get on back to work."

They walked slowly toward the entrance to the winding security line where only ticketed passengers were allowed. Bobby took her hand and squeezed it, looping his fingers through hers.

"Look, Mary Kate, I'm proud of what you're doing, no matter what stupid things I might have said. If you get to the top of that mountain, that's fantastic. But if you don't, that's fantastic too. I'm going to love you either way. The biggest thing is for you to take care of yourself."

She turned into his arms. He always gave good hugs, the kind that made her feel warm and safe. If she knew one thing for certain about Bobby, it was that he would never deliberately hurt her, no matter how clumsy his words or deeds.

"I know this is important to you, Mary Kate. But when you get back, we need to start thinking about the things that are important to both of us."

Though she knew he hadn't mean anything bad by that, it still rubbed her the wrong way, like so many other things he had said this morning. If it was important to her, it should be important to both of them.

"I want you to think about us while you're gone. When you get this out of your system, we'll go off to Myrtle Beach so we can talk about our future."

Out of her system? Like an intestinal bug? She didn't want to think about their miserable relationship for the next sixteen days, her first and probably only trip to Africa. She wanted to go and have a good time.

"I really love you, Mary Kate, and I think we ought to be engaged by the time school starts."

She pushed back from his embrace to read his face. This was it, then. The second and last time he would ask—which meant she needed to answer this time. She would have preferred to see a loving or hopeful gaze…something sweet and maybe even intimate. What she got was earnest, the ever-practical Bobby Britton.

"I should go." The growing security line appeared as her imminent salvation.

"I love you, sweetheart."

"I love you too." She hugged him again hard and kissed him quickly on the lips. Then she turned and walked away, resolved to break up with him once and for all as soon as she got home.

Chapter Five

Mary Kate let out a breath of relief as the wheels touched down. The joke her mom had made about having enough in her bags to move here didn't seem so silly once it occurred to her the only way to get home was to get back on a plane.

Her first up-close look at Tanzania was the small terminal flashing by as they slowed to taxi. It reminded her of the cafeteria at the school where she taught, a square building with a flat roof, but this one had a small tower in the center. Despite the crew's commands to remain seated, people were already standing to gather their belongings. She had a small shoulder bag for her money, tickets and passport, and the few things she thought she would need during the flight. Her backpack was crammed into the overhead bin.

When they finally stopped, she stood and stretched in the aisle, amazed to realize her second wind, despite being up all night. She was thrilled to finally be here, not because it was the end of her journey, but the beginning of her African adventure.

At the door she got a blast of hot, humid air, not unlike Georgia on its most miserable summer day. They filed off the plane slowly, descending the stairs onto the steaming tarmac.

She couldn't stop thinking that her feet were walking on a whole new continent, and she tried to commit it all to memory. The Kilimanjaro airport was as antiquated as Hartsfield in Atlanta was modern. Grass grew up through the cracks in the asphalt, and the building could have used a fresh coat of paint.

Through a glass door marked Arrivals, signs in both Swahili and English directed them into two lines, one for visitors to Tanzania, the other for residents returning home. Mary Kate was near the back of her line, which made her worry since she could see their bags being delivered in the room beyond. The last thing she needed was for her things to be stolen off the conveyor while she was stuck in line.

She recognized about a dozen people who had gotten on the plane in Atlanta. One was just ahead of her in the line, a young man with short blond hair that stood up in all directions. She had almost spoken to him in the departure lounge at Johannesburg, but when she saw that he was wearing earphones, she guessed he didn't want to be bothered. That was a nice trick, one she used sometimes on Carol Lee.

She finally reached the front of the line and handed her visa and brand new passport to the agent. He examined both—if one could call a cursory glance an examination—stamped the passport and handed it back without a word. She resisted the urge to page through it right away to check out the stamp, feeling it would make her look like the novice traveler she was.

The first thing she noticed in the baggage claim area was a cluster of people collecting blue bags marked with the name of another tour company. By their accents, she guessed them to be British, or maybe South African. She couldn't tell the difference. An Asian couple in their early thirties held yellow Summit bags like hers, and she turned in time to see a third Summit bag go by, only to be hoisted by the blond man. His face fell when he read the tag, and he placed it back on the conveyor. Mary Kate tugged it off and caught her other canvas bag right behind it. Her feeling of relief was palpable, as was the obvious despair on the man's face.

"I see you got your ugly yellow Summit bag," he said, his face set in a grim smile.

"Yours didn't make it?"

He shook his head. "No, my flight from Denver into Atlanta was late. I guess they didn't have time to make the transfer. At least I won't have any trouble getting through customs."

She couldn't believe he wasn't frantic. "Maybe there are some that haven't come out yet." Just as she said that, the conveyor stopped.

"I'd say that's everything." He held out a hand and she got her first good look at him. He was about her age, maybe a few years older, slightly built and not much taller. "I'm Drew Harper."

"Mary Kate Sasser." Having two first names was not her favorite southern trait. Her friends from college in Savannah knew her as Kate, but all the confusion from her teachers, who had called her Mary, made the whole idea of changing her name more trouble than it was worth.

"I guess I need to go file a claim. You don't happen to speak Swahili, do you?"

"Afraid not."

"I didn't think so. That accent of yours is a dead giveaway. I'll guess Atlanta."

"Close. A couple of hours east in Mooresville."

"What's that near?"

"Nothing at all whatsoever."

He laughed. "Sounds like the Denver airport."

"How's that?"

"It isn't near anything either." Sensing her confusion, he quickly added, "Sorry, that's kind of a local joke."

"What are you going to do about your stuff?"

"Don't know. We don't go up till Monday. Maybe it'll come in on the next plane."

"I hate to tell you this, but there isn't another one from Atlanta until Wednesday."

He made a face. "I forgot about that. I guess I could be an optimist and imagine they got as far as Johannesburg. But since neither of mine made it and both of yours did…" He shook his head, apparently resigned to the likelihood they wouldn't arrive in Tanzania before the start of their trek. "I'm sure I'm not the first person this has happened to. Maybe I can pick up a few things tomorrow."

"Here?" As soon as she said it, she remembered her irritation at Bobby for assuming there wouldn't be 7-Elevens in Tanzania. She had no idea what sort of shops they had near Kilimanjaro, but it made perfect sense someone would sell hiking gear. "You're probably right."

They were joined then by the Asian couple with the Summit bags. "Are you both with Summit?"

Mary Kate felt stupid for being surprised at the man's American accent. "Yes, I'm Mary Kate. This is Drew."

They shook hands as Drew explained about his lost bags. The newcomers were Neal and his wife Mei, from Seattle. Mei was looking over the papers Tom Muncie had sent and noted that the bus to Moshi, which was the base for their expedition, was due in a half hour. That was plenty of time for Drew to file his claim and the rest of them to clear customs.

Customs amounted to handing over the form she had filled out on the plane saying basically that she had nothing illegal in her bags—no drugs, no weapons, no piles of cash or jewelry. From there, she went outside to an open-air café to wait with Neal and Mei.

Mei found a table and promised to watch their things while she read more about the trip. Mary Kate and Neal bought bottled sodas and took the opportunity to stretch their legs along the sidewalk in front of the terminal. Neal finished his drink in about four gulps and covered his mouth to belch. "Did you see the mountain from the plane?"

"God, yes. It scared the crap out of me."

"Me too. Hard to believe we'll all be up there this time next week."

"I hope we'll all be up there. I thought I was ready until I saw it up close."

"Mei said the same thing. We've hiked up to twelve or thirteen thousand feet in the Cascades, but this makes those look like foothills."

Mary Kate was embarrassed to tell him about her climb up Rabun Bald, which wasn't half that high. If they weren't ready for this, she figured she didn't have a prayer. "What made you guys decide to try this?"

"Tom Muncie talked us into it. We met him at a Christmas party last year and he was telling all these great stories. We got excited about it and decided to make it happen."

"That's cool you met Tom." She had talked with the tour organizer on the phone, but had forgotten the main office was in Seattle. "I saw a program on public TV and got excited too. But I couldn't talk anybody into coming with me."

"They'll all be kicking themselves when you get home with pictures."

"Yeah, maybe." Deb was probably the only one who cared. Of course, once Mary Kate got home and broke up with Bobby, Deb would probably be the only one in town talking to her anyway.

"Besides, Tom says a lot of people come by themselves. That list he sent us had people from all over."

Tom had promised to pair her with somebody for the safari part so she wouldn't have to pay the single occupancy rate, but he hadn't worked out anything firm as of the last update. There were eight of them slated to go on safari after the climb, including Neal and Mei, another married couple and three women besides herself. She hoped it was someone interesting since they would be spending a lot of time together.

They reached the end of the walkway and turned back toward the café. In just the few minutes they had been walking, she had already begun to sweat. "Poor Drew," she said, feeling nothing but relief that it was his bag missing and not hers.

"He'll be okay. If the rest of us throw a couple of things into his pile, he'll have enough to make it."

She did a quick mental inventory of what she might be able to share. Drew wasn't much bigger than she was, but it was doubtful he could wear any of her clothes. Still, she could spare some socks and maybe a T-shirt.

Mei looked up from her papers as they joined her. "The others must be coming from Amsterdam. That plane gets in late this afternoon."

"Or they could even be coming in tomorrow," Neal added. "At least we'll get an extra day to rest before we go up."

Drew came out and dropped his backpack next to Mei. "The good news is they have someone here who will watch for the bags when the next plane comes in on Wednesday. The bad news is they lock them in storage until I show up with the claim check."

"So you're screwed, man." Neal summed it up pretty well.

"Basically. But he told me to ask at the hotel about borrowing some things, so I'll try that. All I really need is a sleeping bag, a warm coat…"

"Mei and I probably have a few things you can use. You don't have any issues about wearing women's underwear, do you?"

"None at all," Drew answered deadpan. "That's pretty much what was in my bags."

Mary Kate snorted at that. If first impressions were worth anything, she was going to like these people. "Are you guys doing the safari afterward?"

"Not me," Drew said. "I couldn't get that much time off work."

"I'm off for the whole summer. I teach special ed, emotionally disturbed kids."

"That might come in handy this week," Drew said with a chuckle. Then his voice changed to a more serious tone. "To tell you the truth, I won't be surprised if this turns out to be a lot tougher emotionally than physically."

"I don't see how anything could be tougher than the physical part," Neal said.

"I had a couple of friends who did it last year," Drew explained. "One of them had to turn back on the last night because he got disoriented. He got really depressed about it. He said it was the biggest letdown of his life."

Mary Kate certainly understood that. She would be devastated if she didn't make it to the summit.

"I'd like to get to the top," Neal said, "but I'll be okay with it if I don't. Mei's the one who really wants it. I just came along so we could do this together."

"I've worked hard. I want a payoff," she said.

"It could take more than hard work, though," Drew said. "You never know how a climb's going to go. I did a fourteener with one of my friends a couple of weeks ago. That's a whole mile under Kili, and he was puking his guts out because of the altitude."

A fourteener. Mary Kate gathered that meant a mountain that was fourteen thousand feet high. It was ironic that the folks back in Mooresville were worried about things like her falling off the mountain. By everything she had read, altitude sickness was the biggest threat on the mountain. Vomiting and diarrhea, like what Drew was talking about, were relatively minor as long as they subsided. The bigger worries were pulmonary or cerebral edema, which could be killers for anyone not smart enough to head back down immediately.

Irony aside, it was freaking her out to hear these guys talk about their chances for getting to the top, given their experience walking up real mountains. They probably *parked* higher than Rabun Bald.

A white Toyota bus pulled into the circle in front of the café, its faded paper sign reading "Moshi." Two young black men dressed in ill-fitting workpants and wide-collared dingy white shirts exited and began loading baggage onto the roof of the bus.

Mary Kate waited on the curb until she saw her bags secured on top, studying the whole scene for details that made it unique to Africa. Besides the language difference, there was the bus itself, more utilitarian than comfortable. Such a vehicle would never roll out of Atlanta with luggage piled so casually on top. The windows were down, a sure sign this bus wasn't air conditioned. As hot as the terminal had been inside, she guessed there was no such thing as Freon in Tanzania.

A few dozen people, presumably locals, joined them on the bus. Mary Kate took a window seat and Drew slid in beside her. Neal and Mei sat in front of them, Mei now studying a travel guide.

The narrow road out of the airport was paved, but filled with potholes. Building a road in Tanzania was probably a one-shot deal, she figured, with little maintenance. They turned onto what she guessed was the Tanzanian equivalent of a highway, two lanes wide, but without center and shoulder stripes. Soon they were riding by large open fields dotted with small dome-shaped huts.

"Maasai," Mei explained, turning as she held up her book. "They used to be warriors. Now they herd cattle, which are sacred to them. Most of them wear the traditional red cloths. They're supposed to be very noble."

Neal turned to face them also. "Everywhere we go, Mei reads all about it. I never have to worry about anything because she's going to tell me everything I need to know." He flinched as his wife poked him in the side. "Being married to her is like being in continuing education classes all the time."

"It's true. When I'm not dragging him out on an adventure, he's happy to be just a couch nerd. Sometimes I let him lie there and I go off with my friends."

That was exactly the kind of relationship Mary Kate wanted with Bobby, where they would share the really important things, but give each other the freedom to do their own thing sometimes. It was one thing for Bobby not to want to come, but at least he could have sent her off with his support. Instead, it was as if he was punishing her for wanting to do this, like she wasn't entitled to her own—

Suddenly, the bus hit a speed bump that sent them sailing out of their seats.

"*Samahani,*" the driver called, taking his eyes off the road for an instant to turn around.

"That was probably Swahili for bite me," Drew whispered.

She chuckled and shook her head, feeling a rush of delight at being here with fun and interesting people. This trip was more than just an opportunity for a unique adventure. For Mary Kate, it marked the beginning of her new philosophy—*carpe diem*. It was silly to miss things in life or to want them to be different when all one had to do was "seize the day."

After almost an hour of bouncing over the rugged paved road, the bus finally entered a roundabout in what looked to be a small town. The structures weren't exactly modern, but compared to the Maasai huts, they were castles. Some of the small buildings were wood frame, though most were made of cinderblock. They were painted purple, bright blue or orange, and few were larger than the average garage back home.

"Who goes to View Hotel?" the driver asked.

"That's us," she said, pointing to herself and her three companions.

"You change here to other bus." He gestured.

They collected their backpacks and stepped off the bus. The two young men who had loaded the bags at the airport hopped off and climbed to the top to pass down the gear. Mary Kate got her Summit bag, but not the other duffel.

"Wait! I have one more bag, a green one."

After a fruitless search through the towering pile, the man proposed a solution.

"We take others to their hotel. We bring your bag to the View."

The idea of separating from her things was one she wouldn't consider at all. "No, I'll find it." Before anyone could stop her, she climbed the ladder on the back of the bus, crawled through the bags until she spotted hers peeking out from the bottom of the pile. "This one's mine." She stepped back as the two young men extracted it and passed it down. Another man loaded it on a smaller vehicle, and she climbed aboard, claiming a bench seat all to herself.

Neal turned around and spoke softly. "That was pretty gutsy, Mary Kate. Never mind that you just violated the most sacred laws of their religion."

Her stomach dropped as she tried to figure out if he was kidding or not. If he was, then he did deadpan as well as Drew.

"I read somewhere that women weren't allowed to climb anything that put them higher than men."

Mei saved her from a panic attack. "Don't listen to him. If he ever says he read something, he's lying."

The View Hotel was almost a mile out from the center of town along a road that was rougher than any they had been on so far. Still, it was a wonderful surprise after seeing the simple structures in the center of town.

As they peered out the window, Neal summed up what Mary Kate was thinking. "I don't know about you guys, but I'm relieved."

Tom had described the View Hotel as a family-owned inn with a bar and a restaurant. White with a red roof, it reminded her of one of the old frame homes in Savannah, but larger. It had a wide porch at the entrance and picture windows all across the front. The second floor had a long row of small windows, which Mary Kate assumed were the guest rooms.

Two young men dressed in black pants and crisp white shirts—a sharp contrast to the ones who had handled their bags on the bus—bounded off the porch and began shuttling the bags inside. Mary Kate and the others followed them up the stairs to the lobby, where red velvet benches and chairs added an elegant touch to the rustic ebony floors and long mahogany counter. A portrait of Tanzania's president like one she had seen on display at the airport was mounted prominently on the wall behind a young African woman who greeted them. AAA would probably have given the place two stars, but here in Tanzania, Mary Kate was willing to bet it was one of the finer establishments.

Neal and Mei checked in first and followed a bellman up the stairs. Mary Kate went next, since Drew had to make arrangements to borrow things. She couldn't wait to get a shower and change into fresh clothes. The overnight trip was taking its toll.

She stepped up to the counter and handed over her passport, which she had seen Neal and Mei do. "I'm Mary Kate Sasser. I'm with Summit too."

"Yes, I have it. You are a single for two nights, then another night when you return."

"That's right." Though she had agreed to be paired with someone else for the safari, the single room at the View was only fifteen dollars more a night.

The woman filled out a form by hand, something Mary Kate hadn't seen in years. Apparently, computers hadn't spread to Tanzania yet. "Dinner is from seven o'clock to nine o'clock. Breakfast is from eight thirty to ten o'clock. Electricity is off from ten o'clock each night until seven o'clock in the morning."

Tom had warned them about the periodic interruptions in electricity. Another good reason to shower right away. A bellman picked up both of her duffel bags and started up the stairs.

"Good luck getting what you need," she called to Drew.

"Thanks. It'll all work out."

For his sake, she hoped he was right. She trudged up the stairs behind the bellman, hoping she could stay awake long enough to eat dinner. After that, all bets were off.

Chapter Six

Mary Kate patted her stomach as it rumbled. Sleep had won the battle over hunger the night before, but now she was rested and starving.

When she had closed the door to her room last night, she was struck by a remarkable realization—it was her first night ever to be alone in a hotel. It was hard not to feel like a hick from the sticks, because that's what she was.

The room had twin beds, pushed together so the large mosquito net suspended from the ceiling enclosed both. There was a small bedside table and another table by the door. Each held a candle and a box of matches, the only light available once the electricity was turned off for the night.

The bathroom had a toilet, a sink and a tiled shower stall with no curtain. She had worried at first that she would splash water all over the tiny room, but the joke was on her. At full force, the water poured only in a small stream, and its temperature fluctuated randomly between tepid and cold.

For a fleeting moment, she imagined Bobby at the front desk asking—politely—for other accommodations. She, on the other hand, appreciated the adventure.

At the restaurant downstairs, she found her three comrades already seated. Breakfast was buffet style and featured standard Western fare of scrambled eggs, bacon and bread.

"Somebody got her beauty sleep last night," Drew said.

Mary Kate smiled slightly, trying to figure out if he was flirting or just teasing her about sleeping through dinner. "I only meant to rest my eyes, but my head hit that pillow and that was all she wrote."

Two college-age girls and a young man wearing a Penn State T-shirt checked out the buffet before settling at a small table beside them. Neal leaned back and addressed them. "Are you guys with Summit?"

Their faces lit up and they excitedly moved to the larger table. They were Courtney, Rachel and Kirby, all public health majors who would be heading off after the climb on a four-week internship in a Tanzanian village. Mary Kate envied their experience. She would have loved the chance to work abroad during college, but Savannah State didn't have many opportunities like that for students in the special education department. Besides, that probably would have meant staying in school for an extra semester, which would have kept her from graduating in time to take the job in Mooresville. Her whole life would be different if—

"Mary Kate's been sleeping since we got here," Drew told them.

"That's right. Just four more days of that and I'll be caught up."

Courtney said, "You should have seen Rachel. She slept all the way from Detroit to Amsterdam, then from Amsterdam to here."

"I think I have necrophilia or something," Rachel said.

Everyone in the group exchanged quizzical looks until Kirby said in a gentle but nonetheless patronizing voice, "Honey, I think the word you're searching for is narcolepsy...unless you're trying to tell us that you enjoy having sex with dead people."

Rachel blushed furiously as the group erupted in laughter.

Mary Kate liked the new arrivals immediately.

Neal jerked his thumb in Drew's direction. "Drew's bags didn't come, so if you girls can spare him some of your underwear, he'll be ever so thankful."

"Let's see who we're missing," Mei said, pulling out her document folder. "Ann and Nikki from Minneapolis...Addison, Cyn and Javier from Miami...and Jim and Brad from Dallas. I guess they'll get in this afternoon from Amsterdam."

From the way Kirby had called Rachel honey, Mary Kate guessed they were a couple. That meant Courtney might be up for sharing a tent. She seemed nice, and this was her first trip abroad as well. That would give them a lot to talk about after they turned in.

Drew stood and stretched. "Anyone up for a walk into town? I need to pick up a few things...obviously. And they said there was an Internet café a couple of blocks off that circle where we switched buses."

Everyone seemed eager to send a message to home, and they set out together for the short walk into town. They passed a small stand where an enterprising local was selling sodas and candy. Mei pointed out that locals depended heavily on tourism for their livelihood, so they all stopped for a snack, even though they had just finished breakfast.

Mary Kate was still fascinated by the details she gathered as they walked by the simple shacks that served as homes for whole families. Women, some with babies strapped to their shoulders, scratched in scraggly gardens while older children played nearby. "Wonder where the men are?"

"It's Sunday," Drew said. "They're on the couch drinking a beer, watching the game."

She kicked at him playfully.

Mei walked closer so she could keep her voice low. "Don't laugh. That's probably not far off, at least for the Tanzanian equivalent. The women do all the work at home, even if the husband doesn't have a job." She smacked Neal in the stomach as he nodded. "Don't get any ideas."

Mary Kate loved the lighthearted way Mei and Neal interacted. They had spontaneity, precisely what was missing from her relationship with Bobby. Not only were all her activities with Bobby painstakingly planned, so was the way they communicated with each other. Anything that went outside the lines—like her refusal to take the engagement ring or her interest in coming to Africa—disrupted their flow. Hell, it wasn't just Bobby, she realized. It was practically everyone in her life, with the exception of Deb and her Aunt Jean. No wonder she always felt so hemmed in. The whole path of her life was already drawn, just waiting for her to walk down.

"Earth to Mary Kate."

Startled, she stopped and realized she had continued on past the Internet café.

"It's probably not a big deal, but it might not be a good idea to go off by yourself," Drew said.

"I kind of zoned out there."

They went inside and took a seat on the window ledge. The tiny shop had two tables with computers, four in all. One was occupied by locals, three young men who crowded around the monitor. The others in their group were already logging on.

Mary Kate's thoughts drifted again. To whom would she write, and what would she say? The first answer was clear. No one in her family had e-mail, so that left only Bobby and Deb. When she finally got her turn at the computer, she was surprised to find an e-mail from Bobby already waiting.

Hello, sweetheart! By the time you get this, you'll probably be home, back from "conquering" that big old mountain of yours. I just wanted to send this so you would know how soon I started missing you. Can't wait to have you back in my arms where you belong. Love, Bobby

She read his message three times with growing irritation. The quote marks around the word "conquering" were his little joke, another patronizing putdown. And the idea that she belonged in his arms made her feel like a piece of property. Two could play that game, she thought, hitting the reply key.

Hi, Bobby! I'm writing from an Internet café here in Moshi, the village where we're staying before we start our climb tomorrow. I made it here without any problems at all, just as I knew I would. I've already gotten to know some of the people in my group, including a couple from Seattle. Mei was the one who really wanted to come, but her husband Neal came along to give her moral support and share the experience. They're so nice. I'll write again when I get back down. Tell Mom and Dad I got here okay. Love, Mary Kate

She revised it a couple of times to make it seem less bitchy and sent it off. Then she wrote a quick note to Deb, officially announcing her intention to break up with Bobby as soon as she got home.

Chapter Seven

"...stay on the line. Your call is very important to us..."
Addison flipped through her backpack in search of her itinerary. It was probably useless at this point, but the information on the hotel was there. At the other end of the line, Tom Muncie was scrambling to find her a seat on the next plane to Kilimanjaro.

When she began training five months ago, she hadn't anticipated that the most arduous part of the trip would be getting to the trailhead in time to go up with her group. Cyn's meticulous travel plans had fallen all to hell when her father persuaded her to stop in London on the way over. Since she was now traveling alone, she had forfeited her economy-class ticket to Tanzania through Amsterdam in exchange for first-class to Gatwick and on to Nairobi, courtesy of Reginald. But the Kenya Airways flight had been delayed nine hours for maintenance, which caused her to miss the Kilimanjaro connection. The ticket agent was unable to confirm her on a later flight.

She rolled her eyes at the folly of accepting her father's "invitation" to spend the afternoon with him so he could hear all about the Kilimanjaro quest. He couldn't have cared less about her trip, though he was complimentary of her weight loss. His intent was to show her the office she would occupy at the London headquarters of Global Allied Investments and to introduce her to her future coworkers. He was unfazed by her insistence that she wasn't in any hurry to start the job, showing her also the nearby apartment building where he was prepared to lease a one-bedroom flat. The real topper, as far as Addison was concerned, was his tour through neighboring Soho to remind her of London's lively gay and lesbian community. She had almost laughed aloud at how much that phony gesture must have pained him. He was still holding out hope she would outgrow her lesbian phase.

"Addison?" The crackly voice finally returned on the phone.

"I'm still here."

"Okay, here's what we've got."

She listened in disbelief as Tom outlined an overland bus trip to Arusha where she would transfer to a vehicle bound for Moshi. That would put her at the hotel sometime after ten p.m., but enable her to leave first thing in the morning with her group. Otherwise, she would have to be escorted the next day by porters to a meet-up camp along the route.

"That doesn't sound like much of a choice, Tom."

"It isn't bad. Some of our trekkers opt for the overland route so they can see a little more of the countryside."

Two hundred miles in a third world bus wasn't Addison's idea of a pleasant sightseeing trip, but she didn't like the idea of spending a night in Nairobi either, especially at the airport. She jotted down the details and thanked Tom for his help. There probably weren't many tour operators who would piece things together on the fly at three a.m., the time back in Seattle.

The bus to Arusha wasn't due for another two hours, enough time for a shower in the Simba Lounge, the travelers club for elite passengers on Kenya Airways. She checked with the agent and got the key, shuddering as she endured a rude suggestion from a balding Afrikaner who was waiting for a flight to Cape Town. Inside the lavatory, she double-checked the lock before undressing.

The mirror confirmed her exhaustion, most evident in the way her shoulders slumped forward, making her appear shorter than her five-eight frame. She stood up straight and rolled her neck in a circle to loosen up. It was hard not to admire her own figure, slim and sculpted from hours of running and lifting weights at the Wellness Center on the University of Miami campus. Whether she made it to the summit or not, getting ready for the trip had certainly had its benefits.

She pulled the tie from her hair and shook it free. It never surprised her to get come-ons from men, or women either. She had inherited what she thought were her mother's best features—a golden complexion, full lips and brown eyes that angled slightly from her Peruvian-Japanese ancestry. Celia had called her exotic.

Turning on the spray, she shook away thoughts of her last lover, an aspiring model she had stolen from another woman, only to lose her to someone else. *Lesson learned.*

Thirty minutes later, she emerged from the Simba Lounge refreshed and with a second wind she would undoubtedly need for the home stretch into Moshi. Tom had advised her to stay alert while in the airport and keep to herself. Though it was normally safe for Westerners, he said, the Kenyan capital had suffered political violence recently, and steering clear of crowds was a good idea.

Addison picked up her bus tickets at the window and settled with her bags onto a bench, using her sunglasses and cap to shield her eyes from those around her. When her bus arrived on schedule an hour later, she boarded and took a seat to herself near the back. Too late, she realized she was hungry and that her packages of trail mix were stored in the bottom of her Summit bag.

An hour out of Nairobi, she trained her eyes out the window, hoping to see the giant mountain in the distance. Finally, she gave up in the waning light. A view of the savannah would have to wait, she thought, closing her eyes with fatigue.

A gentle tug of her leg awakened her, and she automatically

jerked her foot to draw her backpack closer. She had looped the shoulder strap around her ankle for safekeeping, and was annoyed but not terribly surprised that someone behind her had attempted to move it. Without turning around, she straightened in her seat to make room for the pack beside her.

At the border, they were guided through immigration and herded onto a different bus. The couple who had been sitting behind her didn't make the transfer, but Addison fought the urge to sleep again, reminded of Tom's warning to stay alert. The last thing she needed—as if her travel fiascos weren't already enough—was to be robbed of her passport and cash.

She transferred again in Arusha, this time to a van with two other passengers. When they reached Moshi, the van stopped at a traffic circle, visible only from their headlights.

"View Hotel?" the driver asked.

"That's me," she said, heaving her backpack over her shoulder. She scanned her surroundings as she stepped out, trying to locate the hotel.

The driver unloaded her duffel and Summit bag from the back of the van and pointed to a road extending from the circle. "View Hotel there."

"Down that road?"

"Yes."

Even in the blackness of night, she could make out a few buildings, none of which were large enough to be a hotel. "How far?"

He pointed into the abyss. "There," he said, clearly struggling with his limited English.

"Can you take me?" she asked, fumbling in her pocket for cash. She hoped she was handing him a five dollar bill, but who could tell in this light?

"*Asante*," he said, his face lighting up in a smile. Then he hastily hopped back into the van and drove off, leaving her standing in the street.

"Shit." Out of options, she hoisted her bags and trudged down the road. Acutely aware she was breaking the promises she had made to her mother to be careful, stay with the group and not go off on her own at night, she tuned in to her surroundings. The street was lined with houses—shacks, really—the faint glow of what she guessed was candlelight emanating from within.

As her eyes grew accustomed to the night, she made out a large compound in the distance nearly a half mile ahead. Three times she stopped to rest, her shoulders screaming in agony with her heavy load each time she started up again.

Suddenly, the sound of male voices made her stop in her tracks. Two shadowy figures were walking toward her. She hated to think the worst, but a woman out alone at night could tempt anyone. Her mind raced to inventory her belongings for something she might use as a weapon. As the men drew closer, her heart pounded with fear.

"Addison Falk?"

She was startled by the sound of her own name. "Yes."

"We are from the View Hotel. Tom Muncie phoned to say you would be taking the late bus from Arusha."

Addison exhaled and dropped her bags, which they quickly picked up. "I wasn't even sure where the hotel was."

"You arrived early or we would have met you in town."

She fell into step with them, trying to slow the shaking in her legs. "It's okay. Thanks for coming."

They bypassed the deserted front desk and went by candlelight to a room on the second floor. There, she dumped her belongings and undressed, finally crawling beneath the mosquito netting to her bed. In moments, she drifted off.

Chapter Eight

Addison completed the hotel's check-in process and stowed her passport in the side pocket of her convertibles, the hiking pants that became shorts when she unzipped the legs.

"The rest of your group is having breakfast," the woman told her, coming around the large mahogany counter to steer her into the restaurant.

Addison counted nine at the table, three men and six women, all laughing and talking like old friends. Her first stop was the buffet, where she filled her plate with scrambled eggs and bread. The meat—whatever it was—looked a bit overcooked, and Cyn had warned her not to eat too many fruits or vegetables. She dropped a teabag into a cup and poured it full of steaming water. Only then did she approach the table, clearing her throat to announce her presence. "Is this the Summit crowd?"

A young man jumped to his feet and pulled out a chair. "Guilty. My name is Drew. And you are…?"

"Addison Falk, from Miami." She had studied the list from Tom Muncie. Drew Harper, she remembered, was from Colorado. The others shouted friendly hellos in unison as she set her plate at the open spot.

Drew gallantly pushed her chair to the table. "I'll make the introductions, Addison from Miami. Now pay attention because you may be tested on this later."

She set down her fork and studied the group, mindful of any clues that would help her match the faces to the names.

"This is Ann, from Minnesota." His accent changed to poke fun at the Scandinavian cadence. "They talk funny there, you know."

"Yah," Addison said in agreement, drawing a laugh from everyone, including Ann. She appeared to be oldest in the group, in her mid-forties.

"The lovely woman next to her is Mei, and the ugly man is her husband, Neal. They're from Seattle. You still with me?"

"Ann, Mei and Neal," she repeated, committing their names to memory.

"Those two at the end of the table are the lovebirds, Kirby and Rachel. Courtney is their chaperone. They all wear clothing that says Penn State in case they get lost."

Addison chuckled, glad she hadn't worn her UM cap. As a frequent world traveler, she had learned to avoid wearing anything that proclaimed she was American.

"And that child next to Courtney is Nikki, niece of Ann, also from Minnesota. At a mere eighteen years old, she is wiser than all of us."

"Kirby, Rachel, Courtney and Nikki."

"And this is Mary Kate, from Jaw-ja," he said. The young woman blushed as Drew butchered what Addison bet was a lovely southern accent. Then he cast Addison a challenging look. "Now it's your turn."

Addison rubbed her hands together and concentrated, remembering not only the introductions, but the additional information Tom had sent in her travel packet. From her work with Miami's business community, she prided herself on being prepared so she could make a good first impression.

"Wait," Drew said. "Chinese fire drill!"

Addison shook her head indulgently as everyone got up and

changed seats. Then one by one she pointed at the expectant faces around the table. "Okay...Nikki from St. Paul, Drew from Aurora, Mei and Neal from Seattle...Ann from St. Paul...Kirby, Rachel and Courtney from State College, Pennsylvania, and"—she looked the southern woman in the eye and smiled—"that makes you Mary Kate Sasser, from...don't tell me...Mooresville, Georgia."

The whole group applauded her triumph as her eyes lingered on Mary Kate. She was pretty—not stunning like the Latina models that adorned South Beach...more like the girl-next-door—slender with short brown hair and small features. Addison couldn't wait to hear her speak in that accent.

"You must have gotten in late last night," Mary Kate said.

Addison related the whole miserable turn of events. "I could use two more days just to catch up on my sleep, but word has it we have a mountain to climb."

"Mary Kate understands all about sleep. She's been doing that a lot. By the way, you didn't happen to bring any extra underwear, did you?" Drew asked.

Everyone laughed at what she knew was her curious expression. "I might be able to spare a sports bra. What size do you wear?"

"Actually, I was thinking more along the lines of long johns, but a sports bra could be kind of fun too."

"Drew's luggage is still back in Atlanta," Mary Kate said. "The hotel found him a sleeping bag and a parka, but we're all pitching in a few extra things so he won't smell so bad."

"Good plan." She stood and motioned for Drew to do the same, wondering if Drew's route through Atlanta had anything to do with being Mary Kate's boyfriend. From their teasing, they seemed familiar. "I have another pair of convertibles you can use if they fit. And an extra fleece pullover."

"Fantastic! Can I kiss you?"

Probably not the boyfriend. "That won't be necessary."

"Can I kiss you anyway?"

"Only in your Larium dreams," she answered, drawing a

raucous round of laughter. Larium was the medicine prescribed to ward off malaria, and she had taken the weekly dosage upon arriving in London. On the subsequent flight to Nairobi, bizarre images had filled her head each time she dozed off.

Neal stood and pulled out his wife's chair. "It's almost time to go. We're supposed to bring down all the stuff we're leaving here so they can lock it up."

"Finish your breakfast. I'll sit with you," Mary Kate said.

Addison liked that idea very much. She checked her watch. "We have about thirty minutes. My stuff's packed already."

"Mine too." Mary Kate nursed a cup of what looked like cocoa. "There was another couple on our list from Miami, but they aren't here."

"Cyn and Javier Juarez…friends of mine," Addison mumbled, her mouth full. "Cyn got pregnant and it was too risky for her to take the shots."

"It's too bad you had to deal with all those travel changes on your own."

"More adventure than I wanted, but at least I got here." She finished her eggs and wiped her mouth with a linen napkin. "I haven't even seen the mountain yet."

"You're kidding." Mary Kate's eyes grew as wide as a child's, causing Addison to grin with delight. "Come out here."

Addison followed her out the front door of the hotel and into the street. The monstrous peak loomed over them and she gasped. "Holy shit."

"My words exactly. They don't call it the View Hotel for nothing."

"There's no fu—there's no freaking way we'll get to the top of that."

"How much do you want it?"

"I want it bad," she said, smiling at Mary Kate's look of determination. "You?"

"That's what I came for."

"All right. We'll get there together." She slapped a high five, just as a bus pulled through the hotel gate. "I bet that's our ride.

We better go in and lock up our stuff."

Twenty minutes later, the hikers were gathered on the front porch, where a tall, muscular black man waited with papers in hand. "Do you have copies of your passport?"

Everyone nodded.

"Good. I am Luke. I will be your trail guide for the trip to the top of Kili. Today, we will drive for three hours to enter the park at Londorossi Gate. Everyone must sign the book and write down the passport number. It is required to enter the park. When we reach the trail, we will hike through the rainforest for four hours to Mti Mkubwa—which means to you Big Tree—where we will camp for the night. You will be tired tonight. Do not forget to drink water, even if you are not thirsty—two liters each day."

Being from Miami, Addison was already in the habit of staying hydrated. Water was prescribed as the best defense against altitude sickness—something about the air pressure and thin air interfering with the way the cells exchanged oxygen. She didn't understand the science the way Javier had explained it, but his message was clear—drink a lot.

"The other thing you must remember is that we go slowly. We say *pole pole*."

That too was in the pamphlet Tom Muncie had sent, Addison recalled, though she hadn't realized until now that it was pronounced *po-lay po-lay*.

As the gear was loaded into the back of the bus, she saw Mary Kate disappear into the small sundries store located near the bar. Addison stalled, letting Drew get on and take a seat. If Mary Kate and Drew were doing this trip together, she didn't want to horn in on anything. But if they weren't, she was the person who interested her most.

Mary Kate emerged, bag in hand, and climbed aboard. Addison whirled her backpack over her shoulder and followed. The bus was large enough that she could have a bench seat to herself. Ann and Nikki were sitting together, already deep in conversation. Kirby and Rachel shared a bench, and Courtney sat behind them, absorbed in a paperback. Mary Kate had taken the seat behind Drew and placed her backpack in the space beside her. Addison took that as a signal she wanted to sit alone and moved toward the empty space beside Drew. Suddenly, Mary Kate looked directly at her and picked up the pack, gesturing toward the open seat.

"Thanks," Addison said, falling in beside her. "When I was stuck at the airport in Nairobi, I called Tom Muncie back in Seattle. He told me I'd be paired up with you for the safari, except he called you Mary."

She sighed. "I know. People don't understand how we do things in the South."

"I like Mary Kate. It's a nice name."

"Thank you, but I think one name ought to be enough for anyone. Addison's an interesting name."

"Very proper British, just like my father, Reginald."

"You don't sound British."

"Miami, born and bred. My mother's from Peru. That makes me a mongrel."

"If you're a mongrel, I'm a…whatever is the most ordinary dog there is. I was born and raised in Mooresville, and both of my parents were too. One of my grandfathers was from the next county. That's practically considered marrying a foreigner where I come from."

Addison chuckled. "Did you guys come by yourself?" She poked Drew in the back to include him in the conversation.

He turned around. "Yeah, I had some friends that did this a couple of years ago. Neither one of them made it to the top, so I wanted to give it a shot."

"I saw it on TV," Mary Kate said. "I tried to get my boyfriend to come, but he wasn't interested…at least not until he realized I was going to do it anyway."

Boyfriend. Addison felt a wave of disappointment as her budding fantasy, which she quickly dismissed as absurd, evaporated. "So why isn't he here?"

Mary Kate frowned and shook her head. "I decided I didn't really want him to come, especially after he waited so long and I made all my plans. All I know is I'm having a good time without him."

"Good for you." To Addison, that didn't sound like much of a relationship.

She smiled to herself as Mary Kate nodded off against the glass, remembering Drew's crack about how she loved to sleep. She peered over her head out the window for her first look at the Tanzanian countryside. It was mostly flat, with a few peaks that seemed to rise out of nothing. What she remembered about Mount Kilimanjaro was that it was more than just the highest peak in the Africa. It was a volcanic creation, not part of a range, and the highest free-standing peak in the world.

An hour later, the bus turned off onto a side road, bouncing them out of their seats as they plowed over one rut after another. Mary Kate woke up as they were passing a small, muddy village.

"Look at that." She pointed to a group of young girls, all walking with large buckets of water perched on their heads. "I thought that was just a postcard."

"Apparently, it's for real. That little one can't be more than three years old." Addison tried to remember some of the development plans she had seen at her father's company. None had addressed improvements in the everyday lives of children and families. Once she signed on with Global Allied, she would steer some of the profits into things like schools and health clinics for villages like this one.

After another hour, they turned again, this time onto a narrow dirt road that meandered through a part of the rainforest that appeared to have been clear cut, as only stumps remained among the lush high grass. Here was stark evidence of the disappearing rainforest, all for the meager livelihood of some of the world's poorest people, who probably had no idea of the worldwide effort against deforestation.

Their route had taken them west of the mountain, where the rainforest obscured their view of the intimidating peak. Since she had never spent much time in the mountains, Addison couldn't help but wonder if she had what it took to get to the summit.

"What kind of training did you guys do for this?" she asked, loud enough for the others to hear.

"I've hiked some in the Rockies," Drew answered, "but I travel a lot for work, so I try to run a few miles every day."

"Yeah, me too," she said. "We don't have a lot of mountains in Miami." None of the mountains near Lima were safe for a young woman hiking alone.

"We run too," Kirby offered, waving a finger to include Rachel, but not Courtney. "We do a couple of miles about three times a week."

"Man, you guys have me worried," Mary Kate said. "I've been using a stair-climber at the gym, but I couldn't run if my life depended on it."

Ann spoke. "Don't worry about it, Mary Kate. We won't have to run here. Nikki and I have been doing the stair-climber too, and I feel like I'm ready."

"You guys might be better off than the rest of us," Rachel said. "Who knows if being able to run on flat ground is going to do us any good? At least you worked on your leg muscles."

Nikki turned around and looked toward the back of the bus where their guide sat with the porters. "What do you think, Luke? How many in the group usually make it to the top?"

He scratched his chin, as if trying to choose his words carefully. "I would say that half of you will reach the summit, maybe more. But I do not know yet who. I can know more in two days."

Addison looked around at her companions. Of the ten, only five.

"Hey, we're missing somebody. Where are the two guys from Dallas?" Mary Kate asked.

No one knew, including Luke, who had expected them also.

The bus lurched to a stop, and Luke got off to open an iron gate. They passed through and pulled in front of a small cinderblock building. He jumped back onto the bus and said, "Leave your things here. This is the ranger station. You have to see the ranger and write your passport number."

One by one, they signed into the log book and walked around, making the most of the chance to stretch their legs. Neal announced that he had found a latrine on the side of the building in case anyone needed to use it.

Addison took her turn in the tiny room. It was totally dark, save a narrow unscreened window near the ceiling. The "toilet" was a mere hole in the floor, approximately six by eight inches.

Mary Kate was the last to go and she gasped for breath as she exited.

"Held your breath, didn't you?" Neal said teasingly. "What if you had passed out, huh? Did you think of that? What if you'd just fallen on your face in there and your arm or leg had gotten stuck in that hole?"

"Stop it! That's disgusting." Mary Kate laughed and tried to cover her ears, but Neal tugged at them playfully.

"I'll tell you what's disgusting. By this time next week, you'll be begging for a bathroom as nice as that one."

Addison grimaced as she acknowledged the likely truth of Neal's words. She had been camping only twice in her whole life, and never without facilities. Yet, because of her somewhat privileged upbringing, she tried not to complain, especially about creature comforts.

"To the bus," Luke commanded, and they herded back into their seats.

Mary Kate reached into her backpack and brought out the mysterious bag she had carried from the hotel shop. In it were two boxes of shortbread cookies, one of which she tossed to the dozen or so porters who sat at the back of the bus. The second box made the rounds of all the hikers, and in moments they were all gone.

"Did you like those, Neal?" she asked innocently.

"They're pretty good," he answered, still chewing.

"I found them on the floor in that bathroom."

Chapter Nine

Mary Kate shifted in her seat to take the pressure off her already-aching back. Despite her continued speculation that the road couldn't possibly get any worse, it had, repeatedly bouncing her against her seatmate.

She found herself utterly fascinated with Addison Falk. At first, it was just the way she looked—she had always loved the contrast of brown eyes with blond hair. Mary Kate had studied her at breakfast, comparing her to some of the really pretty girls she had known at college. Those girls worked at it, but Addison had a natural beauty without even a hint of makeup.

When they had gone outside and slapped hands in a pact to get to the summit, she felt an unusual kinship. It was nice to meet someone so sophisticated and worldly who didn't make her feel like a bumpkin.

But the truly fascinating piece had come when they were stowing their belongings. Among the possessions Addison inventoried for safekeeping was a keychain with a triangle-shaped rainbow, a symbol she recognized from her lesbian friends at Savannah State. Deb had a similar bumper sticker, though she wouldn't put it on her car for fear someone in Mooresville would figure out what it was and bash her windows in.

Addison Falk was nothing like the lesbians Mary Kate had known from her small circle of friends at college, women who seemed to fit a certain profile—short hair, athletic, masculine. Not that all of them were like that, but none was as pretty as Addison.

The bus came to a stop at a small clearing in the lush rainforest. Luke told them to pick up one of the box lunches from behind the driver's seat and find a space outside to eat. That was easier said than done, since the clearing was little more than a pit of mud. Mary Kate rested her backpack on a grassy embankment and leaned against it. She hoped Addison would join her, but she took a spot near the van instead.

"Anyone know what kind of sandwich this used to be?" Drew asked.

Mary Kate was trying to figure that out for herself. "Whatever it was, I think they smeared it on and then scraped it off."

"If I can't tell what it is, I'm not eating it," Courtney said emphatically.

Mary Kate was hungry and ate every bite. Then she washed it down with the extra bottle of water she had packed.

One by one, the fifteen porters assigned to their group loaded up and disappeared into the forest, packing tents, food and other supplies, including a folding table and ten camp stools, and all of the trekkers' gear except what each carried in a daypack. Mary Kate looked down at her attire in wonder—convertible pants, a moisture-wicking polyester T-shirt, a lightweight GORE-TEX rain jacket and two-hundred-dollar boots. She had been practically obsessed with getting just the right equipment, and these porters wore sneakers without socks, cutoff pants and worn cotton T-shirts. No wonder Tom had suggested they leave behind a few items to help out the locals.

Her comrades seemed almost giddy in anticipation of the start of their trek. When Mei herded everyone together for the "before" picture, Mary Kate dug out her digital camera and got Luke to take one for her as well. It was exciting to think the "after" picture would come in only eight days.

"Are you ready?" Luke asked them, heaving an enormous pack onto his broad shoulders.

"Where's the trail?" Kirby asked.

"Follow me," he said, nonplussed. "That is why they call me the guide."

Luke pulled back a large shrub to reveal the narrow trail, a muddy path that started up a steep incline. After only five minutes of walking, Mary Kate was winded and hot. When Luke paused to look back at how everyone was doing, she took off her jacket and tied the sleeves around her waist. Then she found the hose leading to the two-liter water bladder in her backpack and took a deep draw. The hose was the easiest way to both carry and drink water, since she could drink without stopping. The mouthpiece clipped to her shoulder for quick access.

"How high do you think we are?" Courtney asked, also puffing for breath.

"Moshi was at four thousand feet," Mei said. "I think I read the Londorossi Gate was about sixty-five hundred."

"And Big Tree is at ninety-two hundred, so we'll be climbing almost three thousand feet today," Rachel added.

For this section of the hike, they were escorted by an armed ranger. Luke said that was because elephants and water buffaloes frequented certain areas of the rainforest, posing a danger if they charged.

"So how do you keep an elephant from charging?" Neal asked.

Mei groaned in response. "I apologize for bringing along the guy with bad jokes."

That particular joke had made the rounds of Mary Kate's elementary school last year, but she thought it was pretty funny that Neal had brought it up in this context. "I'll bite. How do you keep an elephant from charging?"

"Cut up his credit card."

Mary Kate smiled in appreciation, but Nikki let out a snort when she laughed. Several others mocked her with snorts of their own. Luke simply looked at all of them and shook his head. He probably had no idea what a credit card was.

Courtney and Rachel were directly behind the ranger at the front of the single-file line, followed by Nikki, Ann and Kirby. Mary Kate walked behind Luke, who was in the middle of the pack. After her were Drew, Neal and Mei, with Addison bringing up the rear.

As they walked farther into the rainforest, Mary Kate marveled at the surrounding landscape, a three-dimensional panorama of deep greens. Only occasionally did the sunlight seep beneath the forest canopy, and a fine mist wafted through the valley below. From time to time, Addison would call out "Porter!" and everyone would step off the narrow trail to allow the crewman through. Despite their heavy loads, the porters moved at a much faster pace, hurrying ahead to ready the camp for their arrival. Mary Kate hated to think what a lone porter would do if charged by an angry elephant.

"*Jambo! Asante*," the porter said as he passed. Hello. Thank you.

"*Jambo*," they all answered in unison, quickly picking up the greeting.

Mary Kate glanced over her shoulder, stealing a look at Addison, who had stopped to take pictures. She probably had no idea how pretty she looked against the backdrop of the rainforest. Of course, women like Addison looked great against—

"We stop for a break," Luke announced.

She had been so distracted that she almost plowed right into him. Now standing in a small clearing, she dropped her walking sticks, shed her pack, and rolled her shoulders to stretch.

"Does everyone drink their water?" Luke asked.

Some nodded. Others reached for their bottles. Mary Kate estimated she had drunk a second liter since starting the climb… and her bladder was screaming.

"I think I'll get rid of some water," Kirby said, retreating back down the trail behind a large tree.

"And I think I have penis envy," Rachel mumbled, looking

about for a discreet spot. Walking ahead of the group, she ventured over a small rise where she was hidden from the others.

"I had penis envy when I was younger," Courtney said. "But my mother told me that as long as I had one of these"—she gestured to her lap—"I could have all of those I wanted."

The women laughed, and Drew conceded that she had a point. Luke was unfazed, as if he hadn't understood.

Mary Kate loosened the jacket from her waist and looked around. "I guess I should do that, too. Hey, Rachel, is there another spot over there? Maybe something uphill from where you are?" If she had to pee outside, she didn't want to be downhill from someone else who was doing the same thing.

One by one, they took turns using the makeshift men's and ladies' rooms, though Courtney had second thoughts when Luke cautioned them all to be on the lookout for the green mamba, one of the world's most poisonous snakes.

Once rested, they got underway again. Mary Kate had stepped aside to let Neal and Mei in front she could walk toward the back with Drew and Addison. Addison was telling a story about the airlines losing her luggage in Peru. She had worn her step-father's track suits for three days.

A half hour later, Luke held up his hand to slow them as they walked within thirty yards of a tree that housed a family of black monkeys. Mary Kate snapped a few pictures as the playful primates crawled from limb to limb, hanging upside down to reach out for leaves or to play with a sibling. She doubted anyone back in Mooresville had ever seen such a thing.

Ever since Addison arrived, she had wondered how they would pair up tonight in the two-person tents. Obviously, Neal and Mei would share, as would Ann and Nikki. Rachel would probably go with Kirby, which left two other girls and one guy. Alarmed at the possibility of having to share with Drew, she stepped aside and waited for him to pass.

"Addison?"

"Hey, what's up?"

Mary Kate fell into step in front and talked over her shoulder, keeping her voice low, though they had fallen back out of earshot. "I wanted to ask you something. We're supposed to pair up when we get to camp, and I was wondering if you wanted to share a tent?"

Addison shot her a broad smile. "Sure, but I think Mr. Colorado has other ideas, though I'm not sure he cares if it's you or me."

"Yeah, I know. That's kind of why I was hoping you'd say yes. I thought it might be awkward if he asked. He didn't seem to hear the 'boyfriend' part when we were on the bus."

"Maybe he figured it wasn't too serious if you were here without him."

"Actually, it isn't, but I don't want him to know that." The words echoed in her head, and she realized its double meaning. "Drew, I mean."

Addison chuckled. "Does the boyfriend know it isn't serious?"

"No, he's pretty clueless." She felt guilty immediately for casting Bobby in a bad light. "He's a nice guy, but we don't seem to want the same things."

"You mean like Africa?"

Mary Kate was surprised at Addison's perceptive grasp. "Yeah, but that's just kind of symbolic of everything else. I like to do new things, but Bobby's one of those guys who knows what he wants for breakfast next summer."

"Ah, a creature of habit."

A creature of boredom, she thought. "Yeah, but like I said, he's nice, and he's going to make somebody a terrific husband. Just not me."

"We break here," Luke called again. Their gait so far had been quite slow, and after the initial breathlessness, everyone had managed to adapt, at least enough that they could talk while they climbed.

Courtney was the only one still struggling. "How much farther to the camp?" she asked.

"One hour."

Addison dropped her pack and sat down on the hillside. "I suppose I ought to tell you something before you make up your mind about the tent thing, and I guess the safari part too."

"You mean that you're gay?"

Addison's eyes went wide. "Actually, I was going to say that I snore."

Horrified that she might have been mistaken, Mary Kate felt her face grow hot. "I…"

"No, no. I was just kidding. I don't snore, at least not that I know of. You're right. I was going to tell you that I bat for the other team. I thought I should—"

"I can't believe you did that with a straight face." Mary Kate felt the blood drain from her cheeks. "You just took ten years off my life."

"Sorry, I couldn't resist. How did you know?"

"I saw your keychain back at the hotel." She blew out a breath and tried to relax again. "My best friend has a bumper sticker like that."

"So you're okay with it?"

"Sure. I have lots of lesbian friends."

"Good. Maybe you'll have another one by the time we head home."

"Not if you keep trying to give me a heart attack."

"It was just a little joke," Addison said, batting her eyes innocently.

"Just remember one thing, Addison Falk. Paybacks are a bitch." She almost laughed as Addison gulped. "And I will not deprive you of that experience."

Up ahead, Luke had picked up his pack. That was their signal the break was over.

Mary Kate pushed against the ground to stand. "Ouch!" Her hand was on fire. "What the hell was that?" The burning intensified as she waved her hand back and forth.

Luke hurried back to where they sat. "Nettles," he said simply, his face visibly relaxing.

"Oh, those are supposed to be painful," Ann said.

"They are! What the hell are nettles?" Mary Kate was staring at her hand, looking for stingers or bite marks that would account for this excruciating pain.

Luke pointed to the plant that was near where she was sitting. "These are nettles."

"They've got tiny prickles with some kind of stinging substance," Ann explained. "The sting only lasts about seven minutes, then it's gone."

"Seven minutes!" Mary Kate nearly screamed. The pain was growing worse by the second. It was going to be a very long seven minutes.

"Here, I've got some first-aid cream." Addison took off her pack and dug inside. In moments, she had Mary Kate's hand, gently applying the soothing mixture.

Mary Kate relaxed as the topical anesthetic took effect, and she pulled her pack into place. "Just in case anyone missed that little bit of drama, don't touch the nettles."

"Does this buy me a little forgiveness?" Addison asked quietly.

"You'll have to wait and see."

Chapter Ten

When they dragged into camp, Addison was thrilled to see their tents already set up. Tom had warned them they might have to do that.

Drew stopped in the middle of the camp, clearly waiting for Mary Kate to catch up.

"Which one do you want, Mary Kate?" she called loudly, thinking it best to head off an awkward moment.

"Let's take that one over there," Mary Kate answered, pointing to a small yellow and blue tent on the edge of the campsite.

Addison noticed it was farthest from the latrine. But then again…it was farthest from the latrine. Like everyone else, she had to go.

The latrine was a tall wooden structure, about five feet square, with a wall separating the two sides. The door was actually just an entrance, the right half of the structure. If one were looking down from the top, it would have resembled a capital "G." In the inside compartment, a hole was cut into the floor. Extreme care and concentration were required, as the hole was barely the size of a brick.

The porters had stacked the ten yellow Summit bags in the

center of the campsite. Addison's stood out because it still had the Kenya Airways tag. Already, it was smeared with volcanic silt, fine black dirt that clung like toner from a printer cartridge.

Besides their smaller tents, two larger ones were erected for Luke and the porters. With the flaps open, Addison could see very little in the way of creature comforts. Evidently, the young men who were carrying their equipment and bags were planning to rely on body heat from one another to get through the night. Already, the temperature had dropped substantially, thanks to both the altitude and waning sunlight.

Beside the renowned Big Tree, for which the camp was named, was a third large tent, this one with screens on all four sides where camp stools surrounded a long folding table. A couple of thermoses sat next to tin cups, and assorted flatware lay across a stack of tin plates.

"Hot tea, hot water." The porter known as Gilbert scurried back to the tent he shared with Luke, where he tended something on a camp stove.

Addison poured herself a cup of hot tea to ward off the chill.

Moments later, Gilbert emerged with a five-gallon yellow container filled with warm water. Pouring some into a shallow pan, he rubbed his hands together to show everyone this was for hand washing. Then he laid a funnel atop the container. "To drink tomorrow."

Kirby volunteered to collect the water bladders from inside the backpacks, lining them up in alphabetical order to remember which belonged to whom. Most of the models held two liters. All of the hikers crowded around with their spare water bottles, readying for the next day. Ann presented her clear, one-liter bottle first, holding the funnel as Kirby poured from the jug.

"There's stuff in the water," she said. "The brochure said the water was supposed to be pure."

"We can filter that and drop in some iodine tablets," Addison said, pulling a pouch from her Summit bag.

"I didn't bring any iodine," Ann grumbled. "And I didn't bring any toilet paper either, because Tom said that would be provided too. But Gilbert just told me they didn't have any."

"You're kidding me!" Rachel exclaimed.

"Actually, that would be 'you're shitting me,'" Kirby said, earning him a glare from his girlfriend, but raucous laughter from everyone else.

"I've got plenty of iodine tablets for everyone," Addison said, "but you better be sure you aren't allergic. That would be nasty." Luckily, Cyn had prepared her for both of those needs, but she wasn't about to offer her extra toilet paper. "And I brought some cheesecloth to catch the bugs."

Starting over, Kirby poured bottle after bottle, all through the finely woven filter. To each liter, Addison added a tiny tablet that turned the water light orange. The group effort took almost a half hour, but everyone's water supply was replenished and readied for the hike tomorrow.

Gilbert had started to bring food inside the dining tent. "Eat now."

Three steaming dishes sat on the table, a bowl of boiled potatoes, another containing shell pasta and a third that resembled cabbage. Addison was the first to try the latter and declared it delicious.

"I can't believe you guys are eating that green stuff," Courtney said. "I read that you shouldn't eat anything out of the ground."

Drew scoffed. "Those potatoes you're eating are out of the ground."

"But they had a skin, which was peeled off. You guys go right ahead, but don't come crying to me when you get the runs," she said.

"And don't you come crying to us when you get clogged up," he countered jokingly.

"By the way, if there's anyone who doesn't want their dinner napkin, I'll take it off your hands," Rachel offered demurely.

"Yeah, right," Neal said. "I have a feeling we'll be using dollar bills on our butts before the end of the week."

"And to think, just this morning, we were all being sweet and nice, asking where everybody was from," Mary Kate said, her voice syrupy sweet. "Now it's ten hours later and we're talking about bodily functions at the dinner table."

Addison chuckled to herself at Mary Kate's prissy tone, though she suspected Mary Kate was anything but a prude. From her joke on the bus about the cookies, it was obvious she had a wicked sense of humor, and seemed more than capable of carrying out her payback threat.

Darkness fell soon after dinner, and the temperature plunged, driving everyone inside their tents for the night. Addison unscrewed the valve on her air mattress and it inflated automatically. "I don't know about you, but I'm still a little jet-lagged."

"Yeah, it'll probably take a couple of days to even out." Mary Kate dragged her Summit bag underneath the rain guard of their small tent. "How cold do you think it is?"

"Probably in the upper thirties, but to someone from Miami, it might as well be three." Addison unzipped her sleeping bag and got it ready for easy access once she got undressed. "We probably should keep our backpacks in here. One of the blogs I read said people had things stolen from under their rain guard."

"Who could blame them? It's obvious the people here don't have very much."

Mary Kate was right. It would be bad to be ripped off, but whoever took it probably needed it worse. "Tom said we should consider leaving behind some of our things for the porters. I'll probably leave this sleeping bag and daypack."

"Wow, I hadn't thought about giving them something big like that. I was going to leave a couple of shirts...maybe a jacket."

Addison tugged off her pullover fleece and short-sleeved shirt and squeezed into a thermal top that hugged her skin. "I got most of my stuff second-hand. This is only about the third time in my life I've been in a tent." It took a concerted effort not to peek as Mary Kate changed into her long johns.

"Could have fooled me. You look like you know what you're doing. Nobody else thought to bring the water tablets."

"Yeah, my friend I told you about, the one who got pregnant, she knew somebody who did this trip with Summit last year. She got the lowdown on everything." Addison lowered her voice. "In fact, I'll let you in on a little secret. I brought toilet paper too."

"I'm so glad we're best friends forever, Addison."

"And how convenient that you've forgiven me for giving you a heart attack."

"Totally forgotten."

"I brought camp soap too, so we won't make a mess of the water. I have a vested interest in having my tent mate practice good hygiene."

Mary Kate laughed as she wriggled into her sleeping bag. "I knew we'd be cold up here, but I never dreamed I'd be sleeping in my long johns on our first night. I don't even want to think how cold we're going to be once we get to Barafu." Barafu was the base camp for their ascent on Saturday night.

"Did you know Barafu is Swahili for ice?"

"I don't think I wanted to know that." Mary Kate was inside her bag zipping it up from the inside. "I have some things I can share, too."

"Such as?"

"I brought three dozen energy bars, a box of baby wipes and a bottle of hand sanitizer."

"I brought hand sanitizer too, but baby wipes, what a great idea. And anyone with extra food can definitely be my best friend." Addison's shivering slowed as her body heat warmed the air in her sleeping bag. She could hear Mary Kate's deep, steady breathing, a sign that she had fallen asleep. They would have a lot more opportunities over the next few days to get to know each other, but for now, she was feeling lucky to have hooked up with a tent mate that was fun and easy to talk to. Not to mention cute.

Chapter Eleven

"Who's the moose?" Mary Kate demanded as she entered the dining tent for breakfast. She had been awakened by loud snoring at three a.m.

"Drew!" answered the Penn State crew in unison.

He ducked his head in embarrassment. "I can't help it. I'm supposed to have surgery this fall to fix it."

"What were they going to do?" Kirby asked, picking up two of the dull knives Gilbert had laid out. "Because we might just do it here and save you some money."

Mary Kate was glad she had saved the earplugs she used on the overnight flight from Atlanta. She would never have gotten back to sleep without them.

Addison entered the dining tent and went straight for the thermos containing hot tea. She hadn't spoken a word all morning, which had Mary Kate worrying that she too had snored all night. No one had ever complained of that, but these circumstances were different from anything she had experienced.

"Good morning," Addison finally said with surprising cheer. "Did anyone else hear that elephant singing last night?"

"It was Drew," Nikki said, jerking her thumb in his

direction.

"Couldn't have been. It was like"—she waved a hand in the air—"nature's symphony."

"Very funny," Drew said. "You think just because I'm wearing women's underwear that gives you the right to torment me about a medical condition that's clearly beyond my control."

Addison made a sad face and pretended to play a violin. "You want us to feel sorry for you just because you're wearing satin panties?"

Drew's scowl dissolved immediately into a grin. "If you give me your satin panties, you can say anything you want."

When Gilbert appeared with scrambled eggs, mangos and bread, Mary Kate joined the others in disregard of Courtney's warning about not eating fruit. The dripping mango was too enticing to resist. Only Courtney abstained, gleefully warning them they would pay the ultimate price.

As the hikers ate, the porters efficiently dismantled the camp, folding up the tents and cooking equipment.

"Don't look now, but I think breakfast is over," Mary Kate said. She made a quick trip to the latrine and then waited while the others did the same. She had expected to be sore or tired from the hike yesterday, but she was neither. That was encouraging.

"We go to Shira Plateau," Luke said as they lined up behind him. The air was crisp and damp, and the trail less steep than their climb to Big Tree.

Mary Kate lagged behind to walk next to Addison, who was chatting with Luke.

"...five years I work for Tom Muncie."

"And how many trips have you made up this mountain?"

"This is one hundred three."

"Wow," Mary Kate said. "Have you always made it to the top?"

He shook his head. "Seven times no. I stayed behind with climbers who were sick."

"That's all? Only seven times? Everyone else made it to the top?"

"Oh, no. We have four guides who go to the summit. When climbers become sick, a guide returns with them to camp."

"I get it," Addison said. "So there were seven times when all the other guides had already turned back."

"That is right."

"So who led the other climbers when you turned back?"

"They went ahead from Stella Point. The trail to Uhuru is clear from there."

Mary Kate had studied the map of the mountain and recognized Stella Point as being on the crater rim near the summit. When they stopped for their first break, she noticed Luke scribbling in a notebook. "Do you keep notes on every trip?"

He smiled wryly and nodded. "I watch you."

"What do you mean you watch us?"

"I watch who drinks the water, who eats, who is very tired. It is my job."

"What does that tell you, Luke?" Addison asked. "Can you guess who will get to the summit?"

"Usually. But the most important thing I cannot yet see. Who is confident? Who is determined?"

"Is that what it really takes?"

"The one who believes he can do it—or she can do it—is the one who has prepared. And the one who has prepared does not want to be disappointed."

That made sense to Mary Kate. Most of the people in their group seemed fit, except Courtney, who was winded at every break and groaned each time they resumed. But Mary Kate had been surprised to learn the Penn State trio had booked this summit trek only a month ago, so even though Kirby and Rachel ran a few times a week, they had not trained for the climb the way the others had.

After an hour and a half of winding through the lush rainforest, they suddenly emerged. There was no gradual thinning of the thick green vegetation. They had simply walked through a door into another room of the great outdoors. The accompanying armed ranger bid them farewell with a wave, and Luke took the point.

The brush was still relatively thick on this new terrain, but unlike the lush foliage of the rainforest, it was dry. Only a few of the trees reached higher than ten feet. The canopy that had protected them from the morning sun was gone, and as soon as Luke called for a break, they peeled off their jackets and unzipped the pant legs on their convertibles. Mary Kate laughed inwardly at how she had thought herself so clever for finding all the best gear. Practically everyone else had managed to find the same things.

Late in the morning, the group stepped over a low ridge to discover their dining tent erected in a clearing, with the table and camp stools already set up inside. Gilbert and the porters had hurried ahead to prepare lunch. Courtney made do with peanut butter and bread, but the others—hungry and now confident their systems would withstand the change—devoured the fruits and vegetables too.

Addison had the hot tea to herself once Gilbert delivered a tin of cocoa powder called Milo. "I bet that stuff has cocaine in it. That's why you're all craving it," she said.

"Speaking of drugs…" Drew pulled a small bottle from his pocket. "Is anyone taking Diamox?"

Diamox was a medication that facilitated the oxygen exchange in the blood in case the body didn't adjust on its own to the altitude. Tom had mentioned it in the guide as something climbers had used for years, but he stopped short of recommending it, insisting that going up slowly and drinking a lot of water was sufficient for most.

Mary Kate had gotten a prescription just to cover all her bases. "I brought some, but I haven't taken it yet. I haven't really noticed any effects of the altitude."

"We started it as soon as we got to Moshi," Courtney said. "My doctor said it needed to be in your system two days before it would take effect, so you might want to go ahead and start."

"What are you going to do, Addison?" Mary Kate asked as

they geared up to start the afternoon hike.

"I hadn't planned on taking it. I was hoping the water would be enough."

"But by the time you need it, it might be too late to do any good."

Addison shrugged. "It's a moot point. I didn't bring any."

Mary Kate read the directions on her bottle and washed down her first pill. Addison was right about the water, but the Diamox wouldn't hurt. She wanted every advantage. "I have fourteen pills. I'll share if you want some."

"Nah, I'll take my chances."

Luke loaded up his pack and waited for them to line up. "Before our next break, I promise you a spectacular sight."

Mary Kate shifted her position in the line until she was behind Addison. Though they had few things in common, she liked thinking they might end up with a friendship that lasted beyond this trip. It would be nice to have a close friend who was so different from the people she knew back home, or even from the other small town girls at Savannah State. Ironic that so many of her close friends were—

"Everyone stop!" Luke yelled. When he had their attention, he turned and pointed to the top of the ridge they were climbing. Beyond its crest was a slim band of white. "The mountain."

Mary Kate whipped out her camera and zoomed in on the sight. Given the direction of the trail, it was clear the entire mountain would come into view once they crested the ridge. Here, with only its snowcapped peak visible in the distance, it was tantalizing.

With every step toward the top of the ridge, the mountain grew exponentially larger as it revealed itself. When she finally got her first full view of Kilimanjaro, Mary Kate was awed beyond words.

"Like he said, spectacular," Addison said.

"No kidding." Completely devoid of vegetation, the mountain was gray, its glacier top like icing on a cupcake.

"And it's almost ten thousand more feet to the top."

Luke clicked a series of photos of the group with the mountain in the background, and Mary Kate traded cameras with Addison to get a solo shot.

"Come stand with me," Addison said. "Hey, Drew. Make yourself useful." She handed him her camera and slung her arm over Mary Kate's shoulder.

"I want one of these with my camera too."

"Save your battery. I'll send it to you."

Mary Kate smiled broadly as the camera clicked, practically giddy that Addison was already talking about staying in touch after this trip.

They hoisted their packs and lined up again, but Luke held back, pointing to a cluster of colorful dots about a mile ahead on the plateau. "That is our camp, Shira One."

The remainder of their afternoon hike was easy, and they entered the open flat camp just before three. Mary Kate was glad to get there, but felt good about her stamina. Two days of hiking had gained them six thousand feet in altitude—about seven thousand feet higher than she had ever been in her lifetime—and she wasn't feeling any effects so far. In the next three days, they would hike about fifteen miles, but climb only three thousand feet. Tom had said the slow ascent would be their greatest ally for acclimatization.

"I'm whipped," Ann said, dropping her backpack underneath her rain guard. "I might catch a nap."

"Go ahead. I'll do the water," Nikki said. She joined Mary Kate at the water station. "My aunt was up most of the night. It's going to take her a couple of days to adjust."

Mary Kate nodded with understanding. "I think I slept about ten hours last night, so I should be caught up now." She and Nikki held the water bladders and filter as Drew filled them from the jug Gilbert had provided.

"Hey, Mary Kate! You want your sleeping bag out?" Addison and the others had spread their bags across the tops of the tents to dry the condensation that had gathered overnight.

"Sure, thanks." She liked the camaraderie of their teamwork.

Though they each brought their own experiences to bear, all were novices on the mountain, and their inclination to help each other gave her a sense of security.

Gilbert appeared again and proudly presented them with freshly popped popcorn, which disappeared almost as soon as he set down the enormous bowl. Retreating to the cook tent, he fired up the stove to make more.

"Man, that water's freezing!" Kirby said, rubbing his hands together briskly as he returned from the creek that crossed directly between their campsite and the mountain.

"Water?" Addison ducked inside their tent and returned a few moments later with several items rolled up inside a towel. "I'm feeling kind of grungy. I think I'll try to find a wide spot in this creek and catch a quick bath. Anyone else game?" She locked eyes with Drew and stuck out her tongue. "Besides you."

"Wait for me!" Mary Kate stowed her water and went into their tent for her things.

The other women, all but Ann, also collected towels and a change of clothes, and fell in as Addison led the way.

"What about me?" Drew whined. "I'm grungy too."

"That's right," Neal said. "You stink and you snore. And the naked women don't want anything to do with you."

After ten minutes of hiking downstream across the rocky terrain, they found the perfect spot, a clear, shallow pool about ten feet across, well out of sight of the camp. The pool was fed by a small waterfall above and emptied through a narrow channel at the bottom. The sloping sides gave them a place to sit partially submerged as they washed.

Mary Kate wasn't sure what the others had in mind, but she had spent enough time in locker rooms to be comfortable changing in front of others, but only if they were changing too.

"This was my idea, wasn't it?" Addison said as she eyed the water skeptically. Then she pulled off her boots, socks, pants and shirt. "In for a penny, in for a pound." To that pile, she quickly added her briefs and sports bra, squatting tentatively to slip waist deep into the water's edge.

"How is it?"

"F-f-fine," she answered. "Quite warm, in fact."

"Jesus Christ!" Rachel said as she dipped a toe. "Addison lies."

Studying Addison from behind, Mary Kate was mesmerized by the contrast of the sinewy muscles of her upper body and the curve of her hips. The lesbians she knew who played basketball were either wiry or broad and muscular. Addison had the best combination of all, a body that was both fit and feminine. If Mary Kate were ever going to be attracted to another woman, it would be someone like Addison.

Courtney and Rachel took off their shirts and pants and sat on the rocks next to the water, opting for a sponge bath away from the icy flow. Nikki and Mei gamely stripped down to join Addison in the water, both slinking wide-eyed and gasping into the edge of the frigid pool.

"Be careful," Mei said. "These rocks are slick."

Mary Kate eyed a slab of rock across from Addison that would allow her to sit waist deep like the others. She dropped her towel and change of clothes nearby and bravely shed every stitch, dreading the first touch of the water. Addison echoed Mei's warning as she cautiously inched down the slight incline. Just as her feet settled into the icy flow, they sailed out from under her and she plunged full force to the deepest part of the pool.

"Oh, shit!" she screamed, gasping to draw breath into her frozen lungs. "Oh, shit. Oh, shit. Oh, shit." The slippery incline offered no traction as she tried frantically to pull herself out. She grasped Addison's outstretched hand and noticed that her other hand was covering her mouth. "I can't believe you're laughing at me. What did I tell you about paybacks?"

"I can't help it."

Mary Kate scooted up to sit next to her. She took the offered bar of soap and rubbed it briskly over her tingling skin. "For all you know, I could be injured."

"Are you?"

"No, but that's not the point." She couldn't maintain her

serious tone with everyone on the verge of laughter. "Go ahead and laugh, all of you. But if I see a bug going into your water bottle tomorrow, you can bet your sweet asses I won't be filtering it out."

Nikki hurriedly dried her skin and pulled on her fresh clothes. "I have to hurry back to camp now so I can write all of this in my journal while the picture is still fresh in my mind."

"Very funny!" Mary Kate shouted.

Mei, Courtney and Rachel followed close behind, leaving her alone with Addison.

"Seriously, are you all right? You didn't hurt yourself, did you?" All traces of teasing were gone. Addison had pulled on her pants and shirt and was standing barefoot.

"It's too late to be nice to me now, Addison. I predict your air mattress will spring a leak tonight." Mary Kate finished rinsing and hastily dried her legs. Despite her invigorating plunge, she reveled in the special satisfaction that only being clean could bring. As she stood to pull on fresh panties, she was surprised by the touch of a towel to her back.

"There you go," Addison said, dabbing at the drops of water.

"Thanks." Mary Kate took the towel and dried her front, feeling ridiculous at her sudden rush of self-consciousness. Sure, she had admired Addison's body when she was nude, but she had been discreet about it. Addison didn't even pretend not to look.

"Sorry, I didn't mean to get so personal." Addison winced. "I just thought you'd want your back dried."

"It's okay. I appreciate it," she said, embarrassed to hear the quiver in her voice. She was relieved when Addison sat down to put on her boots, and she used the opportunity to quickly pull on the top to her long johns.

"I'm kind of a touchy-feely person with all my friends. If that makes you uncomfortable, don't be afraid to say so, and I'll shove my hands in my pockets or something."

Mary Kate chuckled, trying to shake the tension. "I told you already. It's too late to be nice to me. I'm poking a hole in your air mattress."

Chapter Twelve

They had been in their tent for over two hours, talking about why they had decided to come to Africa, and their chances for reaching the summit. Addison had explained her quest for the Hunger Coalition, and how everyone else had canceled. "I have to admit, I sort of dreaded coming all by myself, but I'm glad I did."

"I'm glad you did too."

"Right. Otherwise, you'd be sleeping with a moose."

"You mean not sleeping with a moose."

She chuckled. "I'm not sleepy at all tonight." They could hear murmurs from the other tents, a sure sign they weren't the only ones unable to sleep.

"Me neither. I wonder if it has anything to do with the altitude."

"It's probably just the time change. We'll adjust in a day or two, especially with all the hiking."

"Tell me some more about your job in London. I have no idea what an investment banker does." Addison had told her a little about her father's firm.

"I like development projects like the one I worked on last

year for my internship. The Fed—that's the Federal Reserve Bank—it has a branch in Miami, and I helped to oversee one of the community lending projects down in Homestead. The idea was to get a cluster of small businesses off the ground near one of the new subsidized housing projects. The people who live there need these services and the jobs too. I helped to screen the business owners and match them to the right lenders."

"I bet you feel like you're doing something good in the world."

"I told my father I wanted to look for investment opportunities in underdeveloped countries. Unfortunately, I have to prove myself with the conventional projects first, and that could take a few years."

"Still, you're helping to build something. That's important."

"Look at you, teaching kids with behavior problems. That's hard work, and it does a lot of good. I can't imagine many people want to do that."

"Not many do, which means I could go just about anywhere I wanted and find work."

"And you chose to go back home."

Mary Kate sighed. "It seemed like the thing to do at the time, but I sort of wish I'd tried for something different."

"Why didn't you?"

"You have to understand how things are done in small towns. Not many of the kids from my class went to college, and most of the ones who did go didn't finish. They left, got homesick and came back. And what happened to me is that my mom—she teaches biology at the high school—she talked to the superintendent, who talked to the principal at my school, and he called me in Savannah *my junior year* to tell me he'd have a job waiting for me when I finished. I never even bothered to apply anywhere else."

"Do you like it?"

"I guess. But if I had gone to work somewhere else, maybe people wouldn't think they could push me into all this other stuff."

"You mean like your boyfriend?"

"Especially him…well, no. It isn't really that Bobby pushes me. It's more that everybody else expects me to marry him…all of my family, the people at our school."

"He's a teacher too?"

"Assistant principal. My boss, technically."

"I bet that's sticky."

"Not really, but everybody knows everything about our business. And Bobby told all the other teachers that he'd gotten me an engagement ring for Christmas, so when I didn't take it, everybody had to come and tell me what a fool I was."

"Wait a minute. You didn't take his ring, but he's still your boyfriend?"

"I wasn't ready. He said he'd wait, but that when he asked again, that was it. I either said yes, or we broke up."

"So the next time will be an ultimatum."

"Which I got at the airport as I was leaving. He expects an answer when I get home."

"Are you breaking up like you said, or still thinking about it?"

"Both," she said, her voice rising with irritation. "I've made up my mind, but now I'm dreading what everybody's going to say."

"It's your decision. What does anyone else have to do with it?"

"Nothing," she said with a groan. "My mother will probably be the most reasonable about it, but even she's going to remind me that I could do a lot worse than Bobby."

"You could do worse than a lot of people, but that's no reason to marry someone you don't love." Mary Kate probably wouldn't appreciate the comparison, but Addison had felt the same way about her job. It was her decision, and she hated the pressure she got from her father. "Maybe it's time for you to change jobs. You could at least go work at a different school, and you wouldn't have to look at him every day."

"It's not that simple. There are only two elementary schools in all of Hurston County. Even jobs like mine don't come open very often. Once people get tenure, they tend to stay for life."

"Who says you have to stay in Hurston County?" Addison cautioned herself not to join the chorus of people telling Mary Kate what to do. She had probably thought all of this out on her own, and was staying where she was because, deep down, that's where she wanted to be.

"I've thought about maybe checking into openings somewhere else. One of my friends from college teaches in Charleston. That could be fun."

"It's a bigger city, right?"

"Everything's bigger than Mooresville, but I have to stick it out for at least another year. I signed a letter of intent last February, so I'm committed."

"What happens if you change your mind?"

"Nothing really. It's not like they can make you teach there if you don't want to. But it won't look good if you apply to teach somewhere else."

Addison couldn't get a bead on Mary Kate's mindset. On the one hand, she sounded bored and disenchanted with life back in her small town. On the other, she seemed resigned to it, as if it were her unavoidable fate. "Have you thought about what you're going to say to Bobby when you get home?"

"Not really." Mary Kate sighed with what sounded like frustration. "The whole thing's just one big mess."

Addison worried she was making things worse. "I'm sure you'll handle it all just right, Mary Kate. You're too level-headed to do something without knowing how it's going to work out."

"I appreciate you saying that. You have no idea what it feels like to always have people around you who think they know best."

"I do, actually, at least as far as my father is concerned. He's never seen any future for me other than working at his company in London."

"He must have a lot of faith in your work."

That was probably part of it, but Addison was more cynical

about his interest. "Maybe, but I sometimes wonder if getting me to move to London is part of the contest he's been having with my mother for the last ten years. Once I go to London, he feels vindicated. And on top of that, he gets to work on me nonstop about being gay and how that won't fly in the business world."

"Your father doesn't accept you being gay?"

"He goes through the motions, but I think he figures if I'm working for him, he can get me to do other things too, just like what you said about going back to your town. I remember back when he and my mom split up, one of the things they fought about was which one screwed me up."

"You're kidding. How could parents do something like that?"

"I don't know. They fought about everything, really. At least my mom got over it. She even tried to set me up once with some lady who worked for her husband. Of course, that was probably to get me to move to Peru." She snorted. "I make them both sound awful. They love me, but that didn't mean I wasn't a pawn."

"It's interesting when you think about it. We come from totally different places, but our situations are so much alike, with the people back home pulling at us."

"Yeah, maybe we'll both figure it all out here in Africa. At least nobody's breathing down our necks."

"I don't even want to think about it anymore."

Addison took that as her cue to drop it. "You know what I don't want to think about? Having to pee."

Ten seconds of silence was followed by an exasperated sigh, and the sound of Mary Kate's sleeping bag being unzipped. "I hate you."

Chapter Thirteen

Addison was the first one out of their tent, but only because she hadn't slept all night, despite the fact that Mary Kate had gone quiet a couple of hours before daybreak. It was probably the power of suggestion, but more than once, Addison wondered why her air mattress had seemed so flat. A quick check when she sat up confirmed that Mary Kate hadn't made good on her threat.

"You're up early."

She followed the voice to the dining tent, where Ann was smearing peanut butter and marmalade on bread. "Good morning."

"Sleep okay?"

Addison shook her head. "Didn't sleep at all." She was glad to see that Gilbert had already made the tea.

"Sounds like me the night before last. But I think I made up for it."

"Did you hear somebody getting sick last night?"

Ann cocked her head toward the tent behind her. "Yeah, it was one of the girls, either Rachel or Courtney."

"Man, she must have thrown up ten times. I wonder what

was wrong."

"Wouldn't it be something if it was Courtney? She's the only one who hasn't eaten the fruit or vegetables."

"Yeah, but it might be the altitude," Addison said. "Twelve thousand feet is pretty high for somebody who lives in Pennsylvania."

Ann leaned closer and lowered her voice. "Not to mention somebody who didn't train at all. And Nikki said her water bottles were half full last night, so she isn't drinking like she's supposed to."

Addison shook her head, wondering how somebody could be so foolish. "She's taking a big chance."

"I know. It's hard not to get on her case, but I'm on vacation from being somebody's mother on this trip. Thank goodness my niece can take care of herself."

Mary Kate emerged from the tent, bleary-eyed and disheveled. "Something tells me it's going to be a long day." She took a seat at the table, and Ann handed her a slathered piece of bread.

"Looks like lots of us had a rough night," Addison said, nodding in the direction of Drew and Kirby, both of whom were stumbling from their tent. "I don't think we gain any altitude today, so maybe we'll all be back to normal tonight."

Drew pushed by them and poured a cup of tea. "My head's about to explode."

Addison smiled to herself as Ann slipped seamlessly into a mothering role, moving behind him as he sat to gently massage his temples. "Make sure you drink plenty of water today."

One by one, the remaining hikers joined them for breakfast. Even Neal and Mei were subdued, both complaining of a restless night. The Penn State trio appeared, but Courtney stayed well clear of the dining tent.

"She isn't interested in food this morning," Rachel said.

As they wrapped up breakfast, Luke joined them to lay out their day. "We have an easy hike, only three and one-half hours. We gain two hundred meters."

"Seven hundred feet," Mei said.

"We will reach the camp in time for lunch. That is the good news. The bad news is that Shira Two is upon rocks, not as comfortable. The wind blows very hard."

Given how tired they all seemed, Addison doubted that would matter to anyone. Under normal circumstances, she would have hung back to walk with Mary Kate, but after their talk into the wee hours of the morning, she didn't want to be pushy in case Mary Kate wanted a change of company. She was pleased when Mary Kate scooted around Neal and Mei to take the place behind her, but became concerned when she saw her worried expression.

"You okay, Mary Kate?"

"I don't know. I feel kind of numb and tingly. I had trouble holding on to my cup this morning."

"Maybe you slept on your arm or something, pinched a nerve."

She shook her head. "It's in my feet too, like I'm walking on pins and needles."

Addison stopped and pressed her palm to Mary Kate's forehead. "I don't think you have a fever or anything."

Neal and Mei walked around them, leaving them on the trail behind the group.

"I don't feel sick, just numb."

"Did you eat something unusual?" She shook her head, feeling ridiculous. "I know, stupid question. You took that Diamox yesterday. Are there side effects?"

Mary Kate pulled off her pack and dug out the small bottle to check the label. "Here it is…dizziness, blurred vision, stomach upset, numbness in the extremities. So I bet that's what it is."

"You need to stop taking it."

"I only had one yesterday at lunch."

"Good. I bet if you drink up your water, it'll be out of your system soon." She helped Mary Kate with her pack and they quickened their usual pace to close the gap between them and the group, catching up with the others just as Luke called for a break.

"You should eat something too, Mary Kate. Maybe it'll speed up the effects. Try one of your energy bars."

"Good idea." She pulled two from her pack. "You want one?"

"Sure."

Addison propped her pack against a jagged rock to use as a back cushion. The energy bar was a good idea, especially since she was dragging from her sleepless night.

"You know what? I bet we all could use one of these," Mary Kate said.

Addison watched as Mary Kate made the rounds of the group, passing out energy bars. It was nice the way she stopped to give Courtney a pep talk. Mary Kate was a good soul, not like most of the self-centered women Addison had dated.

Shuddering, she recognized something inside her as she compared Mary Kate to women she knew romantically, the familiar sensation that signaled more than just a passing interest. The signs were all there. She had taken to Mary Kate right away, and despite spending their long nights together in the tent, she preferred her company all day as well. *Not good. Not good at all.* Mary Kate was friendly and accepting when it came to lesbians, but that didn't mean she was open to going where Addison's thoughts were headed.

Rachel perched on a nearby rock, her arms crossed to ward off the chilly breeze. Despite the bright sunlight, they were all still in their jackets. "I don't know about you guys, but I'm kind of pissed that Tom didn't give us a little more info in the stuff he sent out. He gave this long list of things we should bring, but then he kept saying to pack light. I don't know if I've brought enough clothes. I nearly froze to death last night, and we're just at twelve thousand feet."

Drew polished off his energy bar and wiped his hands on his pants, the convertibles Addison had given him. "We'll probably have to wear the same clothes the whole time we're out here, just adding something else every day."

"Especially you," Neal said with a chuckle.

"Yeah, yeah. By the time we go to the summit, I'll be wearing all of your clothes at the same time."

"Just imagine what you'll smell like by then," Neal went on. "I hope you at least collected enough underwear to change every day."

"Nah, just half as much. I've just been turning them inside out on the second day."

"That's gross!" Courtney said. "Way too much information."

"And you wonder why you're still single," Kirby said, shaking his head. "Get a clue, man."

At the front of the line, Luke picked up his pack and turned toward the mountain. The others groaned and fell in behind him.

Now conscious of her growing feelings—and of her reluctance to give them rein—Addison hung back to let Mary Kate walk with someone else. As if to torture her, Mary Kate stepped aside to wait, and they fell in step again. Addison secretly loved it, but Mary Kate would probably freak if she had any idea.

One hour later, the hikers climbed onto a rocky mesa, so small the tents were erected with barely a yard between each. Addison looked about quickly and chose the tent in the center, figuring the other tents would shield them from the frigid wind on this exposed ridge.

Again, they spread out their sleeping bags to dry, this time securing them to the tent wires so they wouldn't blow away.

"Whose tent is this one?" Kirby yelled, opening the flap to find two Summit bags already under the rain guard.

"That one's ours," a voice called from the dining tent, where two figures sat huddled against the stiff breeze.

Everyone converged on the tent, surprised to be meeting new arrivals on this, their third day on the trail. From their age difference, Addison guessed they were father and son.

The older man stood, offering his hand. "I'm Jim, and this is my son, Brad. I got delayed on business, so we came up the Machame Trail. Hope you don't mind a couple of extras."

"Are you the guys from Dallas?" Mary Kate asked.

"That's us. We got here yesterday."

Brad stepped forward, his face set in a scowl. "Thank God I'll have somebody new to talk to besides this old guy."

His father raised an eyebrow, but otherwise let the remark slide.

"How you doing, Brat?" Neal held out his hand for a shake.

"It's Brad!" the youth answered indignantly.

Ann got up into his face and sneered menacingly. "*Well, Brad!* What makes you think we want to talk to you?"

Everyone laughed as Brad's face turned red. Finally, he let out a small grin. "Shit. Something tells me I'm in trouble now."

Gilbert entered the tent carrying a pan of hot cream soup. As they ate, Jim told them about the Machame trail, which was similar to their route along Lemosho Glades, but shorter. They had spent one night in the rainforest at Machame Hut before hiking up to Shira Two.

The tension between Jim and his son was palpable, but Brad loosened up a bit as they ate. Nikki peppered him with questions, enough to learn that he too was a recent high school grad, bound for college in the fall.

After lunch, they retreated two by two to their tents to escape the relentless wind.

Mary Kate spread out her sleeping bag and opened her journal. There was barely enough room to sit up inside the tent, and only then, if she leaned toward the center. "I haven't written anything since Big Tree."

"How are your hands and feet?"

She opened and closed her palms a few times. "Fine. The tingling's gone."

"That's a relief."

"Yeah, if that's the only thing I have to deal with, I'll consider myself lucky." Though she felt physically fine for now, she couldn't shake her anxiety that the altitude would suddenly hit her hard. That's what many people had described. "Are you feeling anything at all from the altitude?"

"No, but I'm worried about Courtney. She skipped breakfast

and lunch. I wouldn't be surprised if she turns back tomorrow."

"At least she ate one of the energy bars. She doesn't seem invested in the climb so much, and I can't imagine putting up with it if you aren't having fun."

"Me neither."

Addison gestured at the journal. "So what are you writing in there?"

"Just what we did every day, what we saw, what we ate. I want to be able to tell Deb all about it."

"That's your friend back home?"

"Yeah, the one with the bumper sticker like your keychain."

Despite her earlier warnings to herself to tread carefully, Addison couldn't suppress her desire to know how Mary Kate viewed her. "You writing anything bad about me in there? She might like evil lesbian stories."

"I should tell her that you laughed at me when I fell and hurt myself."

"You did not hurt yourself."

"No, but you didn't know that when you started laughing." With a smug look in place, she began to write. "And if you ever come to Mooresville to visit me, Deb will kick your ass."

"Is that an invitation?"

"Sure, but I should warn you there's nothing to see."

"If I came, it would be to see you." An alarm went off in her head that said she was very close to flirting. "I heard that all of you southerners keep shotguns in your pickup trucks."

"Now just because we don't jet off to London and South America doesn't mean we're all rednecks."

"I deserved that," Addison said, feeling mildly admonished. Snobbery was definitely not on the list of traits she wanted to highlight.

"Besides, I didn't say she'd shoot your ass. We save that for Yankees who come down and try to tell us how to do things, and you don't qualify."

"Lucky me. I don't know about you, but I can't believe I had a bath just last night. I'm filthy again." She held out her hand to show the black dirt that had gathered under her fingernails.

"I have that too, and washing doesn't help."

"It's like soot. I hate to think where else it is."

"That's what the baby wipes are for," Mary Kate said. "Next time you go to the latrine, you should take one."

"Hmm. I was thinking about it being in my ears. What were you thinking about?"

Mary Kate sighed and rolled her eyes. "I can't believe you keep letting me step in it like that. I promise I will pay you back in the worst way."

Addison stretched out on top of her sleeping bag and watched discreetly as Mary Kate scribbled into the small notebook. It was cute how her tongue peeked out the corner of her mouth in concentration. Many things about Mary Kate were cute, she admitted, and she had seen all of them. She didn't look much like the other women Addison had found interesting over the years—nothing at all like either the elegant Pilar or the emaciated Celia. Mary Kate probably wouldn't appreciate hearing that she looked wholesome, but that's exactly what Addison saw. There was nothing about her appearance or the way she carried herself that seemed phony, and that went for her personality as well.

Addison hoped she was giving off that aura to Mary Kate as well. She was used to playing the game in Miami, where everyone was someone else underneath. There was no need for pretense here in Africa.

She was relieved there wasn't any apparent fallout from her blunder the day before at the creek. Whatever had possessed her to pick up Mary Kate's towel and dry her back? It was as if her subconscious had known already what she just realized today. There was no mistaking that the gesture had surprised Mary Kate. It was something she might have done for a lover—or at least for someone familiar—certainly not for a straight woman she barely knew.

Mary Kate suddenly closed her notebook and rolled onto her side facing Addison. "I'm so tired."

"Huh?" Addison realized she had been dozing and sat up.

Their backpacks lay at their feet. "How's your water? I should get it ready for tomorrow."

"I can do it if you want. I only got about three hours of sleep last night, but you didn't get any."

"That's okay. I don't want to fall asleep this afternoon or I'll be up all night again. I thought I'd wait until after dinner."

"That's probably a good idea. It's after four already, so dinner should be ready before long."

They pulled on their boots and crawled outside, where Gilbert was bringing bowls into the empty dining tent. Mary Kate went from one tent to the next calling people to dinner while Addison set up the water station and, with Neal's help, began filling bottles. By the time they finished, dinner was underway.

Luke came in as they were stacking the plates. "Tomorrow is our longest hike, about seven hours. We go to Barranco Hut, which is our most beautiful campsite."

Addison was glad that hadn't been today's hike. She might never have made it.

"We climb three hundred meters tomorrow, but it will not be steep. All must drink the water."

Mei smiled as everyone looked in her direction. "About a thousand feet."

As they scattered toward their respective tents, Nikki tripped over a stake in the narrow pathway between her tent and that of Drew and Kirby. Luckily, Jim was there to catch her elbow before she fell.

"Careful."

"No kidding. You guys better watch your step."

When they crawled back into their tent, Mary Kate pulled out the long johns she had slept in every night so far. "You know, when I packed for this trip, I made up this thing called a two-day rule. I planned on wearing everything in my bag for two days."

"Right, but you gave two pairs of socks and a T-shirt to Drew."

She waved a hand flippantly. "I've got plenty of socks. I rinsed out a pair yesterday. But I hadn't planned on wearing long johns to bed on the very first night. I've only got one more set, so I'm going to have to wear each of them for four days."

"That makes two of us, so I won't complain if you start to smell a little. I'll just put my earplugs in my nose."

"Funny." As usual, Mary Kate left on her sports bra underneath her long-sleeved top, but this time she put her fleece top back on. "I've been changing my underwear every day, though. So if I'm in an accident, please let my mother know that."

Addison quickly tugged on her long johns as well, and then added her convertibles on top. "At least if I have to get up in the night to pee—what am I saying? When I have to get up in the night to pee, I'll be fully dressed."

"If you get up, wake me and I'll go with you."

Addison scooted deep inside her bag and worked the zipper from the inside. Luke was right about the camp being inhospitable, with its rocky ledge and stiff wind. But she was too tired to let that keep her from much-needed sleep.

Chapter Fourteen

"Ow!" Mary Kate was jarred from her sleep by a weight that fell across her hips.

"Shit! Goddamn it!" It was Brad.

"I knew that was going to happen," Addison muttered.

They unzipped their bags and crawled out of their collapsed tent to repair the damage from where he had tripped over one of the ties. Several others awakened at the commotion, and Drew and Jim hurried out to help reset their stakes. Mary Kate and Addison then ventured across the rocky terrain to the latrine before resettling in their tent.

"I don't feel sleepy anymore," Addison said.

"Me neither. But it's four thirty, so we got about ten hours of sleep. I don't think I moved all night."

Even though they were now wide awake, there was nowhere else to be but zipped up inside their sleeping bags, given the cold, howling wind.

"I slept like a baby, except for the nightmare about your friend beating me up."

"You mean Deb?" Mary Kate smiled as she envisioned Addison meeting her friends in Mooresville, something she had said she might actually do. "She's been my best friend since we were in second grade. One day on the playground, she beat the shit out of some boy who was picking on me."

Addison laughed. "I get the impression she likes to fight."

"Not really. She's a sweetheart, but she doesn't take anybody's shit."

"So what's it like for her being a lesbian in a place like Mooresville? Does she have a girlfriend?"

"Oh, no. Mooresville isn't ready for something like that. Hardly anybody knows for sure about Deb, but they all gossip about her like they do."

"Why would they gossip?"

"They don't have anything better to do. Some of them probably still gossip about me too, because that's what started everything back in high school. We used to do everything together. We stayed over at each other's houses. We shot hoops together after school."

"They thought you two were lovers?"

"Yeah, a couple of the girls on our team thought we spent too much time together, and they started that rumor. It got all over school, and since my mom taught there, she heard it one day in the teacher's lounge. She told all the teachers it wasn't true, but then she came home and gave me this big lecture about how the other girls my age were dating, and that people wouldn't be saying stuff like that if I went out with boys. So I eventually got a boyfriend, and—"

"A real boyfriend or one just for show?"

"As real as it gets when you're sixteen, I guess. There isn't much to do in Mooresville, so dating means going to parties or football games together. Nothing serious." Someone from Miami would probably go insane in Mooresville, she thought. "Anyway, Deb and I quit staying over at each other's houses. The funny part was that we were sneaking around anyway to see each other like we really were lovers."

"That's cool you stayed friends, though. I came out to one of my friends in college and you would have thought I had leprosy."

"That's ridiculous. Being gay doesn't make you a different person."

"It does to some people."

Mary Kate reluctantly acknowledged to herself that most people in her hometown would think so. "I don't see what the big deal is, or why it's anybody's business what people do in the privacy of their homes."

"People shouldn't have to be private, though. If I want to walk down the street holding my girlfriend's hand, I should be able to do that without worrying that people are going to treat me differently. The rules ought to be the same for everybody."

Addison's sudden mention of a girlfriend jolted her. "You have a girlfriend?"

"Not right now, but I used to date a woman who did the news on one of the local TV stations, and she wouldn't go anywhere in public with me, not even as a friend, because she was paranoid about what people would think."

"I bet you have the most interesting friends." Now she felt totally silly for telling her boring stories of Mooresville.

Addison snorted. "I didn't say we were friends. Things didn't end very well, if you know what I mean."

"That's too bad."

"Not really, if you look at the big picture. Pilar was a lot older than I was, almost forty. That probably stressed her out more than being a closet lesbian. But I got tired of sneaking around to go see her."

"I don't blame you. But still, it must have been exciting to have a famous girlfriend."

"It kind of takes the shine off it if you can't tell anybody. Finish your story about Deb."

Mary Kate groaned. "There isn't much more. She finally told me one day that she'd had this big crush on me for years. Of course, I didn't feel that way about her, and I know it hurt her feelings. But we both got over it and stayed friends."

"Did you ever think about...? Never mind. That's probably

too personal."

"I actually did wonder…if that's what you're asking." Feeling her face flush, she was glad it was still dark. She had never told anyone about making out with Becky Dugan, but the idea of telling Addison gave her an inexplicable thrill. "I messed around a little with one of the girls on my basketball team in college. We just made out, but I…I guess it wasn't what I wanted. I didn't feel anything."

She bit her lip as she waited for Addison to answer.

"I never told anybody that story before, so when you come visit me, please don't blurt it out in front of my sister. She'd probably faint."

Addison chuckled softly. "I wouldn't tell anything you've shared with me in confidence, Mary Kate."

Mary Kate was touched by the sincerity in her voice. "I know. I already feel like I can trust you."

"You can." Addison squirmed in her bag in order to roll over on her side. Her head was only inches from Mary Kate's. "How did you feel about the other girl?"

"I…well…" she stammered, searching for the right words to describe an experiment without coming off as totally naïve. "She was just a friend, really. I liked her, but…"

"You weren't attracted to her."

"No."

"But you made out with her."

"Yeah, I guess I was curious about how it would feel."

"Have you ever been attracted to another woman? A woman you really wanted to kiss?"

Mary Kate tugged on the zipper to let a little air inside her bag. It excited her to finally have a chance to talk about these things with someone who wouldn't jump to conclusions. "I've had crushes on a couple of girls—friends of mine that I thought were really nice."

"But you never acted on either of those."

"No, they weren't like that."

"How do you know?"

"I just knew. One of them was this girl from high school who had a different boyfriend every week. That was just a little crush, though. The big one was my college roommate. I was a bridesmaid at her wedding."

"Why was she the big one?"

Mary Kate was amazed to hear herself talking about these things with someone she had known only three days. "Jessica, I don't know, she fascinated me. I always felt so lucky that we were friends. Then she met Chuck. They got married during spring break our senior year, and I was really happy for her, but kind of sick about it at the same time."

"You were grieving."

"Yeah, it felt like that."

"Did you feel the same way about your boyfriend? The fascination, I mean."

Mary Kate felt a wave of uneasiness, not so much at the question, but at having to admit the answer was no. "No, that's why I knew the thing with Jessica was just a silly crush. It's like it just comes out of nowhere, and it's a bunch of feelings that don't have any rhyme or reason. You just want to be with somebody all the time."

"I always thought that was love."

"Love's different. Love is something you have to work at so that it grows. You feel confident about planning your future together because you want the same things."

"No, what you're talking about is a relationship. We have to work at those, but nobody should have to work at being in love. And I wouldn't dream of having a relationship with someone I didn't find fascinating."

There was no doubt that fascination was missing from what she felt about Bobby, and that if she had even a hint of it, she could go forward with the life he and her whole family wanted. The problem was that she had been fascinated exactly twice in her life—once with Jessica, and ironically, once with the woman sharing her tent.

Chapter Fifteen

"Sorry, guys," Courtney said with a moan. "I hate that I'm holding everybody up."

Addison zipped up her parka and shoved her hands in the pockets to stave off the chilling wind. They were stuck in camp until a ranger arrived to escort the Penn State trio off the mountain. Courtney had thrown up several times through the night and had a relentless headache. They had decided this morning to descend and spend a few days on a wildlife safari before starting their internships.

"I see a truck," Neal said as he peered through his binoculars across the plain. Luke had said the ranger could drive within two kilometers, but would have to hike from there.

Addison gauged the wind direction and stepped down from the ledge to seek shelter between two boulders.

Mary Kate followed. "Got room for me down there?"

"Sure." She sat on the ground with her back against a rock and motioned for Mary Kate to sit across from her. After their long talk in the wee hours of the morning, she saw Mary Kate in a whole new light, one that—for better or worse—fanned her interest.

"I feel bad for those guys having to turn back, but I'm just glad it's them and not me."

"I know what you mean," Addison said. "Getting this far and not making it to the summit would seriously suck. But we're better prepared than Courtney."

"Yeah, but nobody knows how the altitude's going to affect them. We're still going up, and we have four more nights before we summit. Anything can happen between now and then."

"Are you worried?"

Mary Kate shrugged. "Nervous is probably a better word. I think I'd be sick if I didn't make it to the top."

Addison squeezed her knee and smiled. "I have a feeling you're going to run off and leave us all....unless we all freeze to death here."

"I wish they hadn't taken our tents. I'd be waiting this out in my sleeping bag."

"I heard Luke tell Neal and Mei that the porters were leaving early to get the best campsite at Barranco. There's another trail that crosses there on the way up the Western Breach, so the camp will be crowded."

"The Umbwe Route. I read about it. It's for the more experienced climbers."

"We'll have the Barranco Wall tomorrow, you know."

Mary Kate shook her head. "I can't even think about that. I'm freezing my ass off here, and it's what? About forty-five degrees?"

"The wind makes it colder." Addison nodded in the direction of the mountain. "We're headed onto the mountain today. Once we get off this plateau, we should be out of the wind."

"I hope you're right." Mary Kate's teeth were chattering.

They huddled until the ranger arrived, and then they joined the others in saying goodbye to Courtney, Rachel and Kirby.

As they gathered their packs to start the day's hike, Luke drew them into a circle. "Does anyone else feel doubts about going to Barranco?"

111

"I just scored Kirby's balaclava and gloves, so you're not getting rid of me," Drew said.

"Looks like you're stuck with all of us," Neal added.

Addison studied the faces of her fellow hikers. Only Brad seemed disinterested, but she suspected that had more to do with his father than with the challenge before them. She fell in between Jim and Mary Kate as they got underway. "So what brings you and your doting son to Kilimanjaro?"

He grinned at her exaggerated cheerfulness. "It's his high school graduation present. It was supposed to be a bonding trip, but that isn't happening yet. I may have waited too late."

"Teenagers are funny animals," Mary Kate said.

"Especially when they grow up hearing only one parent's side of things."

Addison related to that. "Are you and his mom divorced?"

"Ten years ago. He's been living with her in Austin. Now that he's eighteen, the visitation rules don't apply anymore. I practically had to drag him here."

Given the circumstances, it was hard for Addison to see why Brad would appreciate being dragged somewhere he didn't want to go, especially since this was supposed to be his graduation gift. "Did you guys train together for the hike?"

"We both play a lot of tennis, so we're in pretty good shape. Brad was ranked ninth in Texas as a junior, but he couldn't hold it when he moved up last year." He flashed his T-shirt, which was emblazoned with an SMU logo. "He's going to play at my alma mater this fall though. I won the conference tournament two years in a row when I was there thirty years ago."

"What kind of work do you do?" Mary Kate asked.

"I used to be a software developer, but I sold my company last year. Now I'm donating my time to build better systems for several of the non-profits in the Dallas area."

Addison couldn't help but see a bit of her overbearing father in Jim, except for the part about giving back to his community after his success. That didn't sound like Reginald Falk at all. Brad was lucky to have a good role model, even if their relationship left much to be desired.

An hour into their hike, they left the plateau, and nearly all of the significant vegetation. The new terrain was like desert, with only an occasional shrub to decorate the mountainside. Even though they were walking slowly, the uphill climb in the brilliant sunshine had Addison sweating. When Luke called the break, she and Mary Kate went behind a boulder to undress so they could take off their long johns.

"Good thing about these rocks, because it doesn't look like we'll be seeing any more bushes," Mary Kate said.

"Who knows how long we'll have boulders to hide behind? From here, it looks pretty barren up toward the summit." She sat on the ground to put her boots back on. "I'd give just about anything for another bath."

"I was thinking the same thing. I thought I'd ask Gilbert to fix me a pan of water when we got to Barranco. Then I could sit in the tent and do a sponge bath."

"That's a great idea," Addison said. "What's that old saying? You wash my back and I'll wash yours."

"I think that's scratch, not wash."

"Same difference."

"Yeah, right. Would you have said that to Drew?"

"Not a chance." Addison grinned broadly and shook her head. She was glad to see the mock scowl on Mary Kate's face, and took it as a sign she wasn't offended by such an obviously flirtatious remark.

They stuffed their clothes down inside their backpacks and returned to the trail. Mei and Neal had also changed, and the others had stowed their jackets. When they started up again, everyone spread out in the line, each seemingly lost in solitary thought. The scenery was the most majestic yet, as they picked their way over three steep crests, then down into broad valleys. In the third valley, Addison's mouth watered the instant she saw the dining tent erected. Gilbert waited with hot cream soup.

The lunch break was shorter than usual, since they were two hours behind schedule for the day. After only forty minutes, they were climbing again.

Addison lagged behind to talk to Mary Kate, who seemed subdued this afternoon. "You're awfully quiet all of a sudden. Is everything all right?"

"Yeah, I'm just thinking about stuff."

"Did it bother you that I asked so many questions this morning?"

"No, I like talking things out with you. You make me put what I'm thinking into words, and that helps me get clear on what I have to do."

"You mean like breaking up with your boyfriend?"

She nodded grimly. "I just dread what everyone is going to say."

"It's not about what they want." She didn't want to add pressure to what Mary Kate already felt, but it sounded as though she needed a bit more encouragement to follow through with what she wanted to do. "I know it's hard to go against people. I talk a big story, but I'm headed to London to work for my father, even though that isn't what I really want. It's just easier to follow the plan."

"Right, but they're going to look at me like I was from another planet if I say something like I can't marry Bobby because I don't find him fascinating."

"No one's entitled to an explanation, Mary Kate. You shouldn't have to justify a decision like that."

"I know." She sighed.

"But you hate to disappoint people."

"Yeah."

"Are you having second thoughts about it?" Addison hoped not. People deserved to be outrageously happy when it came to love, not to feel as if they were being led to the gallows.

"No, I'm just letting it all get to me. I promised myself I wasn't going to think about this while I was here."

"That sounds like a great plan. Just put it out of your head." She looked around at the breathtaking landscape, a mountain to one side and a sprawling rainforest to the other. "When will you ever see something like this again?"

Mary Kate gazed out over the scenery and smiled. "You're so right."

Addison loved how her face lit up. "That's more like it."

They had fallen back, well out of earshot of the others in the group. Still, Mary Kate lowered her voice. "Can I ask you a personal question?"

"Is this going to be like truth or dare?"

"Oh, no. I'm not that brave." She chuckled without looking up. "It's kind of what we were talking about this morning. Did you always know you were gay?"

"I always liked girls. I think I figured out the gay part when I was about fifteen. My parents had just divorced, and they thought I was just trying to get attention."

"What were you doing?"

"Nothing. I just came out and told them. I can still hear my father. 'Oh, for heaven's sake, Addison! Must you be so recalcitrant?'" She did her best British accent.

Mary Kate snorted. "Your father actually called you recalcitrant? My father probably doesn't even know what that means."

"Yeah, I had to carry a dictionary everywhere I went just to understand his insults. My mom wasn't quite that bad, but she thought I was just going through a phase and would grow out of it."

"When did she figure out that wasn't going to happen?"

"Not sure she has," she said, shooting Mary Kate a grin. She was dying to know what was prompting these questions, but was afraid Mary Kate would back off if she prodded.

"Did they ever meet any of your girlfriends?"

"Nobody met Pilar because she wouldn't go anywhere with me."

"That's the TV woman?"

"Yeah, she was my first lover. I was nineteen. She was thirty-eight. Venezuelan. Beautiful, exotic. Our entire relationship happened inside her condo. I felt like I'd just invented sex, and I wanted to tell everybody."

"Is that when you knew for sure then that you wanted to be with women?"

"Oh, yeah. Because I figured out then that sexuality—for me, anyway—wasn't about being touched by someone. That was nice and all, but the thrill I got was from touching her." They walked in silence for several yards, long enough to worry Addison that she had gone overboard with her explanation. "Was that too much information?"

"No." Mary Kate shook her head vehemently, but it was obvious she was flustered. "I was just thinking about what you said...the thrill part."

"Sometimes I don't articulate what I'm thinking very well. What I meant was—"

"Is it just a sexual thing?"

"Of course not. Is being straight just a sexual thing?"

Mary Kate sighed and looked away. "I don't know. You're probably asking the wrong person."

Addison bit her tongue to keep from asking her why. If Mary Kate had doubts about her sexuality, it was better that she express them on her own. The idea of prodding her about it seemed almost predatory now that she had realized her attraction. But if Mary Kate was looking for support, that was a different matter. "If you want to talk anything out, I'm a good listener."

"Be careful what you ask for."

She rested a hand on Mary Kate's shoulder as they slowed. "I can handle it."

The conversation tapered off as they picked up their pace to join the others. As the sun fell, the colorful tents beneath an enormous rock wall were a welcome sight.

Addison handled the water detail with Drew, giving Mary Kate some private time in their tent for a sponge bath. It was tempting to follow suit, but hunger and rest were bigger priorities. Besides, Luke had said their next campsite in the Karanga Valley had a stream, and a real bath trumped a sponge bath every time.

"You guys all right?" Drew asked. "I noticed you hanging

back today."

"We're fine. We just can't walk and talk at the same time." She finished the last water bladder and set it in the line to be claimed. "Have you had any more headaches?"

"Not too bad. You okay?"

"I was worried earlier today that my appetite was leaving me, but I'm starving, so I'd say it's returned with a vengeance."

"I think that bit about losing your appetite is a myth started by the trail companies so you'll have another excuse for being tired of getting potatoes morning, noon and night."

She laughed absently and looked past him at Mary Kate, who was crawling out of their tent. "Feel better?"

Mary Kate joined her as Drew left for the dining tent. "It's an improvement, but I still have on the same ratty long johns."

"You can change tomorrow. Luke says there's a stream at Karanga."

Her eyes grew big. "I don't even want to think how much colder it will be."

"But it only lasts a minute."

Mary Kate snorted. "So does being clean."

"Good point."

They headed into the dining tent, where Gilbert had left a bowl of oxtail soup in the center of the table.

"Anyone else thinking about tomorrow morning already?" Nikki said, looking over her shoulder at the infamous Barranco Wall.

Addison had studied the wall, a six-hundred-foot tower of rocks and outcroppings. Though it appeared to be almost vertical, she could barely see pieces of the trail that zigzagged to the top.

Gilbert entered again carrying more food. As they ate, they inventoried their various maladies, ranging from Neal's mild headache to Ann's upset stomach to Brad's blisters.

"I can't believe you brought tennis socks," Jim said, shaking his head.

From where she was sitting, Addison could see Brad flip his father the bird beneath the table. "Brad, I have a first-aid kit with some cream and bandages. You can use whatever you need and give it back to me in the morning."

"Thanks. It's nice that someone cares," he said, directing his sarcasm in his father's direction.

Addison felt sorry for him. Though her own upbringing had been filled with the acrimony of her parents' withering relationship and divorce, she had always known she was loved and cared for. Brad clearly had doubts, and she hoped Jim would use this trip to heal the rift between them.

The rest of dinner was relatively quiet, a likely sign folks were tired from the long hike. Addison and Mary Kate turned in as soon as they finished eating.

"I don't know about you, but that wall intimidates the hell out of me," Mary Kate said as she climbed into her sleeping bag. "I've been trying not to think about it, but I bet I have bad dreams."

"Don't worry. I walked over there while you were taking a bath. It isn't as steep as it looks from here. It zigzags around a lot of the rocks and shrubs."

"That's a relief. I told my mother there was zero chance of me falling off a cliff."

"It's nice she worries about you," Addison said, still thinking about Brad and Jim. She settled into position and zipped her bag up to her chin. "We'll go up together tomorrow. You can dream about something else."

Chapter Sixteen

Mary Kate was glad to see she wasn't the only one having butterflies over the Barranco Wall. Addison's assurances the night before had helped her sleep, but seeing the wall up close for herself this morning reignited her anxiety. For the most part, the trail zigzagged just as Addison had said, but there were several places where the only way to ascend was to climb the rocks. If she stayed focused on just getting to the next rock, she was fine. It was looking over her shoulder at the sheer drop-offs her mother had warned her about that unnerved her.

"Take my hand," Addison said as she leaned down. Her other hand gripped a sturdy shrub.

Mary Kate was glad for the help, and occasionally returned the favor by giving Addison's backside a push. The first time she had done that had prompted a wide-eyed grin.

"Here comes another big rock," Addison said, low enough so no one else would hear. "Will you put your hand on my butt again?"

"No problem." Mary Kate slapped her rear firmly.

"Careful. I might like that."

She laughed, amused not only by Addison's playful inferences, but by the openness of her teasing. It was flirtatious, but not in a threatening way. "You need to keep your mind on what you're doing. Do I have to remind you about my mother's nightmare?"

The trail of hikers spanned over a hundred vertical feet, with Luke at the top and Nikki and Ann close on his heels. He turned often to help them to the next level, much as Addison was doing for Mary Kate, and Neal for Mei. Jim was navigating the trail on his own, and Brad walked with Drew at the back of the line.

For Mary Kate, the trickiest part—besides the looming cliff—was the effect of her backpack. It would have been relatively simple if she only had to judge how much energy was needed to leap from one rock to another and how much give was required in the recovery. But all of her mental calculations were thrown off-kilter by the twenty-pound pack riding above her center of gravity. Simple hops from one rock to the next required the utmost concentration.

Interspersed in their precarious efforts was the constant stream of porters, who scrambled ahead without pause, even as they carried roughly eighty pounds each. When the hikers bunched up in a bottleneck, the porters forged their own path on the adjacent, steeper rocks.

One hour into the climb, they reached the halfway point. Addison tugged Mary Kate onto a wide ledge, where they collapsed with the others, sweating and sucking wind.

"This isn't a six-hundred-foot wall," Jim said breathlessly. "It's a hundred six-foot walls, and we've only done fifty of them."

"Remind me of that tonight. I'm going to write that in my book," Nikki wheezed.

Luke let them rest for twenty minutes, which passed too soon for Ann. "Go on without me. Send a helicopter," she said.

Addison was the first one forward. "Are you okay?"

"Yeah, I'm just whining. I'll get there."

"We'll move up behind you, Brad and me," Drew said.

Pushing and pulling, they worked together for another hour until finally they stood atop the high ridge at 13,300 feet, the highest they had been yet. The view behind them was majestic, as a thick cloud cover followed their tracks, totally obscuring not only their campsite below, but the entire plateau beyond.

"Just think, if we'd left a day later, we'd be hiking today in the rain," Addison said.

"It was like this from the plane when we flew in. The glacier stuck out at the top, but everything else was covered in clouds."

At this altitude, the mountain terrain resembled one of the moonscape photos in the library at her elementary school. They were directly beneath the towering glacier, which topped out over a mile above where they currently stood. But they were close, and two days from now, they would be on their way down.

Luke nodded in the direction of a distant peak rising high above the clouds. "Mount Meru."

"I read somewhere that's the second highest mountain in Africa," Neal said.

Mei rolled her eyes and sighed. "I told him that three minutes ago when we got to the top of the ridge."

"Let's get another picture together," Addison said, handing her camera to Brad.

Mary Kate smiled as Addison's arm went around her waist. She returned the gesture, giving her an extra squeeze. There was a reason she wasn't threatened by her familiarity—because she welcomed it. "Thanks for not letting me fall off a cliff."

"I've gotten used to you."

Luke picked up his pack and led them across the ridge. "Down is more difficult."

"Down?" Brad practically screamed. "Why did we climb all that way if we were just going to give it all back? Let's go on up the mountain."

The Western Breach loomed above them, veering sharply upward from the ridge, but Mary Kate couldn't imagine doing something that required more skill than the Barranco Wall. "We're supposed to hike high and sleep low. That's how we get acclimated."

"But it isn't how we get to the top."

"Knock it off, Brad. These people don't want to hear you

121

whine," his father said.

Addison caught up with the red-faced teenager and said something no one else could hear. He nodded and hurried ahead in the line, positioning himself between Ann and Nikki.

"What was that all about?" Mary Kate asked.

"I just told him Ann and Nikki probably needed his help. I thought it might take the sting out of having his dad yell at him in front of everybody."

"That was a good move."

"Jim needs to take another look at his son. He only sees the bad things, the times he comes up short. That's not right."

Mary Kate recognized that feeling from the kids in her classroom, the ones whose behavior problems kept them from doing well in the mainstream. Everyone was always yelling at them, they said, so Mary Kate worked hard to give them plenty of positive reinforcement. "Did you figure that out all on your own?"

Addison scowled. "I lived it. From the time I was a kid, nothing I did was quite good enough for Reginald Falk. Even when I got all A's in school, he stayed after me to play the piano better, or to put in extra laps at the pool before the swim meet. Whatever I did, he wanted more."

"I'm sure he's proud of you."

"Of course he's proud. He made me in his own image— Addison Falk, snotty investment banker."

"That's ridiculous. You don't have a snotty bone in your body."

"That's because I haven't completely given in to him yet. I will eventually. And he'll treat me just like Jim treats Brad—dress me down in front of others, nitpick every little thing I do, and tell me every day how he would have done it differently." The hurt in her voice was undisguised.

"Then don't do it. Don't give in. Make your own way, and do what you want."

"I wish it was that easy. I sent out some résumés, but I'm running out of time."

Mary Kate listened in disbelief as Addison told of how her father had put her home up for sale to force her hand. "If you need more time, you can come to Mooresville and stay with me while you keep looking. But don't take his job because you think you're out of options. Your career ought to be your decision, not his." She realized with irony that her arguments sounded just like the ones Addison had given her yesterday when they talked about why she needed to break up with Bobby.

"If all that sounds familiar…" Addison spun her hand in a circle, as if prompting Mary Kate to finish her sentence.

"I know. I was just thinking the same thing."

"Sounds like we both have to fight against the grain." She jumped down from a rock and turned to help cushion Mary Kate's landing. "It sucks when other people run our lives."

"I'm fighting already just by coming here."

"And aren't you glad you did?"

"You're kidding, right? This is the most amazing experience I've ever had."

"People are happiest when they make their own decisions. Even if we screw up, that's better than marching to somebody else's drum."

As they stumbled down from the ridge, Mary Kate considered all the criticism she had gotten over the past six months. It was nothing compared to what she would get for breaking up with Bobby, but once that was done the pressure would be off. No amount of scorn from her family and coworkers could be worse than the stress from feeling the walls close in on her life.

More resolved than ever, she let herself relax fully to enjoy what was here. As they spread out along the trail, she took in the remarkable scenery of the mountainside. Small shrubs and large boulders dotted the terrain, becoming more plentiful as they hiked across a broad valley toward another ridge. In under an hour, they descended into the Karanga Valley campsite, lush from the stream that tumbled through a line of trees. The warm sun was a sharp contrast to the frigid wind at Shira Two.

Gilbert prepared lunch while the men took their turn in the

woods, getting their first bath since leaving the View Hotel.

"Man, that's cold!" Drew proclaimed as he emerged, his hair dripping.

Neal stumbled from the woods behind him. "No wonder. Ten minutes ago, that water was a glacier."

Mary Kate had discovered that for herself when she took the opportunity to wash out the long johns she had worn for the past four nights. She had another pair that were heavier, but perhaps too heavy for their last night on the mountain at Millennium Hut, which was in the rainforest. As she draped her long johns over her tent to dry, Addison came out with a towel and a change of clothing.

"Ladies?"

Mei groaned and gathered up her things.

Ann looked around with skepticism. "I probably should. I'd hate for Nikki to get back to Minnesota and tell everyone I was the only one in the group to go the whole time without a bath."

Mary Kate fell in with the line as they trudged up the hillside into the trees. Because of the steep incline, there were no large pools like the one at Shira One.

"I need to find a waterfall so I can wash my hair," Addison said. "I used to be sort of blond."

"You couldn't pay me to put my head in that cold water," Ann said, claiming a small rock next to the creek. Nikki and Mei sat nearby and started pulling off their clothes.

Mary Kate wanted to stick with Addison, but only if she was welcome. "You want company or privacy?"

"Come on." When they had moved out of earshot of the others, she turned back and grinned. "We can talk about that back washing thing again."

"You're full of yourself today, aren't you?"

"I can't help it. I got all wound up from you touching my butt."

Mary Kate shook her head and smiled. Though flattered by the flirtation, she was pretty sure it wasn't serious, which left her with no idea how to respond to Addison's innuendos.

They climbed nearly a hundred feet higher before finding a stream of water tumbling between the rocks into a pool no larger than a bathtub. It was perfect for hair washing. Perfect, that is, if the water were sixty degrees warmer, Mary Kate thought.

Without getting undressed, Addison loosened the tie that had held her long hair back since its last washing at the Shira One campsite. Tipping her head forward, she gasped as she soaked it in the icy stream. She broke off a small piece of camp soap and began to lather.

"I have a feeling this is going to be the fastest bath of my life," Mary Kate said, as she dipped her own head under the frigid running water. She took the other piece of soap and started to scrub the dirt from her scalp.

"I know, but it'll be worth it. Remember how nice it felt the other night to be clean, even if it only lasted an hour or two?" Addison rinsed her hair of the thick black sludge and started to lather again. "I bet I could wash it ten times without getting all the dirt out."

"Two is all I can stand." Mary Kate rinsed and scrubbed again. At least her hair was short, she thought as she dried it briskly with a towel.

Addison pulled off her soaking shirt and sports bra and began to wash her upper body with a soapy cloth. "Jesus, that water's cold."

Mary Kate was captivated by the sight of Addison's breasts, which she hadn't seen clearly at Shira One. They were high and round, with rose-colored nipples stiff from the chilled water. Watching Addison's soapy hands slide over them gave her an inexplicable rush, and she forced herself to look away, but not before Addison caught her.

"See something you like, Mary Kate?"

She shuddered hard as her face filled with heat. "I was..."

"I'm just yanking your chain," Addison said, a hint of a smile on her face. She rinsed her cloth and soaped it again. "You'll be my friend forever if you'll wash my back."

Grateful for the chance to move out of Addison's line of sight, she hurried behind her and started to scrub. Her mind worked quickly to explain why she had stared. "You must have done a lot of weights to get ready for this. Your shoulders are ripped."

"I noticed yours too. But then I always try to check out a girl's shoulders when she's nude." She flashed a mischievous grin over her shoulder.

"I was not checking you out." Embarrassed by the quake in her voice, she tried a playful tack. "Who says you're my type anyway?"

"Aha! So you do have a type."

"That's not what I said."

"But you like my shoulders."

In frustration, Mary Kate scraped the washcloth roughly across Addison's back. "You have a very nice body. Is that what you wanted to hear?"

"That'll do." She rose suddenly and pushed off her pants to stand completely naked. Then she briskly soaped her legs and pubic region.

Mary Kate willed herself to look everywhere but at Addison. Now more self-conscious than ever, she busied herself with drying her hair again to postpone getting undressed.

Thoroughly lathered, Addison scooted toward the small pool. "Now for the fun part." She let out a muted scream as she backed under the waterfall, rapidly rinsed the soap from her skin and slid out. "If my heart doesn't start again on its own, will you call nine-one-one?"

"On what? My shoe?" She looked up just as Addison tossed her towel to the ground. In all the years she had spent in locker rooms, she had never been so conscious of being in the company of a naked woman. Addison had a gorgeous body.

"You want me to do your back?"

"No!" She hadn't meant to shout, but the idea of Addison touching her now was more than she could stand. "This water's too cold for that."

The air between them was noticeably thick with tension as Addison quickly tugged on fresh clothes, lightweight convertibles, and a T-shirt. "Are you okay, Mary Kate? Sometimes I get carried away with kidding and stuff. If I went too far, I'm sorry."

So her flirtations had only been a game. "It's okay. I'm fine." Except that now she couldn't make eye contact at all.

Addison stood quietly, as if waiting for her to come clean on what she was feeling. "Do you want me to stay up here until you're done, or head on back so you can have some privacy?"

Being alone to deal with her confusion had a lot of appeal, but she didn't want to make matters worse by running Addison off. "You can stay or go. I'm fine either way."

After a long moment of silence, Addison started back down the hill.

Mary Kate felt sick to her stomach. All day, she had enjoyed Addison's attention and playfulness, and instead of being honest with herself about it, she had run from it like a scared child. Now Addison was back in camp feeling as if she had done something wrong.

Chapter Seventeen

Addison was relieved to find that most of the others in camp had staked out their own space, spreading their sleeping bags in the sun. She needed solitude as well, especially given the foul mood that was welling up inside.

When she saw the uncomfortable look on Mary Kate's face up at the stream, she knew she had taken her teasing too far. It wasn't enough for her that Mary Kate had laughed and played along with her silly flirtations all day. She had to push it, because deep down, she had wanted to see if Mary Kate was interested. Not only was Mary Kate obviously not interested, she now had every reason to freak out.

Mary Kate suddenly emerged from the woods, freshly scrubbed and dressed now in hiking shorts and a long-sleeved crew neck shirt. She deposited her dirty clothes in her Summit bag, and then turned to walk directly toward Addison with her sleeping bag.

Addison braced for an unpleasant confrontation, though she was anxious to get it over with. If she was lucky, they would clear the air and limp along as friends. Whatever the case, she hoped Mary Kate wouldn't want to switch tent mates.

"I don't think being clean ever felt this good," Mary Kate said, sprawling on the ground beside her.

"I wonder how long it will last."

"Fifteen minutes? This silt gets on everything."

Addison nodded, satisfied that the small talk was Mary Kate's way of glossing over their awkward exchange. If that's what it took, she would follow that lead. "We won't get another one until—"

"Addison, I'm sorry."

They exchanged questioning looks.

"What could you possibly be sorry for? I was the one who was out of line."

"No, you weren't. I was…just what you said." She shook her head and sighed. "I was looking at you, and you caught me. And instead of owning up to it—which I couldn't even do in my own head—I freaked out."

Addison fluttered at the admission. Her first inclination was to lighten the mood with a glib remark, but Mary Kate was clearly upset. "Do you want to talk about it?"

"I don't even know where to start."

"What is it that's bothering you? Did I make you uncomfortable?"

She shook her head. "Not you, Addison. If anything…"

"Talk to me."

"I really like you a lot," she said bluntly, studying her hands to avoid making eye contact.

"Good, because I feel the same way," Addison answered without hesitation. "But I don't want that to cause you grief."

"It isn't grief. It's just…I don't know what to think." She huffed softly. "What does it say about me that all of my closest relationships have been with women? That the person I wanted to kiss most was my roommate? Or that I'm glad it's been you flirting with me and not Drew?" Her voice shook with obvious trepidation. "I'm beginning to think I might actually be gay."

"Maybe, maybe not. But what if you are? You said yourself that being gay doesn't make you a different person."

"What I meant was that it shouldn't make me see other people differently. That's not the same as feeling different about myself."

Addison gave her a scolding look to say she wasn't buying that. "What are you feeling right now?"

"I guess a little embarrassed."

"Why? Should I be embarrassed too?"

Mary Kate shook her head and looked away again.

"You don't have to feel that way with me," Addison said. "You can talk about anything you want and it stays between us."

"I know."

"Look, I really am sorry for putting you on the spot today. You've made this trip so much fun for me, and I don't want anything to ruin that."

"You didn't do anything wrong. I just freaked out is all—at myself, not at you."

"You shouldn't freak out about it. I was just playing around." Addison chuckled gently. "I can behave myself. No matter how sweet you are, I promise to resist your charms."

Mary Kate finally smiled. "I think the question is whether or not I can behave. I was the one who got caught peeking."

"Yeah, well, I peeked the other day at the creek, but you didn't catch me."

They both laughed, breaking the tension between them once and for all, just in time to greet Drew, who was making the rounds to share a bag of candy. Though she wished they had a few more minutes to talk privately, Addison felt good about where things now stood, and it seemed Mary Kate did also.

When the sun fell behind the ridge, the air chilled noticeably. Addison fetched her fleece pullover, and Mary Kate's too, as they gathered in the tent for dinner.

Gilbert surprised them with a menu they all agreed was inventive, especially considering the shelf life of anything with protein in it had long since passed. The first course was French toast with marmalade. Next was a mixture of peppers and carrots, and piping hot french fries, which disappeared as soon as he set them down. For dessert, he produced a plate of fried banana pastries.

Jim, who was sitting directly across from his son, nodded over his shoulder. "Your sleeping bag just blew in the dirt." When Brad turned his head to look, Jim swiped the last bite of his pastry and shoved it in his mouth.

"Aw, man!"

Fearing an angry outburst from the youth, Addison laughed heartily and the others joined in.

Brad finally followed suit. "You better watch it, old man. You'll find a mamba in your sleeping bag."

As they were finishing dinner, Luke came in to brief them on what the next day would bring. "We leave tomorrow morning at nine o'clock. We have a long day to get to Barafu Hut. It is like Shira Two, but much colder and with many rocks."

Addison shuddered to think a campsite could be colder than their night on the ridge.

"When we reach the camp, we will eat and go to sleep. I wake you at eleven o'clock to climb. If you help each other, we will all be standing at Stella Point by sunrise."

"And how many of us do you think will make it all the way to the summit?" Drew asked.

Luke's eyes moved from one face to the next as he weighed his response. "All of you will reach the crater rim at Stella Point. Who goes on to the summit is up to you. Then we return to Barafu to break camp."

"We're finally here," Nikki said quietly. "I mean, I know it's not Everest or anything like that, but this is the biggest mountain I'll ever climb."

"I know what you mean," Ann said. "Tomorrow's the day we've been working toward for six months." She laid her hand in the center of the table, palm down.

Mary Kate covered it, and Addison covered both. One by one, all nine built a tower of hands as a show of solidarity.

When their meeting broke up, Addison and Mary Kate got situated inside their tent, both changing into clean long johns for the cold night ahead.

"I can't believe it's finally time to go up," Mary Kate said. "Are you feeling any effects at all from the altitude?"

"Nothing. How about you?"

"None. I keep expecting to. Every little twinge in my head makes me think I'm getting a headache, but then it passes. Same thing with my stomach."

"It's probably just nerves. I heard Luke tell Nikki that the climb to Stella Point was the toughest part because it was long and steep, but it wasn't anything like the Barranco Wall."

"That's a relief. Can you imagine trying that at night?"

Addison settled into her sleeping bag. "What about everything else? Are you feeling all right with where we left things this afternoon?"

"I'm as okay as I can be, considering I started the day with a pretty good idea of who I was, and now I'm going to bed without a clue."

"You'll figure it out."

"You know what I can't stand? That all of those gossips back in Mooresville might have been right about me."

"I don't think you know that yet. Give it some time." Addison held in check her excitement about Mary Kate's musings. Though she would have loved letting their relationship take its course, she didn't want to take advantage of Mary Kate's confusion and doubt. But they had a solid foundation now upon which to build a relationship, whatever that might be.

"But isn't your sexuality supposed to be fundamental? I should know this about myself."

"I don't know that many lesbians who always knew. Most of us went through the motions with everyone else until we figured out something was wrong."

Mary Kate sighed heavily. "Something's definitely wrong."

"No, it isn't. That was a bad choice of words. It isn't wrong, not for me, and who knows? Maybe not for you. But it's like being a square peg when most of the holes are round. And we don't realize it until we finally find one that fits."

"But you found it when you were a teenager. I'm twenty-four years old, and I'm just now getting around to looking for it."

"That doesn't mean anything. I know lesbians who were married twenty years before they came out. Most of them say they had a lot of pressure to conform when they were growing up, just like you did."

"But your parents—"

"My parents didn't like it, but they knew that wouldn't stop me."

"That's right. You were recalcitrant."

Addison chuckled. "I also didn't have friends from school whispering about me, or worries about a job. Miami has tons of gay people. I don't even stick out."

"I understand perfectly why people just conform. It's so much easier."

Addison was saddened to hear the resignation in Mary Kate's voice. "It might be easier in the short run, but if it isn't your true path, you waste a lot of living."

"Do your friends feel that way? The ones who were married twenty years?"

"I think some of them do. The ones who had kids are all happy they did, but they're happier now with who they are." Addison squirmed deeper into her sleeping bag. "Jesus, it's cold tonight."

"I drank all my water before two o'clock so I wouldn't have to get up tonight."

Addison squeezed her eyes tightly shut and tried in vain to drive the urge from her brain. "I hate you."

Mary Kate unzipped her bag. "If it makes you feel any better, I just jinxed myself too."

Chapter Eighteen

Mary Kate stirred in her bag, hovering between waking and sleep. A quick blink told her it was daylight, time to get up and start the day.

"Good morning."

She opened one eye and saw Addison only inches from her face. That's when she realized she had drifted in the night to the center of the tent, well into Addison's space. "Uh-oh." She wiggled her hips to move away.

"It's okay. I think we're on a slight hill and you just slid down. If I'd been on that side, I would have done the same thing."

"I squashed you."

"You kept me warm."

They heard chatter from the dining tent and got dressed.

Gilbert had toasted the now-stale bread in a hot skillet, but it didn't improve the taste. Either their appetites had left them at this altitude, or they had simply grown weary of the repetitive breakfast fare.

Luke appeared in the dining tent to encourage them to eat. "You will need energy for the climb tonight."

Mary Kate made a face, but nonetheless accepted a peanut

butter sandwich from Ann.

Mei entered the tent, her face lined with worry. "Neal didn't sleep last night."

"Is he okay?"

"I think so. But he's going to be very tired tonight." She slathered peanut butter and marmalade between two pieces of bread and took it back to their tent.

"I didn't sleep too well either," Drew said. "But I guess a little is better than none at all."

Mary Kate couldn't help but be disappointed at the sluggishness of her fellow climbers. This was their big day, and no one else seemed to be up for it. She followed Addison into their tent. "Everyone's dragging today."

"You might have been the only one to get any sleep last night. I don't know what the problem was, but I don't think I slept more than an hour or two."

"Addison, you're going to be exhausted."

"I hope not. I ate a lot more than I wanted so I'd have a little extra energy."

"You can have my energy bars too, whatever you need." She felt guilty that sliding into Addison had kept her awake.

"Thanks. Maybe I'll be able to fall asleep when we get to Barafu."

They were ready to go by seven thirty, but Luke held them in camp, explaining that they needed to give last night's summiting party time to vacate the campsite at Barafu Hut.

The high walls that formed the Karanga Valley shielded the camp from the morning sun, but when it peeked over the eastern ridge, they climbed one by one to the high rocks on the western side to get warm as they waited.

Except for the persistent chill, Mary Kate felt good today, wearing clean clothes from head to toe for the first time since Shira One. She was dressed in lightweight black fleece pants, a moisture-wicking shirt, with a bright green fleece pullover that hugged her torso snugly. When the sun finally cleared the valley wall, she lowered her wraparound shades and basked in the thawing warmth.

Addison was the last to emerge from the tent, and she tossed her filthy Summit bag into the pile in the center of camp. She too was wearing form-fitting fleece pants, but wore a looser fleece top over a lightweight turtleneck.

Mary Kate stared from behind the shelter of her sunglasses as Addison bent over to retrieve her backpack from underneath the rain guard.

"Wow!" Drew also admired the sight.

"Wow is right," echoed Jim.

Mary Kate's first inclination was to scold the men for their Neanderthal objectification of women. Instead, she chuckled softly with relief that she hadn't said "wow" aloud herself. Addison had an allure that completely transcended gender. Before falling asleep the night before, she had let her mind wander to what it would be like to kiss her, and if she did, whether Addison would be interested in more. For an instant, she had even imagined Addison touching her intimately.

"I can't believe I wasted all those hours last night that I could have been asleep," Addison said, taking a seat between Mary Kate and Drew. "I guess I've grown so used to hearing Drew snore that now I can't sleep without it."

"Very funny," he said.

"Are you sure it wasn't because I crushed you in the tent?" Mary Kate asked softly.

Addison leaned closer, and in a voice only Mary Kate could hear, said, "It may have been one of the reasons I stayed awake, but only so I could enjoy it."

Mary Kate squeezed her lips together, but couldn't suppress her smile. "You can't stop yourself. You are a hopeless flirt."

"Just being honest." She gestured below as Luke strapped on his backpack. It was finally time to start their day.

They began with a steep climb, but upon reaching the ridge top, immediately descended into another valley, this one almost three miles across.

Though they walked silently most of the morning, Mary

Kate kept an eye on Addison, just in case she struggled from being overtired. As they pulled out from their first break, Drew moved close behind her.

"How are you feeling, Mary Kate?"

"Pretty good. I keep expecting to start feeling the altitude, but so far, nothing. Too bad there isn't any wood up here to knock on." They had left behind all vegetation in the Karanga Valley.

"I wanted to talk to you about something, but I don't want you to say anything. Okay?"

She was surprised by his serious look, and couldn't imagine what sort of secret he might tell. "Sure."

"I didn't tell anyone this morning, but the reason I was up all night was because I got this awful headache again. I'm kind of worried about it."

"Did you take something? I think Addison has some aspirin."

"It's gone for now. But this happened before when I went up Pikes Peak in two days."

"What did you do?"

"I came right back down and it went away. But I'm a little worried because we were only at thirteen thousand feet last night, and we're headed way higher than that tonight."

"You should tell Luke."

"No, I don't want him to know. If he thinks it's going to be a problem, he might not let me go up. I'd rather make that decision myself, you know?"

"I understand. But I'm not going to let you do something stupid."

"You're not going to rat me out, are you?"

"No." She walked backward to address him face-to-face. "I won't say anything to Luke, because I wouldn't want anyone else making my decisions either. But I am going to watch you, and you better not be stubborn about it if it's obvious you should go back down. That peak isn't worth dying for, you know."

"That's why I wanted to tell you, so you'd watch. Kind of like the friend that tells people when they've had too much to drink."

"We'll watch each other—you, me and Addison. Deal?"

"Deal."

True to her word, she bit her tongue during their next break when Luke made the rounds asking everyone to come clean about how they were feeling. Nikki admitted to having headaches, and Neal lost his lunch, but neither felt the problems were serious enough to turn back. Drew casually indicated that he was feeling fine. When they pulled out again, Mary Kate waited to walk with Addison, who was smiling and humming to herself.

"You're in a pretty good mood for someone who didn't get any sleep last night."

"What gives you that idea?"

"Because every time I look at you, you're smiling."

"Maybe that's because I smile every time you look at me."

Mary Kate laughed at that comeback. "You can't keep that charm of yours inside at all, can you?"

"I try. My little voice tells me to behave, but I don't listen very well. How would you handle somebody like that in your classroom?"

"I'd probably show her a lot of positive reinforcement whenever she exhibited appropriate behavior."

"I respond to positive reinforcement."

"I can tell." It was nice to have all the tension of yesterday behind them. If anything, the awkward scene from the creek had helped her get clear on what she was feeling. Her fascination with Addison was growing by the minute, and she was definitely entertaining the idea of following it wherever it led. The electricity between them was unquestionable.

The last leg of their hike took them across another broad valley before their ascent to the Barafu campsite. The glacier loomed above them. In all, they would gain two thousand feet today, still leaving them four thousand feet below the summit.

Halfway up the ridge to Barafu, Mary Kate was gasping for air. *Pole pole* was still the mantra, and she forced herself to drink all of the water in her pouch, even though she wasn't at all thirsty.

When they crested the ridge, the sight before them nearly stole their breath. Luke waited at the top, corralling the group as he pointed to the long incline that led to the glacier. "Up there is Stella Point. It is a six-kilometer walk from here, and is one thousand meters higher. We will stand there at sunrise. Gilbert has dinner ready now, and you should eat, then rest. I will wake you at eleven. It will be very cold."

Barafu Hut was home to three dozen tents this night, including a larger one for three new guides from Summit Trail and Safari who would accompany the group up the mountain. Mary Kate remembered what Luke had said about needing more experienced guides on hand as escorts for the summit, especially to watch for signs of distress among the climbers.

The tents were packed closely together on the rocky ledge, the support wires wrapped around rocks or simply whipping in the growing wind. Addison chose the one farthest from the single latrine and dropped her pack underneath the rain guard. "I'm whipped. I'm going to head on to sleep."

"You should eat something first," Mary Kate said.

She shook her head. "I'd rather go up without food than sleep."

"Okay. I have five more energy bars. That'll get us through the night." Mary Kate helped her spread out her sleeping bag. "Lay out your stuff for tonight so you can get dressed fast. I'll do the water."

Addison nodded absently and began to rummage through her bag.

Mary Kate joined the others in the dining tent, where Gilbert had set out a bowl of pasta with a chunky brown sauce that only the men would eat. The Milo was gone, the tea tepid and the conversation subdued. When they finished their meal, she worked the water detail with Jim and Brad before finally joining Addison in the tent.

As quietly as possible, she readied her gear. The first order of business was to change into her heaviest long johns, her thickest fleece pants, and the form-fitting green fleece top she had worn all day. Then she put on her last pair of clean socks, adding the dirty ones as a second layer. At the foot of their tent alongside Addison's gear, she laid out her gaiters, gloves, hat, balaclava and a fleece ear band. To the side, she set her insulated pants and jacket, which would protect her from the wind.

Her parka, which she hadn't yet worn, had several large pockets inside, including one that would hold her water bladder. If she packed her energy bars, sunglasses and water inside the jacket, she wouldn't need her backpack at all. That would definitely make the climb easier.

Luke had warned them to expect temperatures in the single digits by eleven o'clock. Mary Kate followed Mei's advice of pushing Addison's camera—which they were now sharing—a flashlight and both water bladders to the bottom of her sleeping bag so they would stay warm.

With her last check, she could feel her excitement grow. In five hours, they would start their final push upward to stand on that glacial peak she had seen from the plane. It was hard to imagine sleeping, but she knew she had to get some rest at least.

As she squirmed into her bag, she heard a muffled voice.

"You can sleep next to me if you want."

So she did.

Chapter Nineteen

Mary Kate shifted carefully in her bag so as not to wake Addison. It was nice to know at least one of them was getting the sleep she needed. Her lighted watch read a quarter to eleven. Luke would be rousing them soon to start the climb to Stella Point.

In the dark, quiet hours, she had examined her feelings about the woman next to her. It was clear from Addison's overtures that the invitation was there. If she wanted it, they could take this to the next level, whether just a kiss or some sort of mutual exploration. Perhaps they would even have sex.

It wasn't as if she'd never had casual sex, but it had been quite a while, since Jessica's wedding three years ago. Ushers and champagne, always a dangerous combination. And before that, there had been Keith, her prom escort, whom she never dated again.

The more she thought about having a sexual encounter with Addison, the more she found herself both excited and intrigued. If ever she were going to do something like this, what better place to do it than halfway across the world from Mooresville, Georgia? No one would ever know about it unless she told them, and she seriously doubted that she would say a word to anyone, not even Deb. Mary Kate was attracted to Addison in a way she had never been drawn to anyone…including Jessica. Every detail of her life was fascinating, her jetting between London and Peru, her famous ex-lover.

"It is eleven o'clock now," Luke called, his deep voice rumbling into the night. "Neal?"

"We're awake," Mei answered.

She could hear him move from tent to tent. He finally reached theirs and called out her name.

"We're up." She unzipped her bag and gently shook Addison's shoulder. "It's time."

Addison groaned, but sat up and scooted from her bag, stretching her limbs to shake off the sleep. "I think I slept the whole time."

"I think you did too. Are you ready for this?"

"Yeah. How about you?"

"I didn't sleep, but I'm ready to go." She dug the two water bladders from her sleeping bag. "Here's your water."

"Ah, warmed by your feet. How nice."

"Would you rather have a block of ice?"

"Point taken." Like Mary Kate, Addison had slept in her thickest long johns and middle layer. Piece by piece, they dressed like jousters, covering nearly every exposed inch.

Before they exited the tent, Addison gripped Mary Kate's gloved hand with her own. "Good luck tonight. I'm there if you need me, okay?"

Mary Kate pulled her into a tight hug. "Thanks. Let's go get that mountain."

As they gathered near the trailhead, she made her way over to Drew. In a low voice, she asked, "How's your headache?"

"I'm good. Looks like a go."

"Okay, but I'm watching you."

He grinned at her. "I'm watching you too."

The full moon lit up the entire mountain in a magnificent spectacle, the glacier on top glowing like neon. Luke lined them up, asking that they try to keep the same order all the way to the top. Nikki and Ann were first, followed by Lazaro, one of the three new guides joining them on this last leg. Neal, Mei and Drew were next, then the guide, Eric. Mary Kate and Addison followed, just in front of Jim and Brad. Mohammed brought up the rear.

"Turn off your lights," Luke said.

The guides wore head lanterns, but none was lit. One by one, the flashlights were stowed, leaving only the full moon to light the ridge. Within minutes, they were acclimated to the darkness around them.

"Use your light only if you feel you must have it."

With Luke in the lead, the path was easy to follow. After walking very slowly for only a half hour, he stopped at a place where boulders lined the trail. "We will break every half hour for five minutes. You should drink."

"I don't know about you guys, but I think I wore too many clothes," Ann said.

Mary Kate also felt damp with perspiration from exertion.

Five minutes passed quickly, and they were underway again. The pace was very slow, even slower than it had been throughout the trip. It reminded Mary Kate of when she had first learned to count seconds. *One Mississippi, two Mississippi, three...* For this climb, she took a step, counted two full seconds, took another step, two more seconds. With each step, she would plant one of her walking sticks slightly ahead. This rhythm seemed to serve her well. She still hadn't noticed the effects of the thin air, but she concentrated on taking a breath after each step to make sure it wouldn't hit her all at once.

"We break."

The half hour had passed in what seemed like ten minutes.

Mary Kate reached inside her jacket for the bite valve to her water bladder. She wasn't thirsty, but Luke insisted they would need the water tonight.

"It's getting colder," Addison said softly.

"I thought it was just me."

"No, we've already climbed a couple of thousand feet higher."

Again, the break was short and they started up. Mary Kate lost count of how many times they stopped, deciding it was best not to know how much farther they had to walk. Her watch was buried underneath four layers, and it didn't really matter anyway. She was getting very tired, and the temperature had continued to fall as they climbed. With her fleece cap pulled low over her ears, she dropped the ear band over her balaclava to add a layer of cover to her mouth and nose. Her breath crystallized inside the fleece, but it was warmer than if she left it exposed to the night air.

"My water's frozen," Addison said at their next break, fingering the tube that ran from her backpack. "I forgot to blow it back through the tube after our last break."

"Have some of mine," Mary Kate said, tugging the bite valve from inside her jacket.

"I can't take your water. You might not have enough."

"I've got plenty. We'll drink yours on the way back down."

"It's a deal." She lowered her head to Mary Kate's neck and took a long pull through the tube.

"Hey, my water tube's frozen up," Drew said.

"Over here." Mary Kate extended her offer.

As he drank, Addison rolled his water tube between her fingers until the ice broke up enough to force it back into the bladder. Then he returned the favor.

From their break, the trail grew steeper, zigzagging between the rocks. The path was covered with scree, loose volcanic gravel that made it difficult to get traction. For every two steps the climbers took, a half-step was lost on the slide.

At the very back of the line, Brad complained that he couldn't go on. He was obviously struggling with every breath and step, to say nothing of the cold.

"I'm sorry he's being such a whiner," Jim said, out of earshot of his son.

"He's doing pretty well for somebody who didn't really train for climbing a mountain," Addison said between gasps. "He probably hasn't focused on getting to the top like the rest of us had. That's what Luke said we'd have to do."

"But he never follows anything through all the way. I was hoping this would be something that would motivate him."

Mary Kate thought of her students. "You've got to help him believe he can do it."

"Oh, my God! Look at that," Ann shouted.

All heads turned to see what had her so excited. It was the glacier, now on their immediate left, a stunning three stories tall.

Mary Kate looked up toward Stella Point. The crater rim was only a hundred yards ahead, clearly visible not only in the moonlight, but also from the glow that crept along the eastern sky. She could make out the silhouettes of several other hikers traversing the ridge from another route.

"We're going to make it," she said, turning to grin at Addison.

But her confidence waned as the mountain made its last effort to keep them from its summit. Now on the steepest part of the trail, every step took a colossal effort, and no breath was deep enough to deliver the oxygen her body needed. She plodded on, occasionally feeling Addison's hand on her back as she slid backward in the scree.

In the last half hour, the sky grew light, and as the group finally peeked over the ridge into the massive crater of Kilimanjaro, a brilliant orange sun tasted the horizon. Mary Kate fished inside her jacket for Addison's camera, hoping the battery had held at what Luke estimated was thirty degrees below zero on the Celsius scale.

"Minus twenty-two," Mei said just before she threw up.

Luke pointed to a trail that circled to the left. "The summit is there. It is one hour or more, three hundred meters higher, but not steep. If you feel strong, you should continue. Anyone who feels pain in the chest or head should return to camp."

The hikers exchanged tentative looks before Mei finally

spoke. "I need to go back down."

Neal put his arm around her shoulder and gave her a light hug. "I'll go with you, honey."

"No, you should go on."

"I don't want to. This is our trip. We're going to do it together."

"I'm going back down too," Brad said, "as soon as I rest here for a week."

"You did a good job, son. I'm proud of you for not giving up."

Mary Kate felt her eyes fill with tears.

"This is it for me too," Drew said. "My head's pounding like a jackhammer."

In the light of day, she saw his eyes, filled with blood from ruptured vessels. "Drew! Are you all right?"

"It happens from the altitude," Luke said, pointing to Neal. "His are red too. It is good they go back." He signaled to Lazaro to escort them down the mountain. "The rest of you should try to go to Uhuru. I will wait here in case anyone else needs help."

Mary Kate and Addison began to pick their way along the icy path. After their brief stop at Stella Point, they were rejuvenated for the final push. "We're going to make it, Addison."

"We both said we would."

Jim caught up with them. "That was good advice about Brad. I sometimes get caught up in wanting him to be perfect, and I lose sight of what a good kid he really is."

Addison stopped and gave him a stern look. "I bet he'd be really proud of himself if he made it as far as you did."

He looked at her quizzically. "You think I should turn back too?"

"It's pretty hard for a kid to grow up in the shadow of a father as successful as you. If he knows he's never going to measure up, he'll eventually quit trying."

Jim nodded as he weighed their words. "Maybe you're right. So get us a good picture, okay?"

Turning again toward the peak, they continued, stabbing

their walking sticks into the hardened snow to gain footing along the slick path. Mary Kate was thrilled with how her body was handling the altitude. "I can't believe this, Addison. I'm not feeling the thin air at all."

Not getting an answer, she turned to find Addison standing perfectly still, almost thirty yards back. As quickly as she could on the icy surface, she hurried back.

"Addison?"

"I'm fine. I just panicked or something because I couldn't get air."

"Do you need to go back?" Forgetting the summit completely, Mary Kate prepared herself to turn back so she could see Addison to safety.

"No, I'm fine. Really, I just freaked for a minute and I waited here until it passed. I feel okay physically. Let's go."

"Do you swear?"

"I swear." Addison lowered her balaclava and shot her a confident smile.

"Here, put one of your sticks away." Mary Kate did the same and offered an elbow. They took the remainder of their steps in tandem, arriving before any of the others in their group. A brown wooden sign marked the summit.

CONGRATULATIONS YOU ARE NOW AT
UHURU PEAK, TANZANIA, 5895M. AMSL.
AFRICA'S HIGHEST POINT WORLD'S HIGHEST
FREE-STANDING MOUNTAIN ONE OF WORLD'S
LARGEST VOLCANOES.
WELCOME

"I can't believe we're here." Mary Kate felt a surge of excitement. This was by far the most exhilarating moment of her life. She thought back to the moment her plane had tilted to yield her first image of the mountain. Her spirit soared as she quietly celebrated the personal conquest of that most intimidating sight.

Addison put an arm around her shoulder and gave her a congratulatory hug. "We made it, Mary Kate. All those hours of training, all that grief you put up with from everybody else, and this is the payoff."

"The top of Africa."

Addison dropped her backpack and took out a strip of cloth. "Can you take my picture with this? I need to prove I made it." She pulled up her balaclava and stood before the marker with a small banner that showed the amount she raised for the Hunger Coalition.

Mary Kate snapped the photo then removed her face coverings too and handed the camera to the guide Mohammed so she could stand with Addison before the sign. After a couple of shots, she posed alone and stepped out of the way for the others who arrived.

"You'll never believe who's following me," Ann said breathlessly as she reached the summit. "Nikki talked him into coming the rest of the way."

Nikki and Brad joined them, with Jim close on their heels.

"We caught this old man sneaking back," Brad said playfully. "He dragged my ass this far, so I dragged his the rest of the way."

Jim shook his head and bent over to grasp his knees. "I'm too old for this shit."

Mary Kate posed for one last group photo, and then tucked her balaclava into her jacket. Either the temperatures were climbing, or she had gotten used to the cold.

"You ready to head back?" Addison asked.

"Sure." As they walked side by side down the gentle slope, she pored over what it had taken to get her here. There were the countless days in the gym getting her body fit for the climb, and the ten days she had rested a sore knee, worrying that it might keep her from going. The two thousand dollars from her Aunt Jean. The warm-up hike with Deb. Most of all, there was the fear about not reaching the top that had been her near constant companions for six months. Now all of the challenges had been met, and all of the rewards obtained.

Luke was waiting as promised when they reached Stella Point. "We go back on this side." He indicated a steep slope alongside the zigzag path they had climbed. The slope was topped with scree and extended for what looked like a couple of miles. There was no need for a guide, as the colored specks in the distance marked Barafu Hut.

"We're going to bust our asses all the way back," Addison said as the hikers gathered at the top.

"I do not know that expression, but other climbers have used it before." The sly smile on his face suggested in fact that he knew the expression very well. "They also say they get little rocks up the...wazoo?"

"Yippee," Mary Kate said without enthusiasm. "Here goes nothing."

She started to walk slowly down the mountain, with Addison only a few steps back. Within twenty yards, her feet flew out from under her and she slid.

"You okay?"

"Yeah. Something tells me that's the first of many." The temperature had warmed considerably with the climbing sun, and she opened the underarm vents in her parka. Despite the heat, she was glad for the padding from the extra clothing.

They stopped to lengthen their sticks for the descent, allowing Brad and Jim to pass. Mary Kate noticed the change in her gait immediately, because it took pressure off her knees.

Three hours later, they entered the dining tent, sore from tumbling and sliding, their knees like jelly. Drew, Neal and Mei, all feeling better after their descent, were waiting with high fives and hugs. Luke then steered them to their tents to change into lightweight clothes so the porters could strike camp and hurry on ahead with their belongings.

Gilbert delivered boiled potatoes and cabbage, along with the last of the stale bread and peanut butter. As soon as they finished eating, Luke lined them up and started their descent. What had been *pole pole* was now *haraka*, Swahili for fast.

"It means get the hell off this mountain!" Neal said.

The descent wasn't steep, but for Mary Kate, it seemed relentless. The constant pounding took a fierce toll on her knees and lower back, and she struggled to find the best position for her backpack, which pulled on her shoulders and neck.

It hadn't occurred to her until now that the routes on and off the mountain seemed to be one-way, since they never met anyone coming from the other direction. During their first break, Luke explained that only the Marangu route, the most popular path for tourists, was used for both the climb and retreat. By park rules, their Millennium Route was for descending parties only. Unlike the trails toward the summit, this one was wide enough for pairs to walk abreast.

"You still feeling good, Mary Kate?" Addison stepped up to walk beside her.

"I can't believe it." She stopped and turned around to face the mountain. "I mean, look at that. We were all the way up there just a few hours ago." The summit seemed even more daunting and farther away now than it had since it first came into view the day they hiked to Shira One. This angle showed more of the glacier, the most majestic view yet.

"I know what you mean. It's almost surreal."

"That's a good word for it." She was feeling tired from being up all night, but the satisfaction from reaching the peak kept her pumping.

"This is probably going to sound corny, but I'm really glad I got the chance to do this with you. You made it special."

"It doesn't sound corny at all." In fact, the words warmed her so much she wished she could take Addison's hand. Instead, she settled for a pat on the shoulder.

"So what's the first thing you're going to do when we get back to the hotel tomorrow?"

"You're kidding, right?"

"I mean after your bath," Addison said with a chuckle.

"Another bath. What about you?"

"I'll probably be picking the scree out of my wazoo."

Mary Kate grinned, stopping short of offering to help.

"Imagine what hot water will feel like."

"Ha! Don't get your hopes up. The first night I was at the View, we didn't have any hot water. What do you think will happen when all nine of us try to turn it on at the same time?"

"We could always double up," Addison said, feigning innocence.

Before Mary Kate could respond, Brad suddenly dropped his backpack and darted off the trail to the left.

"You little shit!" Jim dropped his pack also, running in pursuit as the rest of the group tried to figure out what was happening.

In moments, father and son were rolling on the ground, laughing hysterically until Brad finally cried "Uncle!" It was a welcome sight after four days of tension between the two. Finally, they returned to pick up their packs, still laughing, but not sharing what had triggered the chase.

"Drew said there was an Internet café in Moshi," Addison said when they picked up their pace again.

"Yeah, there is. In fact, I want to go send a note to Deb and let her know I made it."

"Sure. I can send a note to my dad, and to my friends back in Miami. You're not going to write your family?"

"Nobody has e-mail. I'll shoot Bobby a quick note and he'll tell them." It suddenly struck her that she hadn't thought of Bobby all day.

"I bet he'll be proud of you."

"Pffft." She waved her hand dismissively. "That'll last about eight seconds. Then he'll be ready to forget all about it."

"We break," Luke said. They had been hiking for almost two hours straight and were on the fringe of the rainforest.

A dark green hut stood to the side of the clearing, and Jim made his way over to investigate. A moment later he let out a whoop.

A window in the hut was propped open to reveal a cooler stocked with ice-cold Coca-Cola. Luke laughed as he watched their eyes light up at the sight. One American dollar bought two

Cokes, thus Jim's twenty-dollar bill bought a round for the hikers and each of the porters as they straggled through.

Still using Addison's camera, Mary Kate got a spectacular picture of all of the hikers sitting side by side on a long bench with their Cokes, the mountain looming in the distant background. Luke then took their cameras and snapped pictures of the whole group.

"This is the after picture," Ann said, reminding them of when they had gathered at Londorossi Gate.

Mary Kate handed the camera to Nikki. "Would you mind getting a picture of Addison and me?" In what had become their customary stance, they posed with their arms around each other.

"Okay, say...peeing outside."

They laughed just as she snapped the photo.

Brad and Drew went back for seconds and treated everyone to a burping serenade. The collective mood was celebratory, with everyone still riding high from their overnight hike.

Refreshed and rested, they hiked another hour and a half into the rainforest before reaching Millennium Hut, by far the muddiest camp they had seen on this trek. All five of their tents were huddled together—way too close to the latrine for Mary Kate's liking—underneath a stand of wispy trees with branches that brushed the rain guards. Exhaustion washed over her as she noted the cold drizzle.

Poor Gilbert got barely a greeting when he brought out the potatoes and soup. After a quiet dinner, they retreated one last time to their tents.

It occurred to Mary Kate that she had been up for thirty-six hours straight, and that Addison had slept only five hours since Barranco. They quickly changed into their long johns, which they had shed after lunch at Barafu.

"I can't believe it's this cold here," Addison grumbled.

"I know. I expected it to be a lot warmer too." Mary Kate got into her bag and, without waiting for an invitation, scooted next to Addison, rolling onto her side to mold their bodies together.

Chapter Twenty

Addison smiled to herself to feel Mary Kate alongside her. Neither of them had moved an inch all night. Her mind drifted to pleasant thoughts of how relaxed they might be in this same position, but without the restricting bags. Thanks to the casual affection Mary Kate had shown since the Karanga Valley, she had given herself permission to speculate about where they might go from here. Sharing a room on the safari might lead them to share even more.

"Hi," Mary Kate whispered as she raised her head for a moment. "You have a dirty face."

Addison smiled. "I hate to be the one to tell you this, but so do you."

Mary Kate chuckled and dropped her head back on Addison's shoulder. "I have a dirty everything."

"There's ice inside our tent," Addison remarked drearily, peering through the hole in her sleeping bag at the frozen condensation.

"Do you realize that when we crawl out this morning, we won't ever have to go back in?"

In an odd way, that realization made Addison sad. She surely wouldn't miss the hard ground, or the cold, or the dirt that pervaded everything she owned. But she had enjoyed sharing the small space with Mary Kate, especially all the hours they had talked into the night.

"And you won't have a tent mate sleeping on top of you every night," Mary Kate added.

"I haven't minded that at all. In case you forgot, I like sleeping close to women."

Mary Kate burrowed against her. "Lucky for you."

A sudden giggling from an adjacent tent broke their intense gaze.

"Hey, everybody! Last one to the bus is a rotten egg!" It was Nikki's voice.

"That's appropriate, since we all smell like rotten eggs," Drew yelled from inside his own tent.

"I'm running off this mountain so fast you guys will be eating my dust!" Brad said.

Ann corrected him. "It's all mud, Brad. There is no dust."

The banter continued between tents for another ten minutes before Mei finally ventured out. "Shit!"

"What?" several voices asked.

"Everything out here's covered in ice, even the stuff under the rain guard."

Addison unzipped their tent to find a thin layer of ice covering their boots and Summit bags. A peek outside the rain guard revealed more. Ice coated the ground and hung from the trees. "I'm ready to get the hell off this mountain," she said with a groan.

"I'm right behind you. One more day of this, and we'll all be weaving baskets."

Breakfast was hard-boiled eggs, delivered to the camp by the same transport that ferried Coca-Cola to the ranger station they had passed on the way down. Mary Kate shared her hand sanitizer, and everyone made the best of it. They packed only one liter of water each, as they no longer needed to worry about acclimatization. Luke guessed they would be off the mountain in three hours.

The exit through the rainforest was somewhat treacherous, since the damp moss growing across the rocks made for slippery passage. Nonetheless, they were making good time. Nikki had positioned herself directly behind Luke today, determined to be the first on the waiting bus.

After their first break, the trail became somewhat muddier. Addison helped Mary Kate navigate the mucky parts, lending a hand to ensure that she didn't lose her footing. Both were glad they had brought two walking sticks. Those with only one were struggling for balance.

"So we're almost there, Luke?" Ann asked. They had been slogging for more than two hours now.

"I think we are…half." He looked at them grimly. "The rain has made the trail difficult. It is certain to get much worse."

The runoff from last night's chilling drizzle had spread through the jungle like a delta, and soon they had no choice but to trudge right through the middle of it. It was miserable and seemed as though it might never end.

The jovial camaraderie of the day before was gone, and all were quiet in their misery. Each had fallen in the mud, most more than once.

Luke stopped them again when they came upon a log that had fallen across the path. It seemed as good a place to break as any.

"Hey, Luke," Brad said. "It isn't like this in the movies. The African guide is supposed to walk ahead and chop down the branches with a machete so the tourists can walk through without any trouble. They don't have mud like this."

Luke shrugged. "I have never seen a movie."

Addison spotted Mary Kate slumped at the end of the sloping log, her back to the others in the group. She gingerly crept over and touched her on the back. "How are you doing?"

Mary Kate shook her head. "Not so good."

It was clear the grueling slog had taken its toll on her spirit. "We'll be out of this soon."

"I sure hope so, because if I thought the next two hours were going to be like the last, I'd just sit here and cry." As the words left her lips, her eyes filled with tears.

"Hey, it's okay." Addison kneeled against the log and drew Mary Kate to her chest. "It's just for a little while longer. I promise you, that feeling you had yesterday morning will be back as soon as we get down."

Mary Kate tried to smile through her tears. She gave Addison a tight squeeze around the waist and whispered her thanks.

Addison looked over her shoulder to see Neal comforting Mei, who was covered with mud past her hips. Ann sat dejected on a muddy rock. Their misery today seemed magnified by the contrast from their elation at the summit.

When Luke stood this time, he offered encouragement. "No more breaks. Now we go to the gate."

"Why don't we walk the rest of the way with Ann?" Addison suggested. "She looks like she could use a little moral support too."

In under an hour, they exited the muddy trail onto a wide dirt road. It too was wet, but here they could easily get their footing. To their surprise, they were met from the other direction by several young boys who escorted them the final half mile to the ranger station. Everyone thought it odd at first, but the youths' friendly presence was a welcome addition. As they rounded the final bend, they got their first view of civilization—such as it was—in the form of several rugged four-wheel drive vehicles and a simple white structure that housed the ranger's station.

The boy who walked with Addison took her arm and led her to a constantly running faucet that splashed onto a concrete slab. Carefully, she held onto a pole as he took out a ragged scrub brush and began to wash the caked mud from her boots and pants.

"Addison! Look at me."

She turned and smiled as Mary Kate took her picture. It was a relief to see her come out of her funk. No one had imagined the descent would have been so emotionally draining.

The boy was thrilled with the two-dollar tip, though probably not as thrilled as Addison was to have her boots and gaiters clean.

Luke directed them to the ranger's logbook, where each one officially signed out of the park, noting the highest point reached. "Tom Muncie will be pleased that all of you reached Stella Point."

"Too bad about Courtney," Mei said.

He shrugged. "There is little we can do for those who do not come to the mountain prepared."

Addison watched the others sign the book, noting the pride of those who had reached the summit. She too was proud of getting there, but this trip had come to mean more than that. She had set out merely to make the most of the experience, one she had hoped to share with her best friends. She had never expected to meet someone like Mary Kate, someone who made her feel things she hadn't felt in a while.

After a one-hour drive through the countryside, the bus pulled into the View Hotel, depositing them, tired and dirty, onto the same front porch where they had gathered expectantly eight days ago. In their last official act as Summit trekkers, they retrieved their belongings and pooled their dollars to generously tip their guide and the team of porters gathered by the bus.

Addison separated her gear, pulling out only the lightweight items. The rest she stuffed in the Summit duffel with her sleeping bag and presented to Luke for distribution to the porters. "I won't have much use for this again."

Mary Kate kept her sleeping bag, but emptied her backpack and added it the growing pile, which now included Jim's boots, and all of Drew's donated hand-me-downs.

Luke then presented each hiker who had reached Uhuru Peak with an official certificate from the Tanzania National Parks department, noting the date and time of their summit, and the age of the climber. The others got a Summit Trail and Safari Company certificate that said they had reached Stella Point.

Addison followed Mary Kate back inside and made arrangements to meet in one hour to walk into town to the

Internet café. Then she retreated to her room on the second floor and turned on the water in her shower. Even with her diminished expectations about the plumbing, she was disappointed. The shower barely managed a trickle, and it was cold. It would have to do.

After thirty minutes of intense scrubbing and a cursory swipe of her legs with a razor, she called it quits, dressing in clean olive green convertibles with a pale yellow T-shirt. Sandals were a welcome change to the boots she had worn since leaving London.

Mary Kate was waiting on the front porch when she came down. She had on khaki Capri pants with a sleeveless white top and sandals. Small gold hoops adorned her ears, and she wore a necklace with a dainty opal pendant. Addison would have proudly taken her anywhere.

She liked very much where things had come since clearing the air in the Karanga Valley. The more they talked, the more she was convinced her interest wasn't one-sided, and there was no reason to rein in what she was feeling. Mary Kate was twenty-four, old enough to know what she wanted, certainly old enough to stop things from going beyond what she could handle.

"There's a little market up here at the corner that sells sodas and candy. I get the feeling they're open just for us."

Indeed, as they approached, a man rushed from his shack to push up the window of the snack stand, and two children suddenly appeared out of nowhere. Addison bought drinks and candy for the children and promised to stop by on the way back to the hotel.

They reached the café and paid the host for two terminals. The connection was sluggish, but eventually, Addison signed into her e-mail account. A quick check showed nothing pressing, and not a single reply to her e-mail inquiries about job opportunities. She typed a short note to each of her parents, letting them know she had reached the summit and was now safe at the hotel in Moshi. Next, she wrote to Cyn and Javier:

Get ready to be jealous. Kili was everything they said it would be and more. Six of us made it to the summit—including yours truly— and some of us are headed out on safari tomorrow. Can't wait to tell you about the "and more" part. Suffice it to say that she's a Georgia peach and we're rooming together over the next few days (and nights). I hope to have more to say when I see you, but if not, I expect to add her to my short list of very good friends. I'll e you again from London, and I can't wait to show you the photos. Love, Addison

"How do you spell Falk?" Mary Kate asked without looking up.

"F-A-L-K. Who are you writing to?"

"Deb. I'm telling her how you laughed at me when I fell in the water, and how you taunted me when I couldn't get up the Barranco Wall."

"Uh-oh. She's going to come beat the shit out of me."

"Why, I do believe you understand Southern culture after all," Mary Kate said, her drawl more pronounced than ever. "I wrote Deb when I got here and told her I was breaking up with Bobby as soon as I got home. You want to hear what she said?"

"Sure." She closed out her connection and slid her chair next to Mary Kate's.

"To my dear, dear, dear, dear friend Mary Kate. You cannot imagine the joy it brings me to hear you say that you are finished with Bobby Britton. In fact, I bought a six-pack of Coors Light to celebrate the blessed event with you, but I drank the whole damn thing in your honor. Can't wait to hear about your trip, and for God's sake, don't bring home any parasites!"

"She sounds like a riot."

"She is. So here's what I told her." She leaned back and read from the screen. "After the eight coldest, dirtiest days of my life, I am back at the hotel in Moshi. With the help of my untrustworthy sidekick, Addison Falk from Miami, I have conquered the highest mountain in Africa. Addison will be visiting Mooresville someday, and I told her you would kick her ass because she laughed at me when I fell in the water. Don't let me down. See you soon."

"I'm in such trouble," Addison said before breaking into a grin.

She closed her connection. "We should go back before it gets dark."

"You aren't going to write Bobby?"

"No, I changed my mind. I promised I'd call him. He's supposed to tell everybody when I'm back down. Besides, he doesn't check his e-mail that often."

"What are you going to say?"

"I don't know. I'll have to wait and see what comes out of my mouth."

When they walked past the snack stand on their way back, eight small children came to greet them, obviously on the recommendation of their two friends. They bought another round of drinks and candy for the children, and barely made it back to the hotel before dark. Mary Kate stopped at the counter and asked to use the phone.

"Good luck," Addison said, wishing for an excuse to hang around. She wanted to hear Mary Kate tell him to get lost.

Chapter Twenty-One

The line crackled, but finally a familiar voice picked up. "Hi, Dreama. It's me, Mary Kate. Can I talk to Bobby?"

The school secretary put her on hold for a few seconds before coming back to the phone to ask excitedly if she was calling from Africa. "Yes, but this is costing me an arm and leg. Is he there?"

She watched the clock. Forty-five seconds.

"Hey, Bobby. It's me. I was just calling to let you know that we're all back down, and I made it all the way...Yeah, it was pretty tough...No, not everybody. Just half of us."

That was it for his questions—was it as hard as she thought, and did everyone make it to the top. Nothing else about her experience. Then he started to tell her something about his softball team. She checked the clock again. Just under a minute.

"Listen, I've only got a few more seconds. This is costing me twenty bucks, but I wanted to let you know, like I said I would." She rolled her eyes as he continued his story, only faster. "Bobby, I have to go. I'll see you at the airport, okay? Don't forget to call Mom and Dad and let them know that I made it to the top and I'm back down. And tell them to call Aunt Jean."

Then he said the dreaded words.

"I love you too. Bye."

Flooded with an array of emotions, she leaned across the counter to hang up the phone. She felt guilty for her last-second pretense, but the stronger feeling was relief to be done with it. It would feel even better once they finally talked about things being over and they could move on from being a couple, maybe even to being good friends. At least now she could spend the next few days not worrying about it.

She found her fellow hikers at a long table on the outdoor patio of the bar. An ice-cold Safari beer sat at an empty spot next to Addison, who was sharing stories with those around her.

As she approached, she noticed something different. Addison's long hair, which had been tied back in a ponytail since the day she arrived, was now loose around her shoulders. Her casual pose—one arm across the back of the empty chair as she leaned across to talk to Ann—was the picture of relaxation. It was a wonderful contrast to the formality she had shown only last week when she first introduced herself to the group.

Mary Kate interrupted their conversation as she took the chair between them and picked up her beer. "Thanks."

"You're welcome. I wasn't sure if you drank beer," Addison said.

"Not often, but sometimes." She took her first sip of the beer labeled Tanzania's finest. "Oh…that's different."

"The second swallow's better, and by the third, it'll be your favorite," Jim said. He sat directly across from his eighteen-year-old son, who was also enjoying a beer.

"How did your phone call go?" Addison whispered.

Mary Kate didn't want to get mired in talk of Bobby tonight. It was a special night with new friends and she wanted to savor their triumph. She was saved by a flicker of the lights, then another, before the entire complex was thrown into total darkness.

"Hey, Drew. You just got better looking," Brad said.

"Very funny, you little rat."

In a few moments, the bar staff appeared with candles for their table. Jim ordered the next round, which Mary Kate quickly waved off. Two beers would have her singing the Dixie Chicks. Around eight o'clock, the restaurant manager appeared to announce that despite the power loss, the buffet was ready and their table was set.

No one ate the boiled potatoes.

Her plate piled high with seasoned fish, tomatoes and freshly-baked bread, Mary Kate commandeered the seat at the far end of the table. Addison joined her at the corner, brushing their knees together as she sat down.

Mary Kate leaned over and whispered, "It's nice to see you so relaxed tonight."

"Hey, I'm from Miami. I can't relax unless I'm warm."

"It looks good on you."

"Thanks." Addison reached under the table to squeeze her knee.

Mary Kate grasped her hand and held it as they waited for the others to join them at the table. She let go only when everyone began to eat.

A lively conversation recapping their trek accompanied dinner, covering every subject from the toilet paper shortage to their mass meltdown in the mud earlier that day. Mary Kate was glad to feel the exhilaration return, and she couldn't wait to get another look at the mountain from the street the next day.

As they finished dinner and sipped tea, Addison's hand wandered back into her lap and she took it. It made her smile to think that no one else at the table knew of their secret sparks.

The candlelight banquet would be the last meal together for the Summit group. Jim, Brad and Drew were heading out for home early in the morning. The others were staying for a wildlife safari, but tomorrow they would split into three groups—Neal and Mei, Ann and Nikki, and Mary Kate and Addison—and not meet again until Saturday at the airport.

Mary Kate wasn't ready for her evening to end, but the others drifted off to their rooms until she and Addison were alone in the restaurant. "You want to walk me to my room?"

"Love to."

It was funny after all their time together in a tent to be heading off to separate rooms, especially since it was only for one night. If she had thought about it sooner, they could have canceled one room and stayed together. And once they were alone in their room, who knows what might have happened?

When she started toward the exit, she reveled in the feel of Addison's hand in the small of her back guiding her through the candlelit restaurant. They reached the lobby and were met by a young girl with a flashlight.

"I take you upstairs to your room," she said.

Carefully, they mounted the stairs and arrived first at Mary Kate's room. Their escort waited until she had located the matches on the nightstand and lit the single deep candle by her bedside.

"I'm all set," she said, resigned that their evening was over.

"Good night," Addison said awkwardly. Then she disappeared in the darkness down the hall.

Mary Kate closed her door and slid the barrel bolt into place, disappointed at having her time with Addison end so abruptly. All evening, she had fantasized about them coming back to her room, talking into the night and finally exploring the feelings that were flickering between them.

She readied for bed in the dim light, relishing the feel of her cool silk pajamas. The soft cotton sheets would be a welcome change from putting on her clothes to climb inside a dirty sleeping bag.

A soft knock stopped her as she leaned to blow out the candle. Pressing against the door, she asked who was there. The answer made her smile, and she threw the bolt.

Addison leaned casually against the doorjamb, holding a candle. She was barefoot, dressed in baggy shorts and a T-shirt.

Mary Kate grasped her wrist and pulled her forcefully into the room. Then she closed the door again and locked them in. "I'm glad you came back."

Addison set her candle on a small table at the foot of the bed. "I thought we should talk about"—she waved her finger between them—"what's going on here, and what we want to do about it."

Mary Kate swallowed hard, suddenly aware she was shaking. "What do you want to do?" She tossed out the question as though giving Addison authority to decide for both of them.

Addison stepped closer and raised her fingertips to brush the hair behind Mary Kate's ear. "I want to make sure we both want the same thing. I don't want to push this if you aren't comfortable with the idea."

Lots of emotions filled her—most were good—but comfort wasn't one of them. "How can I be comfortable with something that's happening for the first time?"

"What is happening?"

She took Addison's hand and pressed it into her cheek. "I've finally met someone I really want to kiss."

Addison's other hand went around her waist and pulled them together. She leaned in, but stopped momentarily, as if asking permission one last time. Then she finally closed, brushing her mouth and tongue softly against Mary Kate's lower lip.

The sensation was almost surreal, as excitement and want coursed through her. Kissing had never felt so personal, so intimate. There was no checklist in the back of her head telling her how far to part her lips or what to do with her tongue, nothing that asked her to try harder to concentrate on the emotions.

As if an afterthought, she became aware of her hands, which had slipped beneath Addison's T-shirt to caress the warm skin of her back. It only made the kiss they shared deeper, more intense.

Breathing heavily, Addison finally left her mouth and moved to the soft skin of her neck.

Mary Kate tipped her head to the side, yielding to the gentle assault and surprising herself with a quiet moan. The heat seemed to rise between them, and she pulled their bodies closer.

Abruptly, Addison stopped and wrapped her in a tight hug, her lips only centimeters from Mary Kate's ear. "I should have known kissing you would make me crazy. I need to go back to my room while I can still walk."

"I don't want you to go." She had never felt a temptation like this, a desire so strong she couldn't turn it off. It was already too late to turn back. "Stay with me."

Even the panic that her invitation evoked felt good, like a congratulatory response to her show of courage. As if to demonstrate her resolve, she blew out Addison's candle and led her to the opening in the mosquito net.

"And we thought we were through with tents," Addison said, her voice shaking slightly as she ducked through the slit and stretched out on the far side of the bed.

Mary Kate followed and closed the gap behind her, lying back against her pillow in surrender. The bedside candle flickered with its yellow glow, casting their silhouettes onto the transparent white netting. Whatever happened next, she wanted to see it clearly.

Addison moved closer, draping her knee between Mary Kate's so their bodies were entwined from head to toe. When she brought their lips together once again for a searing kiss, Mary Kate drove her hips upward with a physical yearning she had never felt before. She pushed her hands through Addison's hair and synchronized her movements to the rocking rhythm of the thigh that pressed against her need.

Again, Addison stilled and buried her face into Mary Kate's neck as if trying to rein in her impulse. "This is going to happen unless you stop it, Mary Kate."

The whispered warning only fueled her hunger. She grasped the edges of Addison's T-shirt and pulled it upward. "I want to feel you."

Addison allowed her shirt to be removed and went to work loosening the buttons on Mary Kate's top. Then she pushed it aside and lowered her body, bringing their warm skin together.

Mary Kate thought she might die from the softness against her. Her hands roamed across the smooth skin of Addison's back, down the dip of her spine and back up the curved sides to start again. Craving the sensation throughout her body, she hooked her fingertips in the waistband of Addison's shorts. "More."

When Addison lifted her body to comply, Mary Kate pushed off her own pajamas. Then she held her breath in exquisite anticipation as their pubic mounds came together. "God, Addison," she murmured, moaning with sheer bliss. Nothing had ever felt so right.

Another kiss followed, this one more urgent than the others, a signal they were past the point of no return. Addison's hand covered and caressed her breast, teasing her nipple into a hardened tip. Then she dropped her head to suck it between her lips.

Mary Kate pushed her chest higher off the bed, willing it deeper into Addison's mouth. She watched as if dreaming while Addison moved from one breast to the other, lavishing a tantalizing touch on the aching peaks.

Too soon, Addison left her breasts, but she didn't stop. Instead, her warm, wet mouth drifted lower to the patch of curly hair.

Mary Kate covered the chill of her moistened breasts with her hands, kneading them in frenzy as her focus shifted to a stronger ache burning from her center. She could feel Addison's warm breath against her thigh, and she instinctively opened her legs.

Addison's tongue swirled through her folds, an intimacy beyond anything she had ever imagined. Every nerve in her body vacated its function to congregate in a single place, where a warm tingling grew more and more intense. When Addison closed her lips over that tiny spot, Mary Kate erupted, a million vibrations rushing like lasers to and from her core.

Nearly frantic with the powerful sensation, she jerked away uncontrollably.

"It's okay. It's okay," Addison whispered, crawling up quickly to envelop her in a calming embrace. "Easy. I've got you."

Mary Kate shuddered again as Addison's thigh pressed against her hypersensitive center. It was too much, and she squirmed to break free.

"Mary Kate, what's wrong?" Addison shifted her body to the side but did not release her grip.

Words could not express what she was feeling—the most

extreme embarrassment she had ever known. How could she ever have convinced herself that what she had felt during sex with Bobby was all she needed? He had never given her anything so intense, a physical and emotional release so profound that it left her weak and pulsing in its wake.

"Please talk to me."

Mary Kate squeezed her eyes tightly shut to hold back tears, her body still trembling from what they had done. She felt like a naïve teenager who'd had sex for the first time.

"Did I hurt you?"

She shook her head and resolved to speak. Addison needed reassurance as much as she did. "I wasn't expecting that. It was…" She drew in a deep breath. "I felt it all over."

As if sensing her vulnerability, Addison pulled the sheet up over them, and then planted feather-like kisses on her brow and eyelids. "It was beautiful."

"I didn't expect it to be so strong. Or to happen so fast." Most of all, she was surprised at how it had rippled suddenly from beneath Addison's lips and spread throughout her whole body. It embarrassed her to think Addison had known her body better than she knew it herself.

"Sometimes it's like that. It can—"

"I never had an orgasm like that before," she blurted, feeling her face heat up as she took in the surprise on Addison's face. "Nobody ever did that to me…with their mouth, I mean."

Addison smiled warmly and slid her body back into place, resting her leg again in its intimate place. "Then I'm glad I was your first. You have the most wonderful taste."

Bobby had kissed her there once, but only for a second or two. She had returned the gesture with a similar lack of enthusiasm, but—

Her panic rose as it suddenly occurred to her that Addison might want the same from her. She didn't think she could do that.

"Will you let me touch you again?" Addison's hand was already caressing her hip. "Please trust me. I'd never do anything to hurt you."

Mary Kate couldn't have refused if she had wanted to. Her body was already rising in need, and when she felt Addison's fingertips teasing her curls, she parted her thighs to grant access.

"This part of you, Mary Kate"—her hand slid through the wetness—"is the warmest"—her lips tugged gently at her earlobe—"and the softest thing I've ever touched." Her finger gently entered the opening and began to stroke.

Though her hips wanted badly to thrust forward and take in more of the probing hand, Mary Kate didn't want to make a fool of herself with another loss of control. Instead, she willed herself to remain still and concentrate on the sensations as Addison added another finger to her depths. Each time they withdrew, a thumb dragged gently across her clitoris, sending a tremor through her midsection.

"Do you want me to stop?"

"No," she whispered as the warmth bubbled up and gathered at the precipice. Suddenly, the walls of her insides clenched and gripped the fingers that filled her. Hot waves spilled over in rapid succession, finally receding to leave her numb.

Addison withdrew her fingers and dropped her forehead on Mary Kate's shoulder. "You have no idea how good it feels to be pulled inside like that. Thank you for trusting me."

"I do trust you." Mary Kate was almost overwhelmed at the rush of emotions over what they had just shared. It was more than just the physical intimacy. Addison had vanquished her fears and doubts with more understanding and tenderness than anyone had ever shown her. "It's like you're looking inside me."

Addison smoothed her hair to the side and delivered another kiss to her brow. "I will if you'll let me."

Chapter Twenty-Two

Addison awakened just after dawn, pleased to find the warm body that had remained in her protective embrace through the night. They had gotten dressed again before falling asleep, and though she feared at times that Mary Kate would ask her to leave, Addison's calming assurances had prevailed.

Mary Kate stirred and then blinked in obvious surprise at finding Addison looking down at her.

"Good morning," Addison said, unable to mask her delight. "I've been waiting for ages for you to wake up so I could tell you about the most remarkable evening I had."

"Remarkable, huh?" Mary Kate nervously fingered her collar.

"Truly." She leaned down and stole a morning kiss. "I hope you enjoyed it as much as I did, because I don't think I could stand it if you didn't."

"You took my breath away."

"I could say the same."

"Except, I mean really. I had no idea…"

"It was beautiful," she said, still hoping to reassure. "Your body was so responsive, so ready. All you had to do was let go."

Mary Kate stroked Addison's chest with her palm. "It wasn't the sort of image I'd want a lover to see, especially the first time."

"Why do you feel you have to project an image? You should always be who you are."

"Nobody wants to look naïve in bed."

So she was still embarrassed. "We've all been there. Besides, I meant what I said about being glad I was the one who shared that with you." She kissed her again, this time on the cheek. "So thank you for waiting." Mary Kate finally smiled, and Addison was flooded with relief.

"Do you think anyone knows about you sneaking down here?"

She shook her head. "It was dark. But I should probably go back and mess up my bed before the housekeeper comes around."

"You really think they care?"

"It's possible. Homosexuality is illegal here."

Mary Kate's eyes grew wide, but then she tipped her head as if pondering something. "It won't be an issue tonight because we'll be sharing a room."

Yes, but would they share a bed? There was no mistaking Mary Kate's uneasiness, and no opportunity for exploring its roots until they were alone again tonight. Addison didn't think she would last all day trying to guess where they stood. "Are you okay about last night?"

Mary Kate stared back at her for several seconds—long seconds, since Addison was waiting anxiously for her reply.

"I just woke up a different person, Addison. It might not be easy for me to understand it all, but I can't change what I know about myself now."

Addison was gripped with uncharacteristic insecurity. "I want to be there with you when you figure it all out."

Mary Kate pulled her down for a gentle kiss. "Good, because I don't think I can do it without you."

That was all the confirmation Addison needed that their

night together had not been a colossal mistake. They said quiet goodbyes, and she tiptoed back to her room unseen.

Three hours later, they stood in the street in front of the hotel with the others, hoping for a break in the clouds that would grant them one last view of Kilimanjaro. The safari guides arrived before it happened, and they piled into their respective vehicles, vowing to meet up again at the airport.

Addison couldn't contain her delight at finally being alone again with Mary Kate—alone except for their driver, John, a thin Tanzanian who spoke barely a word of English. They were situated in the backseat of a rugged Toyota Land Cruiser, the apparent vehicle of choice for private safaris. Their drive took them over a familiar route past the airport turnoff, and then onto a narrow two-lane road riddled with potholes.

"Maasai," John said, pointing at the two red-clad tribesmen amid the small herd of cattle.

"Mei told us on the way into Moshi that the Maasai consider cattle to be sacred," Mary Kate said.

"I read that too. There was a story not long ago about some tribesmen who were so saddened by what happened at the World Trade Center that they gathered twelve of their best cattle and made a gift to the United States ambassador here in Tanzania."

"I'm not surprised. Mei said they were noble."

Addison stepped out of her shoe and trailed her bare foot along the back of Mary Kate's calf, well out of John's line of sight. "So how'd you sleep last night?"

"Not bad." Mary Kate smiled as a faint blush crept up her neck. "You?"

"Okay, I guess. I had a little trouble falling asleep. It was really hot in my room."

Mary Kate nodded seriously. "Maybe it was something you ate."

Addison covered a guffaw and felt her own face heat up. It was tempting to push the game a little further, but the sudden appearance of an ostrich in the field next to them reminded her they had come to view the wildlife on the *outside* of the vehicle.

John seemed to know the secret locations of all the invisible speed bumps and managed to miss the worst ones. Still, they were plentiful, random and not officially marked. In some places, the local warning system was a small stack of rocks on the side of the road. When they turned onto a dirt road, speed bumps were no longer consequential, as the road itself was as rippled as a washboard.

At midday, John pulled into a courtyard of shops and retrieved the three box lunches provided by the View Hotel. He exited the vehicle and opened their door gallantly. Without speaking, he indicated a wide porch that held a half dozen plastic tables and chairs and pointed also in the direction of restrooms and a small bar where they could purchase drinks.

Mary Kate bought Cokes for all three of them while Addison waited at a quiet table in the corner. It was their first opportunity to be truly alone since early this morning.

"Have you been reading my mind all day?"

"Yes, I think I have." Mary Kate laughed. "And the irony is that I've come ten thousand miles to see exotic animals living in their natural habitat, and all I can think about is your foot rubbing my leg."

"I'll try to control myself," Addison said, smiling playfully. "I look forward to spending every minute of the next four days with you, and the fact that we're going to get to see these fascinating things together will just make them all that much better."

"I appreciate everything you did last night."

"Believe me, the pleasure was mine."

"I don't mean just the…you know." She began to blush again. "I mean the way you talked to me. I'm really sorry that I—"

Addison interrupted her with a hand on her arm. "You have nothing to apologize for," she said sincerely. "I care for you very much, and I hope I showed you that."

"You certainly did."

"You're not the only one sorting things out today." She smiled at Mary Kate's quizzical look. "Believe it or not, I woke up a different person too, all because of how you made me feel.

I can't get this silly grin off my face, and it's all I can do to keep my eyes off you."

Mary Kate laughed softly and looked away, clearly embarrassed by the sentiment, but also obviously pleased.

"You might as well get used to it, Mary Kate."

"Then you better hope we don't get arrested."

John signaled for them, and they walked back to the vehicle laughing. It was nice to have the air cleared, Addison thought. They seemed to do that regularly, but it always moved them forward.

Before entering the Lake Manyara Game Reserve, John pulled over and climbed onto the roof of the Land Cruiser. After releasing a catch, he folded back two panels, opening the roof of the vehicle so Addison and Mary Kate could stand for a safe and unobstructed view of the wildlife in their natural setting.

Within a few hundred yards of passing the park gate, they came upon three other vehicles stopped in the middle of the road. The party in front had encountered an elephant in the roadway, and following park rules, had to hold their position until the animal moved along. Unfortunately, the creature wasn't pleased with the motorized challenge to his territory, and after a stubborn standoff, moved to charge the vehicle in front. All of the well-trained drivers responded in unison, reversing gears to back up quickly. Finally, the mighty beast turned into the woods, trampling the bushes and small trees in his path.

"Did you get pictures?" Mary Kate asked excitedly.

"A few, but I couldn't see him very well from here. Why don't we use my camera like we did on the mountain and I'll send them to you on a disc?"

"Or you can take pictures of the animals and I can take pictures of you," Mary Kate suggested, her voice low enough that John couldn't hear. She raised her camera to snap a candid of Addison as she stuck out her tongue. "Now that's what I call a wild animal."

"I'll give you more than a picture," Addison said, feeling certain John couldn't understand them.

When they cleared the elephant's path, they stopped again as a family of baboons crossed the road in front of them...and another...and another. After almost half an hour, they had seen more than two hundred of the creatures, all passing within a few feet of the Land Cruiser. In some instances, the younger baboons rode on the backs of their parents.

Winding through the heavily wooded park, they got a close-up view of a small herd of impalas, then a fleeting glimpse of a dozen or so zebras as they rushed shyly into the bush, and eventually a long-distance look at two adult giraffes by the lake. Several trips around the lake yielded no new species, and finally John left the park for their first game lodge.

As its name suggested, the Ngorongoro Wildlife Lodge overlooked the magnificent Ngorongoro Crater, a natural zoo that spanned sixty square miles. The crater was home to hundreds of species, including zebras, wildebeests, hippos, elephants, lions and the very rare rhinoceros. Tomorrow, they would descend into the game reserve. But tonight, they would be treated to a buffet dinner and a traditional African dance program at the lodge.

Mary Kate waited with their bags while Addison checked in and picked up the key to their room.

"Lights out at ten o'clock, back on at six thirty," she reported. "Our dinner slot is in fifteen minutes, and the show starts an hour later."

"So we have fifteen minutes to freshen up?"

"Or to make out," Addison said innocently. She opened the door to their room to find twin beds separated by a nightstand. Candles and matches were placed around the room for after-hours illumination. Since the crater ledge sat at over seven thousand feet amid dry vegetation, there were no mosquito nets. She took the bags from Mary Kate and tossed them aside.

They fell together onto one of the beds, kissing frantically. Addison resisted the urge to let her hands roam, not wanting to start something they couldn't finish before their scheduled dinner. "I've wanted to do this all day, every time I looked at you."

After several minutes, they tore themselves apart and left the room for dinner. There was a show—dancers, costumes, drums. It was all a blur to Addison.

When they returned to the room, she took a quick shower and slid naked into bed while Mary Kate finished up in the bathroom.

When she emerged, Addison raised the covers and offered the space next to her. By the familiar candlelight, she watched with growing anticipation as Mary Kate dropped her pajamas on the floor and climbed into bed alongside her.

Addison wasted no time in picking up where they had left off the night before, marveling at the easy way they moved together. She could feel Mary Kate respond. Everything she touched or kissed brought a gasp or a tremble, but it was clear she was holding back, as if afraid to let go. "Listen to your body, Mary Kate. It knows what you want. Let go, and I'll keep you safe," she whispered.

Little by little, Mary Kate moved with the stroking hand inside her, her breathing hitching each time her clitoris was teased.

"That's it. I love it when you move with me." Addison pressed her hips to Mary Kate's thigh to quell her own need, which grew exponentially with each rise and fall. Then suddenly, the orgasm ripped through Mary Kate, and she bit into Addison's shoulder to muffle a scream.

"How do you do that?" Mary Kate rasped.

"I told you. Your body knows."

They lay still for several minutes while Mary Kate caught her breath. "Can I touch you?"

The question surprised her, but set her body aflame. "Of course." She fell onto her back as Mary Kate rolled onto her side. A tentative hand stroked her stomach and hip before slowly tracking upward to touch her breast. Addison watched as her nipples darkened and formed peaks. "See how excited that gets me."

Mary Kate explored the shape and feel of her breasts, first

one, then the other, before lowering her head to draw a nipple into her mouth.

"And I love that."

Seemingly confident in this newfound pleasure, Mary Kate devoured her breasts, combining all possible tactics—licking, nibbling, blowing, tugging. Addison was ready to touch herself when finally a hand wandered lower and into the soft curls at the apex of her thighs. When it lingered too long, Addison gently took Mary Kate's wrist and moved it lower.

"Feel what you do to me."

She shuddered as Mary Kate's fingers slid through her slickened folds, and then again as Mary Kate gasped in apparent wonder. In that instant, she realized the magnitude of the moment, her first touch of another woman.

"I want to come for you."

Mary Kate seemed torn between looking into her eyes and watching what her hand was doing. Addison helped her choose.

"See what you're doing. You have so much power over me."

The pressure intensified as she thrust upward into Mary Kate's rhythmic caress, until she could stand it no more. With her thighs stiffened and high off the bed, her climax ripped through her, the pulsing waves receding in its wake.

"Please tell me you like doing that."

Mary Kate answered her with a passion-filled kiss that begged for a new round of sensations.

Chapter Twenty-Three

Mary Kate awoke to find her back spooned against Addison's chest. As with yesterday morning, a protective arm snaked around her midsection, triggering an automatic need to clutch it tightly and draw even closer. If their night at the View Hotel had raised questions, they had been answered repeatedly last night. Addison had touched and tasted her until she nearly cried. She had no idea that her body was capable of the things drawn from her—five powerful climaxes in two days. Even the meager response she had felt with Bobby—which mimicked the simple release she achieved when she touched herself—was something she had managed only two or three times in a whole year of sporadic sexual relations, and added together, they didn't equal the excitement she felt just from kissing Addison.

It had never been intimacy with Bobby, she realized. There were barriers to her body that she hadn't known existed until Addison broke them down. Addison had shown patience, coaxing her again to relax and to listen to what her body wanted. And what her body wanted from Addison was to be consumed.

She shuddered at the thought that entered her head as they had blown out the candle and given in to exhaustion. This is what she wanted to feel when she finally fell in love.

That idea had her soaring and sinking before she finally drifted off to sleep. It wasn't necessary to set emotional boundaries, because their return on Saturday was a boundary unto itself. What they had here in Africa would have to end at the Kilimanjaro airport. Addison would go on to her exciting lesbian life in London, and she would go back to Mooresville to end things with Bobby and remake her life into something simple, something that would let her find a man who could make her feel this way.

She wasn't free to pursue this kind of love, even if by some miracle Addison felt the same way. Her stomach knotted to imagine the uproar such a decision would cause, not only between her and her family, but for all of them as they dealt with the fallout from others in their small town. She couldn't put them through something like that. There was nothing Addison had shown her that she couldn't have with someone else, now that she knew how it felt.

A pair of soft lips on her shoulder announced that Addison was awake. Turning to greet smiling eyes, she shook off her complicated thoughts. "Good morning."

Addison answered with a kiss to the top of her head. "I like this," she said. "Waking up with you."

Mary Kate snuggled closer, remembering their last morning at Millennium Hut. Lying together nude was warm and sensuous, but that didn't make it natural for her, no matter how good it felt. Life was unfair like that, attaching kinks to everything so that nothing was perfect.

As they lay quietly, Addison stroked her skin in an intimate way that wasn't overtly sexual. From time to time, she would pause to kiss a particular spot or study it as though committing it to memory. Had it been anyone else, Mary Kate might have felt self-conscious under such scrutiny. But in their time together, on the mountain and here in bed, Addison had given her nothing but comforting reassurance, never once asking her to be someone she wasn't. All she had asked was that Mary Kate surrender, not

179

to her, but to herself.

She had done so willingly, and had found a side of herself she hadn't known existed, though she was left now with more questions than answers. What would it be like to go back home and have this secret between them? Would their friendship always include a sexual pull, even if they never gave in to it again? She knew already that she wouldn't feel drawn to Bobby that way once they parted, but this intimacy with Addison was deeper.

At seven sharp, Addison's watch chimed and they pulled themselves reluctantly from bed. "This reminds me of those people who need a vacation to get over their vacation," Addison said.

"Because we've spent ours climbing a mountain?"

"No, because sleeping with you leaves me knackered."

"Knackered. I've heard Brits use that. It means tired, right?"

"It's kind of a raunchy slang for being tired after sex. Very fitting."

All through breakfast, Mary Kate played the word over and over in her head. They had confessed to caring for each other, but Addison probably saw it the same way she did—an exciting sexual interlude, one they could enjoy without guilt or expectations.

"You're quiet," Addison said as they climbed into their vehicle.

"I'm knackered too," she said, nervously checking John for any sign of understanding.

From the lodge, they took a long, steep road down into the crater. John was adept at game spotting, and knew the English words for most of the wildlife. Driving away from herds of wildebeests, zebras and Thompson's gazelles, he located a pair of rhinos grazing in the tall grass. Mary Kate got her best view standing atop the vehicle, and with Addison's camera, captured the wonder of seeing the animals in their natural habitat.

When they stopped by a lake to eat the box lunch provided by the lodge, John advised them in his best broken English not to exit the vehicle, because dangerous lions roamed the area at will. However, others were picnicking in the grass by the lake, so they bravely followed suit. Their only encounter with wildlife left them both laughing, as Addison lost her sandwich to a swooping bird while she was taking a photo.

Before they left the crater, John stopped and set the roof panels back into place for the sixty-kilometer drive to the Serengeti. Mary Kate relaxed against the armrest, the gentle jostling almost lulling her to sleep.

"We got some great photos. What will the folks back in Georgia say when they see how close you got to a rhinoceros?"

Mary Kate chuckled. "Who knows if they'll even care? At least my Aunt Jean will get a kick out of it. She always wanted to come to Africa, and she slipped me some money under the table to pay for this part."

"She must be a special lady."

"She's the best. I've always thought I was her favorite, but I actually think all my cousins feel the same way." Mary Kate chuckled as she thought of her aunt. "She's my father's oldest sister, and she helped raise all of her siblings after their mom died. She was like the grandmother we never had."

"That's sweet. I didn't know my grandparents at all. I was always jealous of my friends who had them."

"I was too, but Aunt Jean made up for it. She made a quilt for each of her nieces and nephews to give to them as a wedding present. My sister's the youngest—she's twenty—and she plans to marry the first guy who asks. I got my quilt when I was twenty-two because Aunt Jean said it looked like I wasn't going to get married."

"She gave up on you at twenty-two?" Addison laughed. "On the other hand, you haven't exactly proven her wrong."

"No, I guess I haven't. And I've enjoyed my quilt for two winters already."

"Do you think you'll ever really consider leaving Mooresville? I know we talked about it a little bit on the mountain, and there are things about being there that get under your skin. But could you give up being close to your family?"

When Mary Kate thought about her cousins and Aunt Jean,

it made her realize how much her extended family had meant to her growing up. But at some point, they had taken different paths, and hers was the only one that had led to college. "I think I could, but to be honest, I can't imagine being too far away. Maybe I'll feel different about it after I break up with Bobby."

With a jolt, it suddenly occurred to her that, technically, they were still a couple, and she had been unfaithful. Addison seemed to read her thoughts.

"You've already broken up with Bobby. You just haven't told him yet."

She nodded, uneasy about whether she would have seen it that way had the shoe been on the other foot. "I guess I'll have the whole year to sort things out about work. Who knows what can happen in that much time?"

"Maybe you'll meet someone who makes you want to move away to London," Addison said, batting her eyelashes.

She wasn't serious. Impossible. "I think my family would have me committed before they'd let me move to London." Her stomach fluttered at the thought. Would she do such a thing? No, not even to Miami. That took nerve she didn't have. She had pushed all reasonable limits just to come to Africa on her own, and that didn't even count the fallout over Bobby.

"But if you moved out of Mooresville—no matter where you went—you'd at least have your own life."

"I'll never have a life without my family, no matter where I live."

"That's not what I meant. I'm talking about having a life outside of the one they have planned for you."

"Breaking up with Bobby's going to burst that bubble. I don't have to leave for that."

"But say you did." She shifted in the seat so they were facing each other. "Where would you go if you left tomorrow?"

She shrugged, and before she could think how to respond, Addison changed her question.

"What's important to you now? What kind of life do you want to live?"

A storm of emotion washed over her, too much to comprehend. She shook her head and looked away.

"Have you been listening to yourself at all these last few days, Mary Kate?" Addison touched her chin and forced her to make eye contact. "Not just to your words, but to everything. I think the answers are there if you'll just pay attention to them."

Where? In her body's response to Addison's touch? "I hate to break it to you, but that part of me isn't the most important thing in my life," she said, sounding more irritated than she had intended.

Addison recoiled, blowing out a breath and turning to look out the window. After an extended silence, she finally spoke, her mood deflated. "I'm sorry. I obviously need to butt out."

"Maasai," John shouted, pointing to a group that had gathered along the side of the road. They were boys, all clad in black and turquoise, with painted white faces.

Mary Kate reached for Addison's camera.

John rolled down his window and talked to the boys in Swahili. "One dollar," he said after striking a bargain.

Addison produced a couple of bills. One of the youths peeked inside the vehicle and resumed negotiations, raising the ante.

"Water too," John added, indicating their bottle on the backseat.

They made the trade and got pictures, then continued the trip in awkward silence. Mary Kate wanted to cry with frustration. Addison hadn't said or done anything wrong, certainly not enough to warrant being snapped at. The curt response had come from a morass of conflicting emotion, of wishing these last few days could be more than just a sexual romp, but knowing there was no room for the kind of romantic attraction she felt. It was easier just to deny the feelings than to face not being able to act on them. "You didn't say anything wrong, Addison. I've got a lot going on in my head."

"I know, and I promised you I'd listen if you wanted to talk about it. I also promised myself I wouldn't add to the chorus of people telling you what to do."

"I know you don't mean it the way they do. I'm just edgy about making a move because everyone in Mooresville is going to have an opinion about it."

"You mean about you and Bobby?"

"About Bobby. About my job." She sighed. "Everything. I'm sorry if I sounded bitchy."

"It's okay." She jerked her head in the direction of John. "This isn't exactly the best place to be talking about this anyway."

To signal the end of the episode, they began pointing out interesting sights along the roadside. The Serengeti terrain was different from what they had seen at the lake and at the crater, more desert-like with occasional stands of trees and boulders that lent shade to a variety of species. Plants were brown and yellow. Even the green leaves held a thick coat of grayish dust.

It was here they got their best look at a lion, lazily stretched alongside the roadway, seemingly oblivious to their presence. From the top of the Land Cruiser, they were close enough to count the whiskers on his face. For almost a half hour, they watched quietly as he regally ignored them.

"I hope we see a cheetah," Mary Kate said, slumping into her seat as they moved on to the next stand of trees. It was tiresome to balance for a long period of time while standing on the seat.

"And a leopard. Those are rarely spotted in the wild."

"I thought they were always spotted." Her play on words earned her a gentle kick.

Near sunset, they pulled into the Seronera Wildlife Lodge, where they were scheduled to stay for the next two nights. The lodge incorporated the indigenous rock into its architecture, and was home to thousands of gerbil-like rodents that huddled along the walkways and windowsills.

Mary Kate shuddered uncontrollably. "Heebie-jeebies," she said, imagining they were walking among rats.

"Try not to think about it."

Their room was similar to the one at the crater lodge, twin beds on either side of a nightstand. After their conversation in the car, Mary Kate wasn't sure what the night would bring. Addison didn't seem to know either, and she dropped her bag on the floor by the door instead of choosing a bed.

"Tom's reviews said the food here was the best of all the lodges."

The centerpiece of the buffet dinner at the Seronera Lodge was barbecued pork ribs, made even more interesting by the suggestion from a tablemate from Australia that the meat was likely from a wild warthog rather than a farm-raised pig. Whatever the source, they ate their fill and headed back to their room to shower before the hot water was turned off at eight thirty. The desert ride had left them dusty, and the sun had sapped their energy.

"Your nose is sunburned," Addison said as Mary Kate exited the bathroom, wrapped in a towel.

"I'm not surprised. I should probably wear a hat tomorrow."

"I have sunscreen if you want it."

Mary Kate hated their stilted conversation. It was clear that Addison was being careful not to stir up another hornet's nest with personal talk. "I never thought you were telling me what to do, Addison." She sighed and sank onto the bed. "You make me think about things I'd rather run from."

Addison took a seat directly across from her so they could talk. "Look, I'm sorry about what I said. I wasn't trying to suggest that sex was the answer to everything. I guess I just wanted you to realize that you didn't have to be stuck with that life anymore." She ran her hands through her hair anxiously. "And I wanted you to ask yourself if you needed what we have together. Because I do."

"Addison…"

"I'm not saying either one of us is ready to make a big leap, but I'd be lying if I said I hadn't thought about how we might be able to make this work."

Mary Kate would be lying also to say she hadn't entertained such a fantasy. But that had been back when they were on the mountain, when she had dismissed it as one-sided, thinking Addison could never find someone like her interesting enough to be more than a friend. Since then, she had held her fantasies in check believing they had no place to go. "What could you possibly see in someone like me?"

Addison leaned forward, resting her elbows on her knees. "I see such a lovely person, like a pearl no one else has found. I hear you talk about the people back in Mooresville, and I can't believe anyone would try to shape you into someone else, or that they wouldn't be lined up to be with you."

Mary Kate stared at her in disbelief. No one, not even Bobby, had ever said such beautiful things.

"So at the risk of telling you what to do, I really want you to start thinking about where we're going to go from here. If you feel anything at all about me like I feel about you, and I don't mean just sexually. I mean if you're falling in love with me, then what's happening between us is worth keeping. We'll find a way to be together."

Falling in love. So it wasn't one-sided after all. Mary Kate held out her arms. "Come here." If they were really falling in love, that changed everything. She dropped back onto the bed underneath Addison's weight. In moments, their towels lay on the floor and they were off to the races again.

When they finally blew out the candle, Mary Kate allowed herself to imagine a different scenario, one that had her jetting off every few months to visit Addison in London. The very idea of that almost freaked her out, but if this was love, then everything was on the table. She would worry later about what to tell people—if she told them anything at all.

Chapter Twenty-Four

Addison closed her eyes to get a moment's break from the cloud of dust and the blinding sun. She had already decided she would sleep for the entire trip home, and for days after, if necessary, but she wasn't giving up even a minute of her time with Mary Kate. Last night had been another incredible exchange of touching, soaring and cresting. Mary Kate had abandoned most of her inhibitions, even taking the lead at one point as she rolled them toward the candle to watch her own hand at work.

Today, they were sated. They were also exhausted, reminiscent of the mornings after their sleepless nights on Kili.

Click!

Click!

Click!

"You're cruel," she winced as Mary Kate played shutterbug. "I look like death warmed over."

"Not true. You look much better than you did this time last week."

"Okay, let's see. What day is it?"

"Wednesday."

"Wednesday was Shira Two. That was the day after your flying

187

bath exhibition." She laughed as she remembered the image.

"You could at least have the decency to cover your mouth again if you're going to laugh."

"Sorry, I can't help it."

"Cheetah!" John yelled excitedly, veering off the road toward a lone bush in the midst of a speckled plain.

Addison and Mary Kate strained to see what their guide had found so easily, but couldn't make it out until they were nearly on top of the beautiful creature. The spotted coat blended perfectly into the shaded landscape as the lazy cat posed for the curious onlookers.

Addison got a dozen spectacular pictures before several other safari vehicles joined them. John reversed their vehicle, drifting back to the roadway. Signs all over the park warned them not to stray from the marked trails.

"So what's been your favorite sight so far?" Mary Kate asked.

She lofted her eyebrows suggestively. "You mean my second-favorite sight?"

Mary Kate no longer blushed. "Okay, your second."

"I think I liked the baby giraffes best. What about you?"

"I liked seeing all the elephant families, and how they crowded around the little ones to protect them when we came by. I can't believe poachers kill such beautiful animals for profit."

"And then there are the ones who kill for sport. There were some guys on my plane from London who had prepaid as much as thirty thousand dollars for a lion or a cheetah."

"I thought the cheetahs were endangered."

"They are, but in some places that just means there are limits on the number you can kill, so they're higher priced."

"That's just plain sick. I have a hard time swallowing the fact that half the men in Hurston County live for deer season, but at least they eat what they kill."

John suddenly veered off the road again, coming to rest in a heavily wooded area beneath a broad shade tree. "Leopard."

Addison scrambled for her camera, focusing just as the beast sauntered lazily into the woods, his long graceful tail disappearing from view. "Great. Remind me when I download that one that it's a leopard's butt."

"You should get a picture of that," Mary Kate gestured up into the tree, where a half-eaten Thompson's gazelle was wedged snugly into a forked branch. "Leopard lunch."

"Ewww!" Nevertheless, she got a photo.

As quickly as they had veered off, John ventured back onto the roadway, stopping to compare notes with another safari driver. He was clearly proud that his clients had what most safari outfits considered a clean sweep—a rhino, a cheetah and a leopard. The other animals were plentiful and not nearly as elusive.

They got a break from the standard box meal, returning to the Seronera Lodge for the lunch buffet.

"Where do you eat lunch, John?" Mary Kate asked. She made an eating motion.

He gestured to a banana and bottle of water on the front seat, and pointed to a shady parking lot off to the side.

"It isn't fair how these drivers are treated," she groused as they walked into the restaurant. "I wonder if Tom Muncie knows that John slept in his car the other night when the temperature went down to freezing, or that he eats bananas while his customers are leaving food on their plates."

"So let's buy him lunch," Addison said.

"I bet they won't even let him in here."

"We'll get it in a box and take it out to him."

John was the envy of his friends, dining on roast beef and fresh bread, enjoying an ice-cold Coke. "Rhino, cheetah and leopard," he said with a smile, assuming this was his reward for doing a good job.

"How do you feel about leaving Miami?" Mary Kate asked as they sat down to lunch.

Addison grew wistful at the thought of the sign in her front yard. "It's funny. I've always liked it there because of my friends. But when my parents split up, it honestly didn't feel as much like home anymore."

189

"I think I'd feel the same way if my folks ever left Mooresville."

"My best friends are probably leaving too, the ones who were supposed to come with me on this trip. They want to raise their family in Puerto Rico. I can't blame them."

"You don't sound all that attached for someone who's lived there all her life."

She shrugged. "I'm adaptable. Roots are more about people than places, but I guess I'll go back for visits."

"So let's suppose we met someday in Miami—I'm not saying we will, but if we did—what would we do?"

"Everything. We'd go to the Everglades, to the Keys. We'd hit South Beach and Little Havana. We'd snorkel, sail. Something different every day."

"Sounds wonderful."

"And what would we do if I came to Mooresville?"

"Nothing that exciting, that's for sure." Still, her face lit up as she talked. "First, I'd drag you over to meet my Aunt Jean. She'd get a kick out of you, especially if you were telling her stories about me busting my ass in the water. She'd love that."

Addison laughed. "I'd enjoy that too."

"And then I'd show you all of the sights, like my grandpa's barn where we used to play when we were kids, and my school." She stole a piece of mango from Addison's plate. "We'd drive up to Lake Hampton and make out."

"Is that where you went with all your boyfriends?"

"Just one." She visibly shuddered. "For a second there, I went back. It was horrible."

"When do you start back to school?"

"Third week in August."

Addison did a few mental calculations. "Maybe I can come for a few days before then, before I go to London."

"That soon?" By the look on her face, she was alarmed.

Addison backpedaled. "Or some other time, or maybe we just meet somewhere like Jacksonville."

"Sorry, I was just trying to think what else I have to do before school starts. Most of all I need to settle things with Bobby."

The specter of Bobby reared its ugly head again, as it had done nearly every time Mary Kate started thinking about going home. Addison couldn't imagine feeling so oppressed, not even under her father's schemes.

What twisted her stomach was Mary Kate's subtle reluctance to make firm plans, as if she feared she would change her mind once she got home. Only last night, they had confessed to one another they were falling in love, and today Mary Kate was doling out hospitality as if it were in short supply. Something was bothering her. Perhaps it was only the anxiety of the breakup. Maybe she needed to get that behind her before she could let herself think about a new life.

Addison's rational side told her to give Mary Kate the time to work this out on her own. It was wrong to push her, even if giving her too much space meant this new love they felt would fizzle. If it truly was real, it would persevere. If not, she would have to accept that she was only a player in Mary Kate's self-discovery. A bittersweet memory for both of them.

The lodge staged a show in the bar after dinner, much like the one they had seen their first night, with costumed African dancers moving gracefully to a drumbeat. Addison was so distracted by her thoughts that she was suddenly compelled to leave.

"I'm going back to the room. Enjoy the show."

She was lighting the candle in anticipation of lights out when Mary Kate came through the door. "What's wrong?"

She shook her head, unable to articulate her concerns. "It just doesn't feel right, Mary Kate. I don't think we're being honest with each other about what this means."

"I'm being as honest as I can. What do you want?"

Addison sighed. "We should be talking about what we're going to do about our feelings. But when I said that about coming to see you, you acted like—"

"I know where you're going with this. I can explain…probably not very well, but I swear to you I'm being honest."

"That's all I ask."

"I freaked out. I tried to imagine how I was going to explain to my family who you were, and why you were coming to visit so soon when we'd just spent two weeks together."

"Do they know every little thing you do?"

Mary Kate threw up her arms in frustration. "You don't understand. We talk to each other practically every day."

So the issue wasn't Bobby, but paranoia about what to tell her family. "I don't want to sneak around, Mary Kate. I already had one girlfriend who kept me shoved in her closet, and I don't deal with it very well."

"Well, I've never had a girlfriend at all, so pardon me if it takes a few minutes to get used to the idea."

Addison slumped on the bed, feeling ridiculous. "You're right. I'm just hauling around old baggage."

Mary Kate knelt in front of her and grasped her hands. "I don't want things to end here, Addison. We've started something that feels better than anything that's ever happened to me, and I want to see where it goes. But I have to figure out how to make all the pieces fit. And it doesn't help matters that you're getting ready to move to London."

"I know, but we have to find a way to do this." How ironic that her father was as much a problem as Mary Kate's family. "I've never felt like this before, Mary Kate. I always knew the other women I was with were temporary, but I feel like you and I really have something. I don't want to screw anything up by—"

Mary Kate cut her off with a searing kiss, and Addison suddenly found herself being driven backward onto the bed. She abandoned trying to understand what was happening in favor of helping it happen. In only seconds, both of them were nude with Mary Kate still on top, kissing her ravenously. A hand slid through her wetness and she gasped, aching for the touch.

Mary Kate's mouth followed her hand, and before Addison knew what was happening, a warm tongue stroked the length of her center. For her first time, Mary Kate seemed to know exactly what she was doing.

Addison moaned her encouragement, and writhed in utter

bliss when Mary Kate found a rhythm with her tongue that matched the pumping of her two fingers inside. She held out as long as she could to enjoy the sensations, but finally spilled over when Mary Kate added clitoris sucking to her sexual repertoire.

"Oh, my God…oh, my God." She held out an arm as Mary Kate scooted up to lie beside her. "You've killed me."

Mary Kate chuckled. "I understand you now."

"What do you mean?"

"It's about the things I want to do to you that define who I am, not the things you do to me." She snuggled closer and let out a contented sigh. "But those things matter too."

Chapter Twenty-Five

Mary Kate relaxed in the backseat as John took a circuitous route from the park, apparently hoping to spot something of interest on their last day of safari. They were headed to Tanganiere, a game preserve in the rainforest that was dominated by a few hundred elephants. The safari had been everything she hoped. Now that they had seen the rarest of species, anything else would be a bonus.

That bonus came in the form of another cheetah, sunning herself on a boulder. John parked within thirty yards of the magnificent spectacle, and Mary Kate used Addison's zoom lens to snap one picture after another.

Addison watched through binoculars, and was the first to spot the two cubs tumbling in the bush nearby. If they saw nothing else today, this made the whole day worth it.

Mary Kate traded that camera for her own and clicked off several photos of Addison as she watched the family at play. Her growing feelings were undeniable, as was the fact that she could never feel sexual excitement for any man the way she did for Addison. Learning that about herself had been worth it, no matter what happened to them next.

No matter what happened…

The anxiety about what to do with this discovery once she returned to Mooresville roiled her stomach. If there was one thing she wanted less than a life with Bobby, it was a life like Deb's. Even if she could learn to handle the gossip and constant fear of harassment, she couldn't stand the thought of inflicting that on her family. And while her mother would almost certainly stand up for her, she would always feel like a disappointment.

Then there was the matter of her job, which she would probably lose. And she would never be able to show her face at—

"I don't think I've ever seen anything sweeter than that," Addison said, lowering herself back into the vehicle.

John drove well away from the mother cat before stopping to close the hatch. Then for the next two hours they drove through the savanna, which was home to herds of zebras, impalas and Thomson's gazelles.

Addison scrolled through the photos on her digital camera. "Remember that first day when we were so disappointed because the zebras ran into the bush before we could get a picture?"

Mary Kate chuckled. "How many have we seen since then? Five thousand?"

"Easily."

John stopped for lunch at a roadside tourist stand, where a throng of women pressed against their car offering handmade beaded and leather bracelets. She and Addison bought several at a few dollars each, spreading their business to everyone in the group.

"So tell me how we're going to do this, you with the big ideas," Mary Kate said as they sat down at a table in the corner.

"How we're going to do what?"

"How we're going to take all of this back home and make it work."

Addison smiled. "For starters, I think you should come to Miami for a week or two before my house sells. Can you do that?"

"My folks will go nuts if I leave town again." That was an indisputable fact of life, as was her paltry bank account.

"Do you have a better idea?"

She sighed dejectedly. "No. They're going to be nuts anyway after I dump Bobby, so it probably won't make any difference. How long do you think it would take me to hitchhike?"

"I have a shitload of frequent flyer miles. I'll send you a ticket."

"Those are yours."

"To spend however I like. If you want me to come to Mooresville instead, I'll do it."

"You'll be bored out of your mind."

"I'm coming to see you, not the barn. In fact, I won't care if we don't even leave your apartment."

Mary Kate was already thinking ahead about the hoops she and Bobby had jumped through to keep everyone out of their business. For one thing, there was Mrs. Winkler, who had the apartment right underneath. She went to their church and knew practically everyone in town. Then there was Donna Rogers, who taught third grade at her school. Their front doors were caddy-corner, so Donna could watch everyone who came and went. "Maybe we should go camping."

Addison looked at her as if she had grown a second head. "I do not plan on camping again in this decade, thank you very much." She reached over and squeezed her wrist. "I know you dread this, Mary Kate." She held up a hand. "Not that I blame you. I'm sure it's hard. But if this is who you are, you're going to have to own up to it eventually."

"Or hide it."

Addison shook her head. "I can't handle the hiding part again."

Though she understood Addison's frustration about secrecy, she didn't think it was unreasonable to want a little time to ease into things. "This isn't going to be the first thing out of my mouth when I get home. It has to be the right time."

"I know, I know." Her face softened. "Let's make a deal, okay?

This is our last day here, and I don't want us to spend it getting worked up about this. I'll promise not to push for too much too soon, and you promise not to freak out."

Mary Kate was grateful for the reprieve. Harping on this all day was almost as bad as Bobby telling her to think about him while she was gone. It just wasn't how she wanted to spend her time. "I think having fun today is a great idea."

The afternoon tour took them through jungle-like terrain, where they saw families of elephants at every turn. John pointed out a lion in the distance which neither of them could see, even with binoculars.

Mary Kate was glad to arrive at Sopa, their final lodge, and by far the most luxurious. The rooms were large, with two double beds encased in mosquito netting, a sofa, and the most modern bathroom they had seen.

Addison dropped her bag beside the couch. "Why don't we go for an early dinner? Then we can come back and relax. We have to be ready for John at six thirty."

Despite the vow to make their last day fun, a cloud seemed to hang over their table as they ate in near silence.

"Do you think you'll ever come back to Africa?" Addison asked as they walked back to their room.

"It's funny you ask. I was thinking this afternoon about how I imagined this would be the trip of a lifetime for me. Now I feel like it's just the beginning."

"What else is on your list?"

"Lots of things. Maybe London."

Addison grinned. "I would love to show you London."

"It'll take me at least a year to save up the money."

"Unless you take me up on my offer of frequent flyer miles. Then you could come at Christmas."

That actually sounded workable.

"And if you get this hiking bug again, there's always Machu Picchu. We could tie that in to going down to visit my mom."

Mary Kate chuckled at the invitation. "We can't even agree on when to visit each other at home, and now you have me meeting your mother."

Addison slid the key in their door. "I'm just throwing out ideas, hoping you'll bite on something."

"Lock the door, and I'll give you something else to bite on."

They quickly undressed and climbed into one of the beds, sealing the net behind them.

Mary Kate assumed the position that had grown so familiar in only a few days, on her back with Addison's leg draped between hers. Solemn brown eyes seemed to pin her in place.

A warm hand began a gentle caress of her skin from thigh to breast and back again. "I want to memorize you."

She closed her eyes and gave up her body to a near-torturous exploration that finally culminated in an intimate touch. Though wet and ready, she had learned to temper her need to make it last.

"You need this, Mary Kate," Addison whispered as she stroked her deep inside. "It's who you are."

She lay awake long after they made love, studying Addison as she slept. Nothing in her whole life had felt as good to her as the love they shared. Now their time was slipping away. No matter how much either of them wanted it, a life together with Addison in London and her in Georgia seemed impossible, even if she somehow found the courage to try.

Chapter Twenty-Six

Addison sighed as she watched the passengers from Johannesburg make their way down the staircase and through the door marked Arrivals. Who would have guessed that flights into such an out of the way place would be on time? That meant Mary Kate would be leaving right on schedule, in less than an hour.

It was probably just as well. She had run out of things to say once they reached a point where everything made Mary Kate cry. Both of them had slept poorly after the tacit suggestion that the Sopa Lodge might be their last night as lovers. As she lay awake, she played out their parting in her mind's eye, vowing to remain upbeat and hopeful, regardless of her sense of dread. As much as she hated to admit it, she understood Mary Kate's doubts about trying to turn this chance meeting into a relationship. It was a lot to ask of someone who had discovered only days ago that she wasn't the woman she had lived her whole life to be.

"I wonder how long it'll be before we board," Mary Kate said, grasping Addison's hand beneath the jacket that spread across their laps.

"Are you ready?"

She shook her head. "No, I could sit here like this all day."

Addison knew she didn't mean it, but she appreciated the sentiment. Once they parted, the pressure about their future would be off. "What? You aren't looking forward to spending the next twenty hours in a space smaller than a sleeping bag?"

Mary Kate chuckled. "As long as we don't bounce around, I'll survive."

"You'll be home this time tomorrow."

"I know. I bet I sleep for three days."

For conversation's sake, she thought about asking if Bobby was picking her up at the airport, but Bobby was the last thing she wanted to hear about. "I'll probably sleep all the way home."

"I would too if I were flying first class like you."

"Yeah, having Reginald Falk for a father comes with a few advantages. But I won't get back to Miami until late tomorrow afternoon." The way her life was going right this minute, she expected to find a Sold sign in the yard and a pile of rejection letters on the floor behind the mail slot.

Her stomach knotted as the operations crew gathered at the podium. It appeared their boarding announcement was only minutes away.

She touched her booted foot to Mary Kate's as they both stared at the floor. "I miss you already."

"You're going to make me cry again."

"We certainly don't need any more of that."

Obviously fighting tears, Mary Kate leaned close so that only Addison could hear. "I want you to know that I love you, and that this has been the most wonderful two weeks of my life. If I can find a way to do this, Addison, I will. But if I can't..."

Addison felt her own tears welling and remembered her vow to leave things upbeat. "Don't think about your family or Bobby or me. Just decide what's best for you and be proud of yourself for taking charge. That's the whole reason you came on this trip."

Mary Kate wiped her cheeks and nodded grimly.

Addison shuddered as the boarding announcement came. "You have my phone number, right?" It was the third time she had asked.

"Yes."

The line had shortened to only a few people, prompting the hostess to make a second call.

"You have to go."

Mary Kate pulled her to her feet and they hugged each other tightly. "I miss you already too."

Addison drew in a deep breath to stifle her tears. "I love you. Don't forget."

Mary Kate planted a quick kiss on her lips and whispered, "I love you too." She looked over her shoulder and waved twice before exiting, and once more when she reached the top of the stairs.

Addison slumped back in her chair and watched as the door closed, the stairs were hauled away, and the plane rolled away from the window toward the end of the runway. Like Mary Kate, she was saying goodbye to the best two weeks she had ever spent. If she managed not to cry any more today, it would be a miracle.

"Addison!"

She turned to see Ann and Nikki coming through the security station. Nikki darted off to the restroom, while Ann came to take the seat Mary Kate had just vacated.

"You ready to go home?"

"Hardly," Addison said. "I don't even know where home is anymore."

"Oh, that's right. You're moving to London."

"Looks that way." With thoughts of working for her father, her day just kept getting worse. "Off to be Reginald's lackey."

"Where's Mary Kate?"

"You just missed her." Though a part of her wanted to wallow in her misery, another part welcomed a distraction from the empty feeling of watching Mary Kate leave.

"Did you two have a good time?"

"Yeah, we did. How about you?"

"Mostly okay. Nikki got food poisoning on the second night, so she missed a day on safari. But we saw a lot."

"Food poisoning," she said, shaking her head. "You know, considering the odds, it's kind of amazing more of us didn't get sick."

"Yeah, but who knows what parasites we're carrying home? Three weeks from now we could all be hospitalized."

"Oh, that reminds me. It's Larium day." Addison reached into her backpack for her pills and bottle of water. "I hope Mary Kate remembers hers."

"When will you two get to see each other again?"

Addison was surprised by the question, since she thought they had been relatively discreet. Maybe someone had seen her coming from Mary Kate's room after all. "We talked about a visit, but nothing for sure."

"I got the idea it was working out pretty well," she said, patting Addison's hand.

Addison momentarily debated deflecting the remark, but her curiosity got the best of her. "How did you know?"

"Are you kidding? The sparks were flying off both of you that first day at breakfast."

"No way."

"Way," she said, nodding emphatically.

"Jeez!" She covered her face with her hands. "Did everybody know?"

"I don't think Brad did, but Nikki told him."

"So much for privacy."

"Look, you can't spend eight days as close as we all were and not notice things like that. You two were always hanging back or running off together. That's what people do when they fall in love."

Addison could feel her face growing red.

"My oldest son was the same way with his"—she made quote marks in the air—"best friend. I knew they were in love with each other before they did."

"Your son is gay?"

"Yep."

Nikki joined them, but buried her nose in a paperback.

"I don't know what's going to happen, Ann. This is all new for Mary Kate, and her family might not be able to handle it. It isn't exactly what they had planned."

"Pffft. Hardly anybody gets what they plan. Besides, it's not their life."

"I know. I told her all those things, but she's worried about disappointing them."

"Jumping out of the nest is hard enough without having your parents hold on to you. But you'll both have to do it eventually if you're going to be your own person." She pulled off her vest and dropped it on her seat. "Watch my stuff. I have to find a bush."

Addison chuckled at her reference to the trail. She wished Ann had gotten here sooner so Mary Kate could have heard her talk about loving her gay son. And that leaving the nest part, if Mary Kate wanted to be her own person...

"...*you'll both have to do it.*" That's what Ann had said, that it wasn't just Mary Kate. She too had to jump out of her father's nest to be her own person.

Another plane came to rest on the tarmac where Mary Kate's had been. This one was Kenya Airways, Addison's flight to Nairobi. It was going to be a long, miserable trip, and there was nothing to look forward to at home.

Chapter Twenty-Seven

Mary Kate closed her window shade to block the morning sun from her personal entertainment screen. She had been tracking their progress on the plane's global positioning system for the past four hours as they approached the east coast of Georgia. She was cramped and cranky, and anxious about what the next few days would bring. One thing was certain, and that was that she couldn't go back to the way things were. She had reached a decision—probably the most important one in her life—and would set it in motion the moment she stepped off the plane.

Her flight out of Kilimanjaro Airport had been the exclamation point on her trip. When they cleared the cloud cover, the majestic summit came into view once again, riveting her thoughts to the enormity of what she had accomplished. Just as when she first saw the peak below their plane, Mary Kate was awed. But this time, she was not intimidated. This time, she owned that mountain, and had proven to herself that no goal, no matter how difficult, was beyond her reach. She didn't have to blindly follow Bobby's dreams, or those of her family. She had stood up to them, and could do it again with confidence.

Ironically, she had given the trek to Uhuru barely a thought since exiting the park at Millennium Gate. It was peculiar that something which had been essential to her sense of self for the past six months had moved so quickly from her consciousness. In her two weeks in Africa, she had conquered the summit, yet it was not what she would remember most about her trip. That distinction belonged to Addison Falk.

She ached to think her first real glimpse of love was over, that the one thing she really wanted was something she couldn't have. In the first place, women from Mooresville, Georgia, didn't just up and run off to London, or anywhere else. Her newfound confidence was about asserting herself to be her own woman among her family and friends, not to be someone else entirely.

In the second place—the most important place—Addison would never be accepted by her family as the person she loved and wanted to build a life with. After the initial disappointment and shame, there would be an agreement by all to pretend things weren't really as they were. Mary Kate would go to Sunday dinner less often, and always alone. Every visit would be a painful reminder that going against the grain in pursuit of her personal happiness had consequences.

Making a life with Addison was impossible without her family's support. To do so, she needed a single-minded determination that being together was worth the cost. If she was wrong—if she and Addison were to fall apart down the road—she would never fully recover the trust of her family, or the respect of the community.

Addison loved her, and she would always cherish that. She, too, loved Addison, but there was nowhere for that love to go.

Addison had awakened her body, and had taught her things about herself that Bobby would never have known. More important, she had stirred the kind of passion that had always been missing in her life, where fascination and desire came together to yield perfect physical expression. Now that she understood her sexuality, she wanted control of it, and would teach Bobby to give her those sensations.

Bobby had other virtues, even if they were tied to a predictable life that felt suffocating at times. He would be principal when

Warner Hughes retired, a job that would take him to retirement. Her family had welcomed him without reservation. Their life was perfectly scripted—a church wedding, three children. Bobby would be a good provider, a family man. Their children would play with Carol Lee's, and their house would have an in ground pool. Like the generation before them, the women would sit in the kitchen and talk while the men watched football in the other room.

"Ladies and gentlemen, in preparation for landing, please bring seat backs and tray tables to their upright and locked positions. Put away all…"

She tipped her seat forward and closed her video screen as the big plane lumbered through its descent. A loud vibration signaled the drop of the landing gear, and she willed herself a dose of courage for what she knew she had to do.

This was the crossroads of her life, and only one path would lead to happiness. She would marry Bobby, probably during the Christmas break so they could have a honeymoon.

Addison was right that she would feel proud of herself for working it through. She would never have to look back on her life with regrets about not trying something different. She had, and it wasn't right for her. This was. She knew because every time she thought of choosing Addison, her anxiety became almost unbearable. Choosing Bobby quieted that.

Numb from her exhausting physical and emotional journeys, she mindlessly followed her fellow passengers through passport control and into the baggage claim area. Balancing her Summit bag and duffel, she walked through the exit marked Nothing to Declare and turned over her form to the customs agent. As she snaked through the hallway toward the arrivals area, she envisioned Bobby's handsome face lighting up with recognition as she emerged. Would he be able to tell that she had been unfaithful?

"Mary Kate!"

She spun in the direction of his voice and immediately found herself enveloped in his strong arms. The kiss that followed surprised her, and she turned her head at the last second to receive it on the cheek.

"I'm so glad you're home. I missed you so bad, I'm not ever going to let you out of my sight again."

She bristled at the possessive inference before accepting it as his way of showing affection. She had intended to accept his proposal in a grand gesture the instant she got off the plane, but this didn't feel like the time. "I've missed you too."

Bobby picked up both bags. "I got here early and got a parking place right by the elevator so we wouldn't have to walk far." All business now, he proceeded toward the elevator. "Everybody's going to be really glad to see you."

"I'll be glad to see them too." It felt good to stretch her legs, but the long walk through the terminal had sapped her strength. When they finally reached the car, all she wanted was to collapse.

Bobby tossed the bags into the trunk while she got into the passenger seat.

"Was it as hard as you thought it would be?"

"Yeah, some parts were a lot tougher than I expected, but I was ready. There were three people in our group who didn't train enough and they had to turn back." That was her way of telling him he might not have made it. "But it was so incredible to be up on top of it all."

"Well, that's what you went for. Did you see lions and stuff?"

"We saw everything. I bet I saw twenty or thirty lions, just out in the wild. And a cheetah with two—"

"We had a little incident with wild animals too." Bobby chuckled as he remembered the tale. "The State Patrol called out to the school on Wednesday morning and told Warner that his fence was down, and he had three bulls running up and down Wilson Mill Road. So me and him jumped in his truck and drove out there. You should have seen us, Mary Kate, waving our arms to get those bulls to go back into the pasture. It was a sight, I tell you."

Stung by his interruption, she leaned back against the headrest and closed her eyes. It didn't surprise her that, where Bobby was concerned, a mother cheetah and her cubs were nothing compared to bulls running loose on the highway. In fact, he was probably no more interested in her trip now than he was before she left.

He drove through the parking garage, winding down several levels until he got into the long line to pay. "I always manage to pick the line that moves the slowest," he grumbled. They were gridlocked in the middle of the garage.

"So what did Mom and Dad say when you told them I made it to the top?" After sitting upright for so long, it felt good to lie back with her feet stretched out.

"You know, I'm not sure I told them about that part. All anybody cared about was you getting down off that mountain okay." He fumbled in the glove compartment for his cell phone. "You ought to call and tell them your plane got here."

"You didn't even tell them I made it to the top?"

"Why don't you tell them, Mary Kate? They'll like hearing that from you."

Bobby just didn't get it. He was a good guy, but he would never get it.

Now overwhelmed with the horror that she had almost made the biggest mistake of her life, Mary Kate had the sudden urge to jump out of the car. She wanted to leave Bobby right here in the garage and run back inside the airport, get on the next plane to Miami, and be there to meet the woman she loved when she walked out of customs. Daring herself to do something so bold, Mary Kate fidgeted with both her seat belt release and the door handle.

"I can't believe it's taking so long," Bobby said as he eased the car forward.

Mary Kate tuned out his irritation and concentrated on relaxing her grip. "I'm going to close my eyes for a little while. I didn't sleep much on the plane."

"That's all right, Mary Kate. I'll wake you up when we get to

Mooresville. Oh, before I forget, I went ahead and got us a room for a week at the Days Inn in Myrtle Beach starting next Saturday. It's not on the ocean, but we can always drive over every day."

A whole week at the Days Inn in Myrtle Beach. *Be still my heart.*

Mary Kate flung her door open, causing the annoying chime to sound in warning. "Pop the trunk. I have to get something."

Bobby complied and stretched his neck to watch her as she hoisted the green duffel over her shoulder.

"Thanks for coming to get me, but I'm not coming home just yet."

"Mary Kate!"

"Look, I'll be back in a couple of weeks. Go on to Myrtle Beach without me, or take your brother or something. I promise I'll come talk to you as soon as I get home." She couldn't say anymore. No matter what, she wasn't going home with him.

Recklessly, she picked her way between the cars that were stacked up at the toll booth, and crossed a stream of oncoming traffic to re-enter the terminal. The line for Hartsfield's major carrier held hundreds of passengers, which meant there was no hope of getting to the ticket counter before Bobby paid his fare, returned to the parking garage and caught up with her. A quick glance at the board revealed another option, and she hurried along the entryway to an agent at the far end.

"I need to get to Miami," she said, slapping her credit card and passport on the counter.

"How many bags?" he asked, not even making eye contact.

"Just these. I'll carry them." She looked over her shoulder nervously for signs of Bobby.

"I can put you on the two thirty that gets in at four, but if you'll go straight to the gate, they might let you on the one that's leaving in twenty minutes."

"Perfect." She fidgeted while he ran her card. She signed the slip quickly and collected her boarding pass. Through the throng of passengers at the main counter, she caught a glimpse of someone who looked like Bobby, and her stomach tightened.

"Is that the only line to get through security?"

He shook his head and pointed in the opposite direction. "You can go in down there, and there won't be as many people."

"Thanks." Without looking back, she lowered her head and walked briskly to the back of the line. As others came behind her, she jockeyed for a position that would keep her out of view. Finally, she presented her ID and boarding pass, and when she collected her things at the far end of the conveyor, she breathed a sigh of relief. Without a ticket, Bobby couldn't follow her in here.

Chapter Twenty-Eight

"Mary Kate."

She shook herself and blinked.

"Wake up. We're here."

Here was in her parents' driveway, a world away from where her dream had taken her. "What time is it?"

"Almost twelve thirty. You slept the whole way."

She sat up and rolled her neck, shaking off a sinking feeling in her stomach as she got her bearings. "I guess I was beat." She got out of the car and heard the front screen door slam.

"There you are!" Her mother stood beaming on the porch.

The whole family appeared, and Mary Kate walked sheepishly to greet them. She hadn't realized it was Sunday and that Bobby was bringing her here instead of to her apartment. "I made it."

"You sure did." Her mother hugged her as the others watched. "Did you have a good time?"

"Yeah, and I got the pictures to prove it."

"I'll get your camera," Bobby said. He plucked it from the pouch on her backpack. "We can look at these before lunch."

Alarmed to realize that her camera held mostly pictures of Addison, she grabbed it from him. "Not yet. I want to download the good ones and put them in a slideshow so you can see them better."

"Let's eat," her father said.

Carol Lee led the way back inside. "I want to hear about the safari. Wayne said he wanted to go to Africa and do that, shoot him a jaguar or something."

"We didn't shoot anything, Carol Lee. We just took pictures." Never mind that jaguars didn't live in Africa.

Dinner was typical Sunday fare, more food than five adults could ever eat. Mary Kate had no appetite for any of it, but gladly accepted a glass of ice-cold sweet tea. Her eyes kept darting to Bobby, who seemed more interested in eating and talking about Myrtle Beach than in hearing about her trip. It was irritating, and she almost said so.

But her problem wasn't with Bobby. He could have been perfect, and she still would have wished her dream had been real. In that flash of subconscious fantasy, she had glimpsed the only path that would lead her to happiness. Once she let herself believe it could happen, the other barriers fell away. No matter how tough they made it, the right road was worth every step.

"You look like you're about to fall asleep, Mary Kate," her mother said. "Why don't you go on back there to your sister's room and get yourself a nap?"

"To tell you the truth, what I'd really like is a hot bath and my own bed. I've been up all night on the plane." She looked at Bobby with pleading eyes, but he didn't take the hint. "Will you run me over to my house, Bobby?"

Her mother pushed back from the table. "Let him eat his lunch, Mary Kate. I'll take you."

She didn't care how she got there, as long as it happened sooner rather than later. She collected her bags and backpack from Bobby's car and tossed them into the bed of her father's pickup, which was in the back of the driveway.

"I appreciate this, Mom."

"It's all right. I can see you're worn out."

"It'll probably take me a couple of days to get back on Georgia time. It was the same way when I got there."

"I bet you were proud of yourself when you got to the top of that mountain."

"I was. I can't even describe it." The ride to her apartment was too short to share the story of their weary overnight push. "It was one week ago today. I can't believe Bobby didn't tell you I made it all the way up."

"Oh, I knew already. I saw Deb at the grocery last week and she told me. Said you sent her an e-mail."

Mary Kate remembered her note, including her declaration to Deb that she was going to break up with Bobby as soon as she got home. No way would Deb have said anything to her mother.

"Did you do much thinking about you and Bobby while you were over there?"

She gave her mother a sidelong look. "Have you taken up mind reading?"

She laughed. "Is that a yes?"

"I thought about him a lot on the way home. I think I've finally made up my mind what to do."

"Just let him down easy, Mary Kate. No point in bruising his ego."

Startled by the assumption, she couldn't resist pushing the envelope. "What would you think if I transferred over to Oak Hill? Or maybe got a job in Newton County? They always have openings."

"You want to leave your school?"

"I've been thinking about it anyway. I never liked the idea of Bobby being my boss. Breaking up with him just makes it that much worse."

"Yeah, I can see that might be touchy. Lord knows I couldn't have worked for your daddy." She pulled into the apartment complex. "Speaking of your daddy, he came over and started your car the other day just to make sure it was okay."

"Good. Tell him I appreciate that." The conversation was surreal. She had just admitted to her mother that she was dumping the best catch in Hurston County, and they were talking about her car.

Her mother turned off the engine, but neither made a move to exit the truck. "When are you going to tell him?"

"I don't want to talk to him while I'm so tired. No telling what I'll say."

"You ought not wait too long, Mary Kate. He told Carol Lee he thought ya'll would be ring shopping this week."

She shook her head in dismay. Where on earth had he gotten that idea? "I never said anything to make him think that, Mom. He told me at the airport that it was time to decide and for me to think about it while I was gone."

They each plucked a bag from the bed of the truck and started up the steps to her apartment. Mary Kate was looking forward to being alone.

"Men only hear what they want to hear, honey. Didn't you know that?"

Mary Kate didn't know anything about men, and she didn't want to study them anymore. "Do you think I'm making a mistake?"

"That's not for me to say. It's between you and Bobby."

"But you're my mother. You're supposed to know me better than anybody." She put her key in the door and opened it, letting out a rush of stale air.

"I think I do, Mary Kate. You never heard me planning what to wear to your wedding, did you?"

"How did you know?"

Her mother took her firmly by the shoulders as they stood in the doorway. "When a girl's in love, she smiles all the time. I don't think I've seen you smile at Bobby since last fall. It was like the thought of getting married scared you half to death."

"It does." Mary Kate felt a wave of shame for dragging this out so long. "I'm worried I'm going to disappoint you and Daddy."

Her mother said nothing, just wrapped her in a comforting hug.

Exhausted and frustrated, Mary Kate began to cry. "I don't

want to marry him."

"It's all right, honey. Just break up with him and be done with it. You're not going to disappoint us. Maybe you'll be ready to settle down in a year or two, or maybe even five years…whatever. People don't get married right out of high school like they used to."

"What if they don't get married at all, Mom?"

"I don't want you to be lonely, honey. And I don't want you to have regrets. But you're only twenty-four years old. That's a long way from having life pass you by." She hugged her again, and spun her toward the bedroom. "If I were you, I'd skip that bath and go straight to bed. You call me tomorrow if you want to talk some more."

"Thanks, Mom."

"You're welcome." She started out the door and stopped. "You reckon I've been gone long enough for somebody else to clean the kitchen?"

Both of them laughed as she left, and Mary Kate collapsed on the couch. Her emotions had been on a roller coaster for the past twenty-four hours. The stress of wanting to please her family had factored in more than she thought, and now that her mother had shown her a little daylight, she wasn't going to waste it.

The new stress was what to do about Addison. Deb had always said lesbians didn't choose between women and men. They chose between women and nothing. Both of those were better than marrying Bobby.

She needed to sleep, but not as much as she needed to talk to Deb. After two rings, her friend answered. "My body is back in Mooresville, but the rest of me hasn't caught up yet."

"Mary Kate! When did you get back?"

"About two hours ago. I'm so tired I can't think, but I wanted to call you before I went to bed."

"I'm glad you did. I can't wait to hear about your trip. You want to get pizza or something tomorrow night?"

She sighed, thinking of her mother's advice to be done with it. "I think I might try to talk to Bobby tomorrow night."

"So you haven't told him yet?"

"It seemed like a bad idea to tell him on the way home. I didn't want to get dumped out on the side of the road."

"Tuesday night, then. And I'm buying, because we're celebrating."

"I'm about to go to bed, but I wanted to ask you something. My mom said she ran into you the other night."

"Right. She caught me buying beer."

Mary Kate chuckled, thinking back to the time her mother had snuck up on them when they were drinking behind the shed. "You didn't happen to say anything about me and Bobby, did you?"

Silence.

"Deb?"

"Not specifically."

"What does that mean?"

"She brought it up. All I told her was that I got an e-mail, and that you'd made it to the top. Then I told her one of the girls you met was coming to visit. I swear I was just making conversation. Then she asked me out of the blue if I thought you were going to get married and I said I didn't think so. I didn't tell her you told me for sure."

"How did she act?"

Deb hissed through her teeth then drew in a deep breath. "Kind of like she expected it. She wanted to know if you ever talked about Jessica anymore."

"Jessica?"

"Look, it's your own business and you don't have to talk to me, even if I am supposed to be your best friend."

"What's my business?"

"Mary Kate, people aren't stupid. I don't know what was going on over there, okay? All I know is that all you talked about for six months was climbing that mountain, but then you sent me an e-mail that was Addison this and Addison that. That's how you used to be about Jessica. You talked about her all the time. Your mother saw it too, and she must have thought the same thing I did."

Though she was alone in her apartment with the curtains drawn, she was blushing furiously. "There was never anything between Jessica and me," she said tightly. She didn't want to talk about Addison.

Several seconds passed before Deb spoke again. "Your mom called me last Christmas when you wouldn't take Bobby's ring. She asked me point-blank if you were gay, and I said I didn't know."

"My mother asked you that?"

"And then she talked about how you were with Jessica, how you came home all depressed after she got married. I told her that you never said anything to me about feeling that way, but I didn't think you were in love with Bobby. I swear that's all I said."

Her heart felt as if it would pound out of her chest. "Addison and I...we fell in love with each other, Deb, but it's all up in the air." This was unbelievable. "Say something."

"I can't talk. I'm wearing this gigantic shit-eating grin."

She let out a muted scream. "You better not be laughing at me. Addison will kick your ass."

"I thought you wanted me to kick hers."

She shook off a happy image of the two women meeting. "What else did my mother say? How did she feel when you talked about it last Christmas?"

"To be honest with you, she wasn't all that thrilled about it, but she didn't want you to marry Bobby if you weren't sure. And she said something about how you never talked with her about this kind of stuff."

That was consistent with the message her mother had given her before she left, and then again today. "But what if I tell her about Addison?"

"She might not like it at first, but it's obvious she's been thinking about it...trying it on. If you ask me, I think she'd want to know."

Mary Kate doubted seriously that her family would accept

Addison as her lover, at least not anytime soon, but for now, she would settle for them not going ballistic. Maybe it would help if she convinced her mother that Addison made her happy. "I need sleep. My brain isn't working anymore. Wish me luck with Bobby, okay?"

The anxiety left her body like a brush fire, flaring up then dying down to smolder. How could she have been so insane to think marrying Bobby was the right path? Her mother was right. She wasn't at a fork in her life, just with Bobby. Ending things with him bought her time to test other waters.

She blew out a raspberry and rolled her eyes. Fires, forks, waters. How many metaphors did she need to make sense of her life? All she wanted was the chance to see if she and Addison could build on what they started. Even if they had to do it long-distance, it was worth a try.

It was a quarter to three, which meant Addison's plane was still in the air.

She located the scrap of paper she had torn from the pad at the Sopa Lodge and dialed the number, which went to voice mail immediately. "Hey, there. I miss you already, and I'm not crying anymore. Call me and help me figure out how we're going to do this. But not now. I'm going to sleep for three days. I love you."

Chapter Twenty-Nine

It was seven a.m. before Mary Kate awoke. Her only interruption had come at six the night before, when Bobby had called to see if she wanted to get dinner. Sleep was more important than food, she had told him, but they firmed up plans to see each other tonight. She had all day to practice what to say.

Food was a priority now. Too bad she hadn't thought to shop for breakfast bars or oatmeal before leaving. No milk, no eggs, no bread. The freezer held Popsicles and two pounds of hamburger. Hitting the drive-thru would require getting dressed, something not on her immediate agenda. She scanned the cabinets again, reluctantly settling on a can of fruit cocktail.

Her bags were stacked beside the door, untouched from when she had dropped them. Practically everything she owned was dirty. She began the tedious task of separating things into small piles, and started the first load in her compact washer. It would take all day to get through this, but she had the time.

The urge to talk with Addison was overpowering, even at the risk of waking her, and she pressed the call button on her cell phone. If only she could wake her with a kiss. "How soon can you get here?"

"Mary Kate?"

"Who else would be asking you that?"

"I listened to your message fifty times. I think I broke my phone."

She could hear the smile in Addison's voice. "I can leave another one if you want, but I'd rather tell you in person."

Addison said that she had come home to find a Contract Pending sign in her yard, and a message from her father saying she had sixty days to make the move to London. "I'm not going to do it, Mary Kate. I'm not going to London. It's time we both took charge of our lives."

"What about your job?"

"I'd rather wait tables in Homestead. Or hell, in Mooresville, Georgia."

"You might have some competition for that job. I can't imagine they'll let me teach any more once they find out I have a girlfriend."

"Did you tell Bobby?"

"Not yet. I'll talk to him tonight. But I talked to my mom a little, and it's not going to be as bad as I thought. Of course, I haven't told her about you yet."

"Just don't tell her I laughed at you when you fell in the water."

Mary Kate couldn't believe how close she had come to throwing this away. "I love you, Addison."

"I love you too."

"What are we going to do?"

"I guess I have to find a job somewhere in the States. I had a couple of interesting bites from the stuff I sent out. I need to call them today and set something up."

"In Miami?"

"I'm not sure. With these big institutions, their openings could be anywhere. I just have to be flexible and remember that anything is better than London. Besides, I like adventure. How about you?"

The way they were talking, Mary Kate was actually starting to believe they could work things out. But there were still obstacles to overcome. "I don't know if I can get out of my contract this year. It's awfully late to be giving notice. They might not be able to find somebody else to take my class."

"We'll work it out, Mary Kate. We don't have to be together to build on this, at least not right now. Just knowing how you feel is enough for now."

"How I feel is that I'm in love with you."

"That's all I need."

Her spirit buoyed by the call, Mary Kate attacked her housework with new vigor. By mid-afternoon, her laundry was done, her apartment aired out and her pantry and refrigerator restocked. Then she took a leisurely bath, talking to the soap dish as if it were Bobby. No matter what his objections, she would heed her mother's advice and keep her reasons free of anything that might hurt his feelings. If life worked out the way she wanted, he would find out about Addison eventually and put it all together. For now, she would skip those details and lay the blame for their demise squarely on her own shoulders.

After a quick dinner, she drove over to Bobby's. They hadn't set a time to meet, but he watched the six o'clock news every night, so she timed her arrival at seven. He met her at the door without a word, leaving her to close it when she stepped inside.

The instant she entered the apartment, she knew something was wrong. The cheerful, accommodating demeanor that sometimes drove her to distraction was nowhere to be found. In its place was a stern formality, much like the one she had seen on those few occasions when he disciplined a student who had misbehaved.

"Is everything okay, Bobby?"

"You wanted to talk. That's why you're here." He pushed his hands into his pockets and rested his hip on the credenza. It was intimidating to see him this way, coiled like a snake set to strike.

Her mind raced to find an explanation for his obvious anger. She had never seen him like this. He had been fine yesterday when she left the house, and again on the phone last night. What could have happened? Had he talked to her mother?

"You know, when you dropped me off at the airport, you asked me to do some thinking while I was gone…thinking about us." She hated the way her voice shook. "I did, and I think we should break up."

She waited for his response, but got only a dark stare.

"I haven't meant to lead you on these last few months. I honestly thought it was all going to work out, but now I realize we don't really want the same things."

This was getting ridiculous. He obviously had something to say, but wanted her to drag it out of him. That was a game she didn't want to play.

Looking at her with obvious contempt, he reached inside the top drawer of the credenza. She felt the blood drain from her face as she saw what was in his hand—her camera.

"Who is she, Mary Kate?"

"Give me that. You had no right to look at my pictures." She lunged to grab it, but he pulled it out of her reach.

"I should have listened to Corey when he told me what people said about you. Now I understand completely why you didn't want me to come to Africa. You two were planning a little rendezvous."

"That's not true. She was one of the people in our group. I didn't even know her until—"

"Ninety-five pictures, Mary Kate. Ninety-five out of a hundred and twelve. If I hadn't seen some zebras in the background, I wouldn't even know you'd been to Africa."

In her mind, she inventoried all of the photos she had taken. Most of them were inside the safari vehicle, either candid shots of Addison watching the scenery, or staged as she mugged with silly faces. None were risqué or suggested more than a friendship. As calmly as she could, she explained herself. "Addison had a better camera than mine. We took all the pictures with her camera and she promised to send them to me. I took those of her just playing around."

His face reddened and he stood up as if to approach her, an

apology already on his lips.

"The tour company paired us up for the safari." She swallowed hard. "And we fell in love with each other."

He stopped in his tracks.

"I wasn't going to tell you, because she didn't have anything to do with you and me. I made up my mind on the way over there that I was going to break up with you when I got back. I even sent Deb an e-mail as soon as I got there. You can ask her if you want."

Clearly anguished, he ran his hands through his hair and turned away, slumping into a chair in the living room.

"I didn't know, Bobby. I thought I was...I just thought it was something I could choose."

"Of course you can choose," he said tersely. "You chose to have relations with me, didn't you?"

"I thought I wanted a husband and kids like everyone else, but I don't. I've had these feelings all my life, wanting more from my girlfriends, but afraid to even think about it."

"You should have been," he muttered. "It's perverted."

She bit her tongue to keep from snapping back. Bobby wasn't spouting things just to hurt her. He believed what he was saying, and nothing she could say would change his mind. "I don't expect you to understand. But under the circumstances, I'd like you to see if you can get me out of my contract for this year, or at least get me a transfer over to Oak Hill."

"You'll be lucky to keep your job at all, Mary Kate. This is going to be a big mess, and I don't really care."

"Would you like that, Bobby? Would you like to tell everybody so they'll all think I'm trash?"

His jaw twitched with anger.

"Look, I don't expect you to feel good about anything right now. But think about what's best for everybody. This is nobody else's business. You don't need to hurt my mom and dad, or Carol Lee. They've always been nice to you, and they're going to have a hard enough time as it is."

Appealing to his sense of kindness toward others seemed to

be having the desired effect. He finally sighed in resignation. "I just don't understand it, Mary Kate. I thought we were good together."

"I thought we were too, most of the time. But there was always something missing for me, and I didn't know what it was. That's why I wouldn't take the ring. I kept waiting for it to fix itself, and it never did." She could almost hear her mother sitting on her shoulder and whispering what she ought to say next. "I should have figured it out sooner. Something had to be wrong if I couldn't make it with a guy as good as you."

He looked at her with new interest.

"Seriously, Bobby. I knew how lucky I was to have you for a boyfriend. Everybody said so. You're smart, you're as sweet as they come and you're the handsomest guy in Hurston County." She definitely had his attention now. "There's only one thing that could have kept me from falling in love with you forever, and that was not being attracted to men. If a woman doesn't like a porterhouse steak like you, don't bother trying to give her a plain old sirloin." She couldn't believe she had actually said that.

Bobby, though, seemed to grasp the analogy. "I really don't want anybody to know about this, Mary Kate."

"I don't plan on taking out an ad in the paper." Nor did she plan to sneak around. "People will probably figure it out eventually, but you'll be married with nine kids by then."

"I don't know if I can get another special ed teacher. We don't get many of those applications."

Mary Kate sat on the ottoman and leaned forward on her knees. "I'll honor my contract if you need me to. But I hope we can find a way to be friends through this. If we're not, it's going to make all the other teachers uncomfortable."

"Fine."

She patted his knee and stood. "I'm really sorry."

Getting no more response, she collected her camera and headed for home.

Chapter Thirty

Addison spun the radio dial in a futile attempt to find something besides country music. Finally, she turned it off and returned her attention to the parking lot. From her space in the corner she could clearly see everyone who came and went.

The building's residents probably wondered who she was and what she was waiting for. She could see from the marked parking space in front of unit three that Mary Kate wasn't home, and even though it wasn't yet dark at eight o'clock, others had their lights on inside already.

She should have told Mary Kate she was coming. Sometimes the wrong people got surprised.

That was the nightmare that played over and over in her head, that Mary Kate would stay with Bobby tonight, either to comfort him or because she had changed her mind. Addison would wait until ten or so, then head back to Atlanta for the night. And probably throw up.

This was the most impulsive thing she had ever done. It had seemed so romantic at the time, as she envisioned swooping Mary Kate into her arms and making love to her all night long.

She had been miserable on the flight home yesterday, certain

Mary Kate would collapse under pressure from her family and friends. The most frustrating part for Addison was knowing Mary Kate was giving up what she really wanted in order to make everyone else happy.

When she had landed in Miami and listened to her messages, she let out a whoop that caused everyone in the first-class cabin to laugh at her obvious good fortune. Most even cheered when she explained why. "She loves me!"

And now she was here in Mooresville, Georgia, with its main street and subdivisions, a school complex that housed K through twelve, and a huge blue water tower with the city's name painted on the side. Thanks to the address on Tom Muncie's information sheets, the navigation system in the rental car had led her right to the door.

She had no idea what Mary Kate drove, but when she saw the white Dodge Neon, she began to smile. Sure enough, it parked at unit three, and Mary Kate got out.

Addison opened her door and called out.

"Oh, my God!"

They met in the center of the lot and hugged.

"I can't believe you're here."

"Me neither. Is it okay?"

"Of course it is." She lowered her voice. "But come inside so I can kiss you."

"Lead the way."

They walked up the stairs and into the apartment, where Mary Kate closed and locked the door. There they greeted like the lovers they were, hotly kissing and reaching inside one another's clothes.

"I missed you," Addison said. She was excited to realize she was actually in Mary Kate's home. Two days ago, this seemed impossible. When they came up for air, they reined in their lust and sat side by side on the couch with their hands entwined.

"You're never going to believe why I'm here."

"I don't even care why you're here. I've had just about the worst evening of my life. Bobby got hold of my camera and saw all those pictures I took of you on the safari. He jumped to conclusions, and he just happened to be right."

What Addison remembered was that those pictures were taken in the company of John, and should have been relatively benign. "There was nothing in there that should have given us away."

"I think he was overwhelmed by the volume."

"What did you tell him?"

"The truth. And that old saying is right. It sets you free."

"You broke up?"

"I would say that's a big ten-four."

She listened as Mary Kate told her story, ending with the likelihood she would stay in her job for another year. Addison had already decided they could work with that.

"Would you like to hear what I'm doing in Mooresville?"

"I assume you came to see me."

"I did, but can I stay the night, by the way?"

"Don't even try to leave. I have plans for you." Mary Kate tightened her grip on Addison's arm.

"Good. I have plans for you too. But I'll need to be out of here early to make my interview." She grinned broadly as Mary Kate digested the news. "I heard from the Fed. They liked my work on the internship and asked me to call them to set up an interview. Their regional office is in Atlanta."

"You might be working in Atlanta?"

"It's possible. They have four openings, and they wanted me to come talk to them right away. I made an appointment for tomorrow morning at eleven and then I got the bright idea to visit my new girlfriend. In fact, I thought she might even come with me…sit in the car and keep me from getting nervous."

"I can do that. That gives me an excuse to postpone talking to my mother."

"Is that going to be tough?"

Mary Kate managed a small smile. "Probably, but not as bad as I thought. Turns out she's been talking to my best friend for a while, and the two of them figured it out before I did."

227

"It happens."

"I need to tell you something real important before we make any big decisions," Mary Kate said seriously.

"I thought we'd already made a big decision."

"We did, but I'm not going to be able to be as open about us as I know you want me to be, at least not right away. It doesn't have anything to do with being ashamed. I just don't want to hurt anybody."

Addison was admittedly disappointed, but after seeing what a truly small town this was, she understood the reluctance. "Is that going to be just a Mooresville thing?"

"Pretty much. All the people that matter are going to know how I feel about you, but I'm not going to be able to walk down Main Street holding your hand. Mooresville just isn't that kind of place."

"I can live with that." She draped her arm around Mary Kate's shoulder. "You know, for all this talk, it's hard to believe we've only known each other for a couple of weeks."

"I know. It feels like a lot longer."

In the back of her head, Addison acknowledged the fear that plagued all lesbians, especially the ones who got involved with women who thought they were straight—that the girlfriend would realize her mistake and go back to men. "It's not such a bad idea that we take our time and ease into things. If I start a new job, I'm going to have to concentrate on that for a while."

"I have a whole month until school starts to help you move."

Addison smiled. "A girl after my own heart."

Mary Kate nestled her head on Addison's shoulder. "I love you."

"It's not going to be easy, Mary Kate."

"Sometimes I wonder if the easy stuff is worth doing. The whole time I was training for Kilimanjaro, I worried about whether or not I was going to make it to the summit. Even when things were going well, I was afraid something would happen, something beyond my control. Then it all just fell into place, you and me, standing at the top."

"You know what I remember? You asked me that morning when we were looking up at the mountain how much I wanted it."

"And you wanted it bad, just like I did."

"That's right. We made a pact to get there, and we did it by working together. Now we just have to ask each other again. How much do you want this, Mary Kate?"

Mary Kate turned and straddled her lap, wrapping both arms around her neck. The look on her face said all the things Addison needed to hear. "I want it bad."

"Then we'll get there. Together."

Publications from
Bella Books, Inc.
The best in contemporary lesbian fiction

P.O. Box 10543, Tallahassee, FL 32302
Phone: 800-729-4992
www.bellabooks.com

WITHOUT WARNING: Book one in the Shaken series by KG MacGregor. *Without Warning* is the story of their courageous journey through adversity, and their promise of steadfast love.
ISBN: 978-1-59493-120-8
$13.95

THE CANDIDATE by Tracey Richardson. Presidential candidate Jane Kincaid had always expected the road to the White House would exact a high personal toll. She just never knew how high until forced to choose between her heart and her political destiny.
ISBN: 978-1-59493-133-8
$13.95

TALL IN THE SADDLE by Karin Kallmaker, Barbara Johnson, Therese Szymanski and Julia Watts. The playful quartet that penned the acclaimed *Once Upon A Dyke* and *Stake Through the Heart* are back and now turning to the Wild (and Very Hot) West to bring you another collection of erotically charged, action-packed tales.
ISBN: 978-1-59493-106-2
$15.95

IN THE NAME OF THE FATHER by Gerri Hill. In this highly anticipated sequel to *Hunter's Way*, Dallas Homicide Detectives Tori Hunter and Samantha Kennedy investigate the murder of a Catholic priest who is found naked and strangled to death.
ISBN: 978-1-59493-108-6
$13.95